UNDER THE EYE
OF THE
BLAZING SUN

Two Adventure Novels and a Romance by
BETTIE WILSON STORY

Chariot Books

Contents

SUMMER OF JUBILEE

Bettie Wilson Story

Illustrated by Arnie Kohn

1

MARTE DRAKE WAS lying on the pier, her chin propped despairingly in her hands, when a strange breezy voice broke into her anxious thoughts.

"A jubilee is coming, you know!"

Just like that. No introduction, no pardons for invading her pier or her thoughts—just "A jubilee is coming!"

She did not move from her outlandish position on the hard gray planks, but as she glanced up she noticed his eyes first. Eyes were important; they could so easily stare at her and stray and turn to pity. . . . His were intimate eyes, open. *He's about my age,* she thought, *fourteen or so. Tall, black hair like mine, crooked grin that says, "I'm in charge of everything I see."* *Except me!* Marte thought. But she did brush her hand through her unmanageable short curls and wished she had paid more attention to the mirror.

The stranger did not leave. "A jubilee is coming!"

She might be a newcomer, but she felt a fierce pride in knowing what jubilees were. Her father had talked about them as far back as she could remember.

Finally she found her voice. "Did you think I would be interested in a jubilee?"

"You will!"

He was certainly sure of himself.

He strode over and stretched out next to her, his head hanging over the murky water. "I'm Brad Baker. I live in the second house down, along with my parents, sister Fran, a black crow. And let's see—assorted chicks, crabs, fish—"

"Strange menagerie!"

"That's not the half of it! If I told you everything that lives with us, we'd be here all afternoon." He pointed to the pier posts below them, crusted with barnacles. "Do you see those tiny soft-shell crabs clinging to the pilings?"

"Yes." She wiped the July sweat from her forehead.

"When they invade the shallows, it's one of the early signs of a jubilee. One's a-coming, all right!"

Excitement welled up inside her despite herself. "You sound like an old-timer."

"What do you know about old-timers? You've

"I'm Brad Baker."

been here only three days, Marte Drake."

He was a snoop too. She breathed in the salty breeze, her chest tight with loneliness. After three days, she still didn't feel at home.

"My father grew up here. Sometimes I think he's still growing up." Now why did she say that? Only it seemed so dreadful, monstrous, and outrageous that when he lost his university job last month, he should uproot them from the only home she had known just because he still dreamed of fish jubilees, devil's holes, and mysterious woods.

"Well, it's good having new people around," Brad said. "By the way, welcome to Alabama and to Bay City."

"Some city!"

Brad grinned. His mouth was not particularly large, but when he grinned, it covered his whole face. "I admit it isn't much of a town," he said. "Where do you come from?"

"A little place, Buena Vista, in a narrow valley high in the mountains."

"And you miss them."

"Of course—I was born there. I know those mountains like the raccoons knew our garbage cans." Marte's voice was tight.

"How did you happen to come here?"

"I told you—my father—" she stopped. No, she wouldn't let Brad's cocky grin pull out all her past, especially that her father had lost his job. What's more, Curtis Drake did not seem to care that English teachers were numerous, not as long as he could live on the eastern shore of Mobile Bay. "It's my mind country," he had explained to her. "I'll never be completely at home till I return there." She thought he had loved *her* mountains.

"Sure, boyhood home and all that stuff." Brad raised himself on his arms as though to do a push-up, then jumped to his feet. "Well, back to the lab. It's all work now so I won't miss the fun of a jubilee. Want to see me off your pier, Marte Drake?"

"Not this time. I was studying the shrimp boats when you came." Studying the shrimp boats, she thought, instead of preparing herself for what was ahead.

Brad did not leave. He speared her against the boards with his steel blue eyes. There was no intimacy in them now.

"Whenever do you plan to get into the water?"

Not only was he a snoop. He was also a spy and a meddler.

Marte tossed her head defiantly. "When I'm ready!"

"It's strange to live on the bay and avoid the water. You aren't doing it because of *that thing,* I hope."

Brad jogged up the pier, the vibrations jumbling Marte's stomach. She didn't want to see him again ever! Who could like someone who made pointed remarks and then vanished? She heard the screen door slam at the second house down and fumed.

That thing! The very idea! Stephanie had never been called a *thing* in her whole life, mainly because she wouldn't stand for it. Marte didn't want to think about Stephanie. After all, Steph was only her artificial left leg, but she seemed to be more. Marte joked about it—how they needed each other, otherwise Steph had no reason to exist—but she would prefer that no one else mention it, especially a perfect stranger who had no business poking his nose in her affairs.

So Brad *had* noticed Stephanie. Marte had thought that if she lay still and didn't walk with him up the pier, perhaps he would not see Steph. Not that she was conspicuous; she was a perfect fit. She looked real, too. And sometimes when Marte was having what she called soul searchings, she talked to Steph; most of the time Steph tried to talk back—now, for instance.

"You never tried to hide me in Buena Vista," Stephanie said crossly.

"Why should I? Everybody knew you and me there." Marte felt touchy. She had not talked outright to Stephanie in months.

At least Brad had not avoided her leg's existence with a bright-faced nervousness.

"Sounds as though he couldn't have reacted any way to suit you," Stephanie reprimanded. Perhaps so. It was a miserable afternoon for another reason: Her cousin, Julia Drake, had landed at the Mobile airport. Marte's mother had driven to meet

14

her. The last time they were together had been a couple of years ago at a family reunion when Marte was twelve and Julia eleven. Neither Marte nor Stephanie had forgotten Julia's unpleasant remarks.

"You must overlook her nastiness," mother had told her. "Julia's mother abandoned her and your Uncle Ben for another man a few weeks ago. We didn't tell you because we thought she would return, but no one has heard from her since."

Now Uncle Ben was dead from a sudden heart attack. Marte's father, who was Julia's new guardian, was bringing her here to live. While Marte felt touched by the terrifying prospect of losing both parents, she would have preferred another cousin to become her "sister."

"We're not going to flinch, Steph. She'll never know that sometimes we're trembling inside," Marte whispered to herself as she gazed far out at the shrimp boats. But even as she set her chin in determination, she longed for the parents she must now share. Her life would never again be the same.

Just as Stephanie was threatening to flip her overboard for feeling sorry for herself, Marte heard three short beeps like a foghorn through the pines. She knew it was time to drag herself up and greet Julia.

Any other time she would dash out to give father a hug and have him swing her around in his arms, despite her fourteen years. She had not seen him since the day she and mother left Buena Vista behind the moving van, and he took a flight to Uncle Ben's funeral in Saint Louis. But now her mind actually centered on Julia; she wished this first meeting were already over   . .

She rose and followed the pier to land, staring at the tan water and then the tan beach sand through the cracks between the weathered planks. As she walked, she felt every nail pounded through to the center support beams. There where the cliff sloped, she passed a tall pine. Its heavy dress of muscadine vines cascaded down like a giant waterfall over the bluff. She stepped across the deep front lawn carpeted over by pine needles, past the white octagonal-shaped gazebo, past the flying-ant hill by the front corner of the porch, past the tall oleander in bloom, and finally to the back of the house where the car was parked.

It was empty.

"Marte!" Father was unloading suitcases from the trunk.

She dashed across the remaining distance. He swung her around as he hugged her, and when he set her down, she looked up into his gray-green eyes specked with gold and brown, framed by wide black brows. Her heart went out to him; Uncle Ben was his closest brother.

Father's eyes glistened suddenly and he hugged her tighter. It was special when they did not need to use words to communicate. Words were so inadequate—like "Where's mom?" which she now asked. That did not say anything—such as, *I want to kiss her for letting me have a minute alone with you . . . and can she tell me how to act around Julia? . . . and if Julia will just accept my leg Stephanie, life will be easier–much easier–but never again the same.* All those feelings prompted the question, "Where's mom?"

"She's inside showing Julia your room."

"Did she tell her we still have most of the unpacking to do?"

"Yes." Father ruffled her dark curls. "How about helping me with these bags?"

Before they had transferred them all to the screened porch that surrounded the house, Jo Drake peered out from the kitchen door.

"Can we help?"

"No. I need the exercise," Curtis Drake answered.

Suddenly Marte was facing Julia. She could not believe her sight. Julia was not the plump, sulky eleven-year-old that Marte remembered. Instead, a grown-up thirteen-year-old stood there, taller than Marte by at least two inches. Julia fingered her long golden hair falling to her waist and waited.

Marte was tongue-tied. She could not go put her arms around Julia. That would start her out all false. Neither did she care to be particularly truth-

17

ful. Julia did not find anything to say either. Why didn't mother and father help them out?

A bluejay fussed overhead in the live oak.

To have something to do, Marte picked up a suitcase. "We'll take your things to my room, Julia. You must be dead tired."

A hen squawked raucously. Loud yells came from the second yard down where two boys sprinted from a large shed. One was Brad Baker. They chased the chicken, yelling directions to each other for heading it off.

"That tall one, Brad, says a jubilee is coming," Marte volunteered.

"Oh?" Mother raised a quizzical eyebrow. She smiled.

"He showed me the soft-shell crabs at the pier," Marte added quickly. "They're swarming in the water."

Brad dived under an azalea bush for the chicken, coming up triumphant.

"What a homecoming if that old bay brings a jubilee my first night home!" Father's normally distinguished face took on a boyish excitement.

Home! . . . her beloved mountains where she could do anything anyone else could. Home was where she did not have to prove herself to anyone.

"Julia, how would you like to spend your first night here on the beach waiting out a jubilee?" father asked. That was his own Midsummer Night's Dream, Marte thought.

18

Julia flipped her golden hair over her shoulder. "Whatever a jubilee is. I guess the beach is as good as sharing a room."

"Who says?" Stephanie wanted to bellow, but Marte stepped on her toes to keep her quiet.

"Do you mind my saying, Aunt Jo, that this is the strangest house I ever saw?" Julia asked as they entered the back door.

"Not at all. Its personality appealed to us—sort of reminded us of ourselves. Can you imagine anything more mixed up than an English-style half-timber, half-brick house, surrounded by a huge screen porch like a beach cottage?"

"No, I can't." One thing about Julia—she spoke her mind.

"Marte, since you set the table and got everything ready for dinner before we returned, why don't you show Julia around?"

Perhaps they could talk if alone. Julia had not spoken directly to Marte yet. Marte showed her the downstairs first: one huge room with a brick chimney in the middle, fireplaces on both the kitchen and living room sides, beamed ceiling, windows all across the front bay side. Mother was right. It was a mixed-up house—but homey, lived-in. You could walk through with your dripping swimsuits, but you certainly wouldn't find it photographed in *House Beautiful*.

19

They stepped over packing boxes to climb the circular wrought-iron staircase to the two bedrooms, her parents' which opened up to an enclosed sunporch on the back, and hers and now Julia's on the front.

Marte plopped down on the windowseat of one of the front dormers. "This windowseat is already one of my favorite spots."

She gazed out through the pines to the pier with its end screened in and its shingled roof forming a high peaked bonnet. It stood out stark and black against the dying sun that tried to sparkle the neutral clouds with brilliant hues. She turned back to Julia standing awkwardly in the center of the room.

"This isn't much of a place yet," she explained, glancing distastefully at most of her belongings still stacked in piles. "But you and I can work together to make it a really great room."

Julia jammed her hands in her jeans pockets.

"Wink at a cloud and it'll disappear," mother used to tell her. Marte winked at Julia, but it did not work! Finally she said, "I'm not very good at one-way conversations—that is, except with Stephanie."

Julia flopped on the bed. "Why don't you stop pretending that leg is somebody? You sound just like a kid."

Marte bit her lip to hold back a retort. "If you—"

"Don't you lecture me!" Julia glared at her, suddenly alive with belligerence. *"I'm* a ballerina! I wouldn't be caught dead with an artificial leg."

Holding her head high, Marte stared out over the brackish bay water smooth with glassy quietness. She heard Stephanie mutter, "Well, I'm glad I don't run in the family." Suddenly Julia was moving around, but Marte kept her gaze out to sea until she heard the bathroom door close. Then she rose and went downstairs. Stephanie stomped on every step.

Marte joined her mother by the stove, where she was stirring the beef stroganoff. "Did I ever say I like frankness? I'm starting an anti-frank campaign."

"Marte, you'll have to be patient. I suspect Julia will take out her bad feelings on you for a variety of reasons."

"I'd like to hear them."

Mother sighed and replaced the lid on the stroganoff. The rest of the house might be a mess, but the kitchen and dining area were in perfect order. Mother often said she did that to make up for not enjoying cooking.

"I could tell you a few, but if you discover the reasons for yourself, perhaps you may understand them—and Julia—better." She hugged Marte. "Now, pour milk for everybody."

Marte got the milk out of the refrigerator and slammed the door, her anger slowly fading. As she passed her mother on the way to the antique oak drum table in the dining corner, she whispered, "I feel sorry for her, but does that mean I have to *like* her?"

Instead of frowning in disapproval, her mother smiled—probably to ease the blow of what she was going to say, Marte thought.

"Pity doesn't help us love," her mother said, giving her a level look.

"What do you mean by that?"

"You'll discover that for yourself."

"Sometimes," Marte admitted as she poured milk into four glasses, "I wish you'd stop forcing me to find so much out for myself!"

Mother was already headed for the front door to ring the dinner bell.

2

DINNER WAS A LIVELY hodgepodge of conversation, with Julia seldom joining in unless asked a direct question. Father had already inspected the soft-shells in the bay and talked with neighbors down the beach. Before midnight, he said, they must get some equipment to the pier. Never mind that they did not own any gigs or nets. Mr. Baker, whom he had met on the beach, said he had enough to supply an army corps. Surely the Drakes could scratch up some tubs and croaker sacks from the garage.

"I'm in the dark. You never have told me what a jubilee is, Uncle Curtis," Julia said, looking halfway interested.

"A few times each summer, the fish, shrimp, crabs—even eels and stingarees—scramble toward the shore. It's a fact—and crabs come right up on the beach as if they were sick of the water. We call that a jubilee by the tubful. If it's a good one we can pick up enough seafood on the beach and in the shallow water to feed us for months."

Father's excitement was contagious, but Marte shivered at the mention of rays. "Don't talk about stingarees!" she said stiffly.

"Why not?" Now Julia was curious.

Mother and father exchanged glances. Had they guessed one of the reasons why she avoided the water? Give her a clear mountain stream anytime with its sparkling ripples, but not the murky bay water where a step might bring disaster.

"There's a question left unanswered," mother said.

"Oh, it—it's just that stingarees frighten me with their whiplike tails." Marte's arms turned goose-pocked.

"They should," father said in his teacher voice. "Their tails are poisonous as a rattlesnake, and their spines are murderous on flesh. But they're actually shy creatures, and they don't strike unless disturbed."

Marte remembered a walk in the shallows around a peninsula when she was eight, the only time her parents had brought her on a visit to Mobile Bay. Father had swooped her into his arms just as her foot was raised to step on the cinnamon-colored flat body of a stingaree. He had only laughed jerkily and said no ray was going to

24

get a swat at such pretty legs, but he held her tightly as he said it.

Now mother was complaining that they wouldn't be fit to get the house in order tomorrow if they stayed up all night keeping watch on the beach.

"Do we have to stay up all night?" Julia blurted.

"We don't want to miss a jubilee," said her aunt, "and unfortunately they happen only between midnight and dawn."

"Oooooooh!" Julia sounded tired already.

Father's brow furrowed. "You're right for most times, Jo. But I remember a Sunday when I was a kid that a jubilee came in the middle of the morning. Your grandfather, girls, was preaching up at Daphne when someone ran into church with the news."

"What happened?"

"Papa's congregation vanished in a few seconds, headed for the beach. Papa ended up following them. He rolled up his pantlegs and joined in the fun."

"What causes a jubilee?"

"We actually don't know for certain. Perhaps too much salt water from the gulf moves into Mobile Bay, or too much fresh water from the nine rivers that pour into it. Some old-timers believe shifting winds crowd the oxygen out and make the bay life sick of the water. And sometimes only crabs come to shore, or just flounders—other times a large variety. For whatever reason, a jubilee makes mighty good eating and hours of fun."

Marte grinned. "Dad has his own theory about what causes jubilees."

"Hush, Marte! The family rule is: Jubilee tales must be told only around the campfire. That's handed down by your Grandfather Drake, so you'll have to live with it. Ben and I and all the older kids in our family did too."

"Okay, I give." Marte was now getting excited. She could at least enjoy the night watch and yet avoid the water. She would capture the fish that came all the way up on the beach. She had heard her father's tales about jubilees all her life. Now she could experience one for herself.

"Don't get carried away," mother said. "Another trick they play is by not coming at all regardless of the signs."

"Or it might come ten miles down the beach," father added dejectedly.

"Do they ever come without any signs at all?"

"Of course! This old bay plays every trick you can imagine on us poor humans."

After dinner father and Marte found two tubs, an ice chest, and two camping lanterns in the garage and carried them to the pier while mother and Julia washed dishes. They then spent a couple of hours unpacking and rearranging furniture.

"I know what's missing!" Marte said and scurried among the boxes until she found one marked

26

Cuckoo Clock. She carefully dug in the straw packing until she had every piece of the brown Bavar-
ian clock laid out on the coffee table. Mother chose
a spot for it on the right side of the chimney. Father
got out his supply box, found a concrete nail, and
hammered it into the brick wall.

"It's beautiful!" Julia said as Marte hung it in
place, then added the top section decorated with
vines and flowers. Last of all she connected the
weights to the three chains—two heavy cone-
shaped weights and one rusty hammerhead.

"A hammerhead? Don't you have another
weight?" Julia puckered her lips and frowned.

"Nope!" Marte dusted it with care. "Dad bought
it in Bavaria when he took some students to
Europe years and years ago. It had only two
weights, so the shopkeeper got the third off
another cuckoo clock."

"Only he must have returned it the minute I left
the shop, because he shipped it with only two
weights."

"Anyway, we like it better this way—it's distinctive!" Marte said. "For a long time we hung a
black trivet on the chain."

Mother joined in, "But the trivet really wasn't
heavy enough."

"Then my set of wrenches hung there—for
years," father said. "Everytime I needed them, I
had to unchain them from the cuckoo clock."

Marte giggled. "This story would make more

sense if only one of us told it. But I found the hammer's head in a junk pile, and it's just the right weight."

Julia said, flipping her hair over her shoulder, "I'd leave the dumb thing off altogether."

She'll have an awful time if she expects everything to be in perfect order in this *house,* Marte thought. She turned the clock hands to the half-hour. The cuckoo sounded simultaneously with the chime. Another door opened and musicians played a German folktune. She did not know how she and Mother had survived three days without the cuckoo clock in place.

It was satisfying to be surrounded in this new house with their familiar belongings. Almost everything they owned had its own story. Some people collected artifacts, Marte decided, just to decorate their home. But the Drakes' things had a long tale behind them. Anyone daring to remark, "That's a lovely painting," or whatever, would end up hearing the story of how the Drakes happened to get it by some unusual circumstances.

"That chain controls the musicians," Marte explained. "The rusty old hammer brings us music every half-hour."

"I like the song," Julia admitted.

"It's a good thing since it's so *loud,*" mother said. "Now to the den. We'll fix it up in this southeast corner where the clock is."

They all pitched in to move the hide-a-bed couch,

28

a leather lounge chair, tables, lamps, and television set. Father promised to build bookcases from floor to ceiling on the outer wall.

"We could have saved a thousand dollars on moving costs if we didn't have all these books," mother said.

Father shook his finger at her. "I've told you ten million times not to exaggerate!"

"Who? Me?"

Julia didn't say anything, but Marte could tell she didn't think she should have to help move furniture. "I'm going upstairs," she said suddenly.

"Don't you girls want to take a nap before midnight?"

"Uh—no," Marte responded quickly, but as soon as Julia was out of sight she headed for the couch in the new den.

"Now, Marte!" her mother reprimanded.

Didn't Julia say she doesn't want to share a room? Does she think she'll have to sleep with Stephanie? Aloud Marte said, "Julia needs some time alone. Doesn't she?"

They did not answer. At least she guessed they did not, because the next thing she knew, her mother was shaking her awake and saying that father had built an irresistible fire on the beach. Already? She looked at the cuckoo clock. It was 12:30 A.M. She lay still and listened for the single chime and the familiar tune.

29

Marte saw what her mother meant by "irresistible" as soon as she reached the pier and looked
down at the beach below. Clustered around the fire
were not only her father and Julia but several
others. She was accustomed to sharing her parents
with students, friends, neighbors; but why must
they attract others as if they had been pulled in by
a fish net—especially at their own campfire? She
slipped the string bag holding graham crackers,
chocolate bars, and marshmallows for "Sa'Mores"
onto her arm and descended the long ladder to the
sand. The water slapped lazily against the pilings.

When she neared the fire, noting the gigs and
nets, tubs and barrels nearby, Marte recognized
Brad Baker among the group. He gazed at her
across the flames in that direct way of his as if no
one existed but the two of them. If he made any
prying remarks about Stephanie this time, she
would feel like letting Steph bop him one.

"We can make room for you," Brad said as he
scooted to one side, "especially if you brought the
makings of Sa'Mores!"

She sat beside him.

The boy who had helped chase the chicken that
afternoon said, "Between two good-looking girls!
Brad gets all the breaks!"

"Yeah, one's my sister. Marte, meet Fran."

"Hey!"

"And Winston McMahan—the smart guy. And
my dad. And Coach Calhoun."

30

"Clustered around the fire were dad, Julia, and several others."

Brad was a younger image of his father, except for a long scar above Mr. Baker's right eyebrow.

Coach Calhoun raked his hands through his hair. "Can you debate, Marte? I've got to fill a vacancy on a debate team by the time school starts."

"I did dramatic readings and monologues in speech contests. Not any debate though."

"Think about it, won't you?"

"Okay."

Brad grinned. "You can replace me. I'm out of the lab too much during debate season—which is most of the year you'll have to admit, coach."

"Confounded 'scientific endeavor.' " Coach raked his hand through his hair again. It was a wonder he wasn't bald.

"What lab?" Marte asked.

"Lab?" Coach Calhoun's tone was less than respectful. "You call that shed out back a lab?"

"It's all I have," Brad responded in a tone that indicated he and coach carried on a running battle about the lab.

"I agree with you, coach." Fran wrinkled her nose as if she had stumbled into rotten seaweed. "Phew—eeeee! I wish you would cart off Brad's little monsters, carcass by carcass and bone by bone."

Marte was confused. "Was that chicken escaping for his life?"

"Not really." Brad put a marshmallow on his

32

stick and began to roast it in the embers.

"*If* the skin graft works. Last week it didn't, and the chick expired," Fran said dramatically.

One of Brad's experiments, Mr. Baker said, was an attempted liver transplant in a kitten. How could he say it so matter-of-factly? Marte wanted to say "Wow!" but thought it might embarrass Brad. After all, *he* wasn't the one talking about his experiments. She looked at Coach Calhoun and said:

"You've lost a debater. Already I can tell you can't compete with that lab."

"Shhhh! Let me live with my dreams a while longer."

"Come on, coach, we were headed gar fishing," Mr. Baker said, rising and starting down the beach. "If you fire huggers fall asleep, we'll yell when the jubilee comes."

"Not when! *If* it comes!" Fran shouted. "I don't know what I'm doing out here anyway. I need my beauty sleep."

"I do too," coach said but followed dutifully behind Mr. Baker, who was climbing the ladder to his pier. Other piers up and down the way were also occupied, some sleeping out the vigil on blankets spread out on the planks.

Marte liked Fran. She looked sensible, but she also probably stayed in the middle of all the fun. Her laugh tinkled like Chinese wind chimes and made Marte feel right at home with her. She

33

wished she could say that about a particular cousin. Julia sat across the fire beside father, watching everyone but saying nothing.

Marte wanted the tall tales to begin. "Dad thinks Paul Bunyan brings the jubilees," she said as a teaser.

"What?"

"That fake?"

Marte pointed to the pine loaded with muscadine vines by their pier. "Bunyan could use that tree as a comb for his beard!"

"Oh, come on, Marte!"

"Ummm, these Sa'Mores are good!" Fran passed the grahams around the circle.

"Bunyan never came this far south," Winston said, twirling his wire-framed glasses. Marte could tell he was the practical one.

"So what? He still roams the forests, so he could appear any place there are trees." Even her mountains could not boast of more forest than this shoreline.

"Since you started this, Marte, you're assigned to tell the first yarn."

"Okay, I'll explain why there are jubilees here and nowhere else." She had been thinking hard all evening to come up with a tale to match one of father's. "It's all because of the Devil's Hole."

"How'd you know about the Devil's Hole?" Fran demanded.

"Dad—"

34

"I used to swim—uh, *around* it when I was a kid," father said.

"What Devil's Hole?" quizzed Julia.

"It's up north a ways where Fly Creek empties into the bay. It's bottomless." Brad placed a marshmallow and half a chocolate bar between two grahams and handed them to Marte.

"You mean you're interested in science, and you actually believe that stuff?" Julia was disgusted.

Brad shrugged. "Why not? We haven't disproved it."

"If you dive into its center, you'll never come up," added Winston solemnly.

"The devil snatches you to deep caverns under the earth," whispered Brad.

"Or maybe you surface in China!"

Fran punched Winston, her long brown hair flaming auburn in the firelight. "Let Marte finish."

"Where was I? Oh, there was a Whirling Whimpus which could turn so fast on its one hoof it became invisible. Remember? It bored itself right into the ground every time it twirled, so Paul Bunyan used it to dig wells."

"What does the Whimpus have to do with the Devil's Hole?"

"He bored it, don't you see? He got carried away and bored all the way through the earth."

"And how is that related to the jubilees?"

Marte could do without Winston's questions.

35

"Uh—well, uh, when the fish and crabs scramble to shore, they're running from the Whirling Whimpus."

"Why?"

"Because the Whimpus is chasing the devil across the bay back to his hole at Fly Creek! So there!"

Everybody hooted.

"Bunyan's just a fake. Anyway, he didn't come here—" Winston began.

"You don't know that!"

"I've got one!" Brad joined in. They all turned their attention to him. "Down the way we used to have a two-hundred-foot cypress right on t'e shore, but such a huge army of crabs marched up it one jubilee that the tree toppled over into the bay. It caused a tidal wave thirty feet high on the Texas coast!"

Mr. Drake clapped Brad on the shoulder. "Welcome to the Society for the Perpetuation of Unretired Liars!"

"Just a bunch of kids' myths!" Julia brushed her hair disdainfully away from her shoulders.

"Facts of make-believe, actually," Mr. Drake said quietly and plopped a marshmallow into his mouth.

'I hope a lobster pinches her toes,' Stephanie muttered to Marte. All Julia did, Marte noted, was to sit back as if waiting for someone to make a mistake—at least according to her standards—

and then she would break out of her silence and let fly with a cutting remark.

"Tell us a folk tale, dad." His stories around the campfire had always been among Marte's favorite memories of their camping trips in the mountains.

"No, this time I'll tell you a story about Ben and me." When he said "Ben," his voice deepened with a richness that reminded Marte of the special way Grandfather Drake (as her father had often told her), who had been a Methodist pastor, always said "church." She pushed back from the warm fire and lay flat on the packed sand. Winston shone his flounder lantern out over the water. It revealed nothing.

"Ben and I were very close, but not always," her father began. "We were close in age and much younger than the other kids, and we were always fighting. Let mama's back turn, and we'd tear into each other. Mama's tears and papa's preachings were like rain on concrete—they never sank in."

Marte gazed up at the moonless sky. She had not heard this story.

Father's husky voice continued. "There came a day, though, when no one was home but Ben and me. What fired our tempers I don't remember. But soon we were tussling and chasing, yanking hair and punching each other with a vengeance. Ben ran into mama's room and rolled across the bed to the floor on the other side. I jumped right on top of his stomach from the bed."

Julia winced. "What happened?"

"He turned white and lay still as death. I thought I'd killed him." Father prodded the hot coals with a pine needle. No one pushed him to continue. Marte could hear the water lap up on the sand. The fire sizzled.

Finally her father sighed. "I knocked the breath out of him, I guess, but for three days whenever mama came in one door I went out the other, until I finally broke down and confessed. Mama wisely knew I'd already been punished enough, but that night in her prayers she thanked God's Holy Spirit for not giving up on me!

"When I thought I had killed him, I realized how much I loved Ben. I'm glad I found it out at an early age. We never fought like that again, but we surely did wait out a lot of jubilees together."

A tightness in Marte's chest, clinging there ever since father had first announced they were leaving Buena Vista, began to loosen a tiny bit. Her parents hadn't changed any; that fact might make this place bearable. She searched for stars through the clouds and thought to herself, *If I live to be a hundred, I'll always remember this*. Especially Dad's deep voice in the night.

Father must have had a reason for sharing this particular incident. Marte glanced at Julia sitting across the firelight. Tears glistened on her cheeks.

3

MARTE COMPLAINED that it was a dumb, fickle bay, passing along all the signs for a jubilee right here on their stretch of shore and then rewarding everyone seven miles down the coast! Mother didn't rub in the fact that she had gone to bed and gotten a good night's sleep. She just quietly smiled whenever someone left for an hour or two to catch up on some missed sleep from the jubilee that never came. She also stopped the cuckoo clock so it would not disturb them.

Marte did not mind feeling sluggish—she decided the fun must be in the waiting. She did not get a jubilee this time, but she had a friend. At least she hoped Fran Baker would be her friend.

It was Brad rather than Fran who appeared that afternoon. Mother was upstairs on the sun porch sorting out all her handcrafts, paints, and easel to fix up a workroom for herself. Father was out on an errand "to buy beds," he said. Julia was asleep on the den couch. Marte answered quickly before

Brad's rattling of the screen door awoke her.

"It's a perfect wind for sailing," he said with his crooked grin. "How about coming along?"

"On a *sail*boat?"

"No, on a banana peel. Come on! Time's a-wasting!"

"But, wait!"

"Why?"

"Well—uh, let me ask mom." She left Brad standing on the porch and dashed upstairs. Surely mother would say no. Mother would understand and protect her from having to go out on the water. . . . But she did not. She gave Marte a long, encouraging look and said quietly, "You can do it, Marte."

All the way back downstairs, Marte searched for ways to get out of going without deliberately lying. Perhaps between here and the pier she could figure out what to say.

"Isn't the lab calling you this afternoon?" she asked as they crossed lawns to the Baker pier.

"Nope—not when a sailing is."

Marte caught sight of a rowboat alongside the sailboat. "Let's take the rowboat instead," she said in a tight voice.

"Oh, have a heart!"

Marte did not budge to climb down the ladder to the platform just above the water where the boats were tied. At least a sailboat wasn't a motorboat, but a tricky wind might make it capsize. . . .

40

"You're white as these sails. Come on, Marte, the boat and the water aren't your enemies."

Maybe not, but they weren't her friends either. . . . The accident that had brought Stephanie into her life assured her of that. Besides, she would never, never, never stay attached to Stephanie in a sailboat.

'Take me off then,' Stephanie demanded, but Marte wasn't about to do such a thing. Unstrap Stephanie in front of a near-stranger and hop down the ladder? She glanced down at her jeans cut away just above the knee.

"What's the matter?" Brad asked.

Must she tell him? If she could use mental telepathy: *I don't know you very well, Brad, but please don't make me tell you.* Her eyes clung to his at the same time that she raised a stubborn chin.

"Don't graft yourself to the pier," Brad said after a long silence. "We'll take the rowboat if that's the only way I can get you on the water."

Marte descended to the platform and crawled hesitantly into the boat. Her father had been successful in getting her in one only three or four times in the past three years.

"You don't have to take me on the water as a project," she said. He handed her an oar, ignoring her remark. They faced each other on separate seats. She dipped the oar into the water and hit the sandy bottom.

"Unfortunately," Brad said, "most of the time

41

it's pretty shallow for a half mile out or more."

They paddled easily against the short choppy waves. Brad leaned over and gazed intently into the water. "There's a stingaree!"

"I don't see a thing—thank goodness."

"You'll get used to this water. Sometimes it's *almost* clear."

Marte shivered. "Do stingarees frighten you?"

Brad's thick dark eyebrows knotted as his arm muscles tightened with the pull of the oar. "No, but I respect them. After all, you can't drop out of life and excitement just because of a little danger. And who would want to?"

Suddenly he stood up, waved his oar, and gave an ear-splitting whistle.

"Sit down!" Marte forced herself not to scream.

Brad sat. He continued one shrill whistle after another.

"You're rocking the boat! Will you stop? I don't see anything out there but dolphins."

"I'm calling them."

Marte covered her ears. "You'll never coax them this close in."

"Who says? I'm the best dolphin caller this side of the Sea of Japan."

And you're an insufferable brag, too, she thought.

They rowed straight out into the bay. "Atta boy!" Three dolphins humped toward them and pushed their heads out of the water about twenty

"Atta boy!"

feet from the boat. They squeaked and grunted and grinned. "They're laughing at us for not sailing," Brad said.

"You mean *you* are."

One dolphin made a splashing dive and nudged the boat on Brad's end, the second following, and then the third to bump them in a game of Follow the Leader. Marte was so excited she forgot to be afraid.

Brad whistled again, and a dolphin raised his grinning face over a wave and nodded at them. In a swift second the three were racing back to the frolicking school in the distance.

Marte rubbed her eyes, unbelieving and speechless. Brad only grinned like the dolphins, turned the boat sideways to the waves, and let the oars idle. The waves slap-galoshed against the side, and Marte tuned herself to the rhythm and watched the dolphins disappear.

Before the tide could beach them on the sand, they picked up the oars and rowed out again. Sometimes they talked; sometimes they didn't. Once she asked him how he had learned to communicate with the dolphins. He answered, "I can do it because I've loved them ever since I was a tiny kid."

A motorboat sounded close by, and Marte turned sharply to see it heading in their direction. Her hands gripped the oar handle until the knuckles turned white. If she could hold tight enough, perhaps she could keep from showing her inner turmoil.

Brad frowned as it slowed down next to them. A voice bellowed out, "What are you doing in a—"

"Marte, meet Roy Biglow," Brad broke in. "Marte Drake, Roy."

"Summer tourist?"

"We just moved here from North Carolina."

"I'm heading up to Fly Creek. You kids want to come along?" Roy's round beet-red face looked as if he were baiting them.

"No!" Marte said before Brad could answer.

"Another time," Brad added.

"See you then!" Roy roared the motor, his boat smacking the waves.

Beads of perspiration popped out on Marte's face.

"You're shaking all over, Marte. What's the matter?"

"I wouldn't like to be in a boat with him—ever!" she said emphatically, and congratulated herself on not being hysterical. She wiped her forehead on her arm sleeve.

Brad cleared his throat. "Roy's just a big mouth, but I wonder what's going on at Fly Creek. I saw Mr. Biglow there the other day with his real-estate partner."

"At the Devil's Hole?"

"No, boating up and down the creek and pointing into the woods. I'm suspicious—but that's a

45

natural feeling where Mr. Biglow is concerned."

"I've never been to the Devil's Hole." Marte's voice was wistful. "Maybe dad—"

"Your dad doesn't want to go, I bet. The Devil's Hole now won't be the same as his childhood memories."

"How do you know?"

"Oh, just a guess. I'm going tomorrow, but I always hike it—sort of a pilgrimage. Want to come along?"

"Is Fran going?"

"Maybe. Julia can too."

"I—I'd like to make my first trip there without Julia."

"Oh? Why?"

"Why do you make it a business to ask hard questions?"

Brad picked up his oar and dipped it in the water. "I always have, Marte. I must ask myself hard questions, too, or I wouldn't get anywhere with my experiments."

"I'm not one of your specimens."

Brad nodded toward her artificial leg. "How'd you lose it?"

She quaked inside. "There you go again with your questions—"

"I know! I'm about as tactful as a Portuguese man-o-war, but it's my nature!"

If she avoided the question, she would just be delaying the answer. Eventually she would have to tell nosey Brad anyway. Her chin stiffened as she gazed directly at him.

"It was a freakish motorboat accident on a mountain lake. I fell too close to the motor blades."

"When, Marte? Were you tiny?"

"No, it happened three years ago."

"I can't believe it!"

"You don't have to."

"But you walk so straight! No one would ever know it isn't real. I mean, it looks so much a part of you, I thought you'd had it from birth."

"How did you know it was artificial then?"

"I had seen you around ever since you moved in, but I didn't know until I came up on your pier yesterday."

"Oh."

"Thanks for telling me."

"That's okay. Stephanie doesn't mind—most of the time."

"Stephanie? Who's Stephanie?"

Marte knocked on her leg. "Stephanie—I named her at the very beginning, although she's had two replacements since I've grown taller."

"Greetings, Stephanie!"

Marte giggled self-consciously. "A lot of times strangers either avoid me, as if they don't want to admit Steph's existence, or they treat me like I'm in the circus or something. Just imagine how they must treat people with *real* handicaps."

"Have I treated you that way?"

47

"No, I think you're just like everybody in Buena Vista. You seem to see me as just me—except you ask too many questions."

"That's me—so don't try to change me either."

Marte wrinkled her nose and blinked her eyes at the same time.

"What a funny face!"

She stared at him. "Oh—just a habit—"

"When you're a little upset?"

"I guess so." Marte gazed at the treelined shore. The tall longleaf pines challenged the sky, and the live oaks spread out their gnarled limbs as if to expand their territory. Gulls swooped by and sandpipers tripped along the beach, running away from each wave that slipped up on the sand and then chasing it back into the bay.

Up the hill from the bluff lay the village. White stucco buildings stood out among the green foliage, and a church tower reached high above the treetops. Except for the piers lining the coast, one would hardly know a village was snuggled among the forest.

Two sailboats passed, and Brad looked after them longingly. Marte knew that if it weren't for Stephanie he would be sailing too. Suddenly she hated this bay that made her feel how different she was.

They docked the boat at the pier's lower platform. Brad lowered a hand into the water. When he stood up, Marte said,

"Thanks for my introduction to the bay." It was a relief to have her maiden voyage behind her.

Brad took her hand and placed something wet and scratchy in it and closed her fingers. "Here's your Distinguished Conduct Medal for your first trip. Next time let's take the sails. Please?"

She opened her hand. A moldy barnacle lay in her palm. The tiny plate that covered its top was shut.

"It needs shining up for the occasion." Brad was watching her face closely. His strong features made him almost handsome, but the most notice-able thing was the intense way he talked and listened—making her feel that she was the most important person in the world. She noticed, though, that he gave everyone that kind of atten-tion.

Marte smiled and held on to the barnacle.

Marte was so excited to tell her parents about Brad's way with dolphins, including all the details she could remember and adding some of her own (a storytelling trait she was picking up from father), that it took a while to realize that they had some-thing to show her. The huge old bed in her room fit like a Scout Troop in a pup tent, father said, so—

Marte dashed upstairs. Julia was putting away clothes in a chest. Marte had eyes only for the beds father had fixed up—old metal-framed singles

49

from a secondhand store. Mother had painted them a deep gold. Father had hung them from the slanted ceiling by large chains, those at the heads much shorter where the roof sloped low. Marte squealed and stretched out on a bed to lay claim to it as it swung gently back and forth. She could see from it through her favorite dormer to a forest of trees out front, the gazebo poised sedately among them, and the bay beyond. In a word, she adored the bed and its location.

"I'll get you matching desks for this back wall," father said. Mother murmured something about how people who said professors weren't practical-minded or couldn't distinguish a hammer from a handcuff just didn't know Curtis Drake.

"As Robert Louis Stevenson would say, I have 'some rudiments of sense.' Right?"

"Something like that." Mother kissed him.

Julia turned her back on her aunt and uncle.

Marte was ready to unpack her belongings immediately and make the room a thing of beauty. Father disappeared to another chore, but mother sat on the bed and helped Julia and Marte make plans. By dinner they had decided to shop for a shag rug and new curtains, erect a bulletin board across the back wall over the desks, and move two small easy chairs up from the living room. Over her clothes chest Marte would arrange all her Van Gogh prints. (Last year her Dutch art teacher's favorite was fellow countryman Van Gogh. He became Marte's favorite too. She ordered several prints from museums her parents had visited the year they had lived in the Netherlands long before she was born.)

Marte went up to bed that night only after her parents had gently insisted. She was disappointed to find Julia still awake. Marte dreaded being alone with her. Julia was standing on her toes with the aid of ballet slippers, her arms spread out like a sea gull's wings. Marte said "Hey" and grabbed her pajamas from under her pillow and scooted to the bathroom. She undressed quickly, slipped off Stephanie and propped her in the corner, and took a hot shower.

"We can't stay in here forever, Steph," she said as she dried off. She put on her pajamas and heaved a sigh, then picked Stephanie up and hopped into the room. Perhaps Julia would keep on with her ballet exercises and not pay her any attention.

"How morbid! Can't you at least put it out of sight instead of on the windowseat?"

"She might run away." Marte glanced at Julia. She did not look in the mood for jokes, so she tried another tactic. "Stephanie likes the view here."

"There's no view at night."

"She counts the stars."

"Oh, for heaven's sakes. I wish you'd face reality for a change."

51

Marte crawled onto her bed, letting it sway by the chains. She studied a cobweb on the ceiling, implored Stephanie to help her, and then said, "Julia, why does Stephanie bother you? She doesn't bother me." Well, most of the time she didn't.

Julia removed her slippers as if they were spun of gold. "She, or *it* rather, doesn't *bother* me. I'm just sick and tired of hearing about it. All anybody can do in our family is rave about glorious Marte and how well adjusted she is."

"Oh? I never heard that—well, actually *I* think everybody takes Steph for granted. I wish you would too." Marte watched Julia wrap the slippers in tissue paper and put them carefully in a drawer. Julia crawled into bed, smoothing out the wrinkles in the sheet she pulled over her.

Marte turned off the lamp.

"Why *should* I?" Julia suddenly demanded. "My mama never took it for granted. 'Why should you pout, Julia? Marte never does, and look at *her!*' " The voice in the darkness was a hateful, shrill mimic. " 'Stop whining, stupid! Marte doesn't whine!' "

Marte sat straight up in bed. "I never saw your mother after my accident. What did she know about me?"

Julia's voice was a sneer. "Everything! According to her she knew everything."

"If that's what she said, I can tell she didn't know

52

me at all."

"I hate false pretending!"

It sounded as if Julia hated everything. "Okay, so I'm perfect."

"I knew it all the time."

I'm so perfect that I'm going to let Stephanie flip you in a mess of eels the first chance she gets, Marte thought. She flopped over, punched her pillow with her fist, and hoped she was having a nightmare.

4

MARTE WAS RELIEVED when father awoke them by banging on the door.

"Breakfast in ten minutes!" He always did that kind of thing when changing plans for the day or gloating over his contributions to breakfast.

Ten minutes—no time to do anything but wash your face and dress. No time to talk or get into an argument, to recall the shrill "Stop whining, stupid—Marte doesn't whine," and no time to remember the early-morning dream from which she had awakened crying. Now she could think about something else.

She waited until Julia went into the bathroom, then quickly slipped on Stephanie and dressed. She was combing her hair when Julia came out.

"I'm going on down. See you in a minute." Marte

would wash her face after breakfast.

"Okay."

Marte had gotten only halfway down the stairs when she thought she heard Stephanie say, 'You're avoiding her.'

"So what, Crossmouth?"

'Quit shrinking up in a shell because you've been hurt.'

"And you mind your own business."

'Ohhhh!' Stephanie stomped. 'You fill me full of wrath and cabbage!'

One thing about Stephanie. She and Steph could have it out with each other and get their bad feelings out of their systems. She wished she and Julia could fight as father and Uncle Ben had done. How would it feel to have Julia sock her? A lot better than picking, cutting, and scratching each other with words.

"Marte, please pour the juice."

"Okay, mom." She now understood why father wanted them downstairs in a hurry. Mother had made her famous biscuits "from scratch"—they deserved to be eaten hot from the oven. Father had cooked everything else—sausage, eggs, and grits.

Marte poured orange juice into glasses.

"I'm so hungry my stomach thinks my throat's cut," father said when Julia joined them. "Now, Julia, you sit here where you can get a hand on these biscuits before I devour them all."

Julia looked still half-asleep. "I'll try."

After the blessing father said, "I haven't gotten a single crab in my baskets."

"If you'd stop breathing down their claws every few minutes, you might have more luck," mother said.

"You're right, Jo. I think we should go on an 'explore,' and then I won't be tempted to check on them so often."

"Don't you have to go to work, Uncle Curtis?" Julia asked, buttering a biscuit with such care that Marte figured it was cold by the time she finished.

Marte concentrated on sprinkling sugar on her grits (which mother usually said ruined them). If father would only say that professors have the summers off . . . . He wouldn't be lying.

"I lost my job at the university—actually, I resigned rather than compromise on a couple of important issues. So we took this opportunity to move back home." How could father look so serene? And why did he have to be so honest?

"Do you mean you don't *have* a job?"

"That's right."

"Then you must intend to live off my money from daddy!"

Marte's knife clattered on her plate. The cuckoo sounded like an idiot in the clock.

"Julia, I explained all this before." Father leaned his elbows on the table and put his fingertips together in his church-steeple pose. That position seemed to bring him patience. "Everything of Ben's is in a trust fund for you. I won't use a penny of your inheritance to provide for you in our home. You're our daughter now. We'll take care of you from our own resources."

"But if you don't have a job, then you must be—I mean, I think you are—"

"Dad's being honest with you and you don't even believe him!" Oh, why did she blurt that out? Stephanie would probably threaten to put her foot in her mouth. But no one seemed to notice her outburst.

"Julia, we don't have any secrets in this family. We could not have moved here if we weren't financially stable. I can't retire in my youth, of course"—he winked at mother with his emphasis on youth—"but as soon as Ben's will is probated, you can see all the official documents for yourself. Any correspondence I receive about your trust funds will be passed on to you. Is that clear?"

Julia didn't say anything. Marte wanted to rage.

Mother passed Julia another fat, juicy sausage and smiled. "I just finished a business course last spring to go with my art. I'd really like to open an arts and crafts shop here in Bay City."

"And I'd like to help her with it."

Marte's gaze flew to her father's face. How could he be father and not teach? Give up his profession and work for mother? It sounded strange.

"Maybe she'll give me time off to do something

I've always wanted—go all over this county listening to the grandchildren of the *real* old-timers and writing down some of their stories."

"Haven't they been written down?"

"Nope, how could they?" Father's eyes sparkled. "We've never had one of Bunyan's blue snows down here from which to extract the ink!"

"Oh," mother groaned. "Maybe I won't need your help with the shop after all."

Not another serious word was spoken during the meal.

Their "explore" turned out to be a trip to Fish River, a few miles east of the bay but flowing into it far south of Bay City. He wanted to show them the loveliest church in the whole countryside, father said. Nestled in a grove of oaks near the riverbank, the Marlow church seemed heavenly—a simple stucco building beautifully maintained deep in a lonesome forestland.

Father walked through all the classrooms, commenting on the new ones since his childhood, and finally entered the sanctuary, where he stood behind the large pulpit and gazed out on an imaginary congregation. A cat in the oak outside that window, he said, had drowned out grandfather's sermon one night. Curtis Drake rubbed his hands all along the pulpit probably just as grandfather had once done, Marte thought, and she wished desperately she could have known him.

Soon they drove to the river where the cable ferry, pulled by hand, was once the only way to cross back and forth. They tromped through the woods and listened to one story after another from father's memories. "The kindest man in all the world lived there." Father pointed downriver a way. "He kept my two baby skunks and fed them with an eye dropper while we were away on a family trip."

"Why didn't daddy talk about these things?" Julia asked.

Father scratched his chin. "I don't know, unless it was too painful. Papa's death was awfully hard on him. We were both in college then. But I think it's more painful when we ignore our heritage— both good and bad."

That sparked a flame of anger in Julia. She flipped her hair back. "I don't care if I ever remember my mama!"

"Why don't we just center on the Drakes, about whom you know very little, I gather. Then perhaps one of these years you'll want to know more about the other side of your family." Father put his arm lightly on Julia's shoulder.

Julia pulled away. "Never!"

Marte wished Julia would not talk that way. It reminded her of the terrible things Julia had said last night about her mother, and it also brought back her strange dream early this morning.

The dream had seemed at first so silly—almost like a fable from long ago. Hundreds of crabs, catfish, flounders, and shrimp were invading the beach. Marte was lying on the sand watching them, exuberant over a jubilee coming at last.

Then one crab, larger than all the others, said in a mumbling grumble, "Why do we run from the water like this? It isn't our nature." Marte was amazed she could understand the language.

The other crabs raised their claws. "Old One, may you live forever, perhaps it is that we have land friends."

"Land friends! Hah!" The larger crab looked thoughtful for a moment. "Very well, I will tell you a story. Once on this shore I met a lovely snake, all gold and brown and ebony, who asked to be my friend. When I readily agreed, entranced by the elegant designs on his skin, he began to wrap himself round and round me.

" 'You hold me too tightly,' I told him. 'Pray tell, land friend, go to my neighbor, the catfish, and he will give you seaweed for dinner.'

"And when I pinched his neck oh so gently with my claws, he slithered over to the catfish and said, 'I want to love you, sea friend.' But again he wrapped himself around my neighbor and squeezed harder and harder.

" 'Oh, but honorable land friend,' gasped the catfish, 'you must meet my neighbor, the stingaree. He will bestow affection on you.' Whereupon the

60

catfish pricked the snake lightly with his whiskers, and the snake slid silently toward the stingaree.

"A clump of seaweed floated across his eyes, and he could not see the stingaree well when he said, 'I want to love you, sea friend.' And the stingaree swam toward him. 'Oh, yes, oh, yes,' he cried.

"But suddenly the seaweed floated away, and the snake could now see the stingaree. He gazed at the stingaree's strong, sharp tail, then straightened out his full length and fled. 'I'll love you, land friend,' the stingaree shouted as he chased after the snake. But the snake only answered with a sigh in the grass. 'I could have liked him,' said the stingaree, and he settled down on the sand."

The listening crabs clacked their claws together, the catfish shook their whiskers, the flounders flopped loudly on their bellies, and the shrimp curled up in little balls.

"Oh, Venerable One, may you live forever," said a timid fiddler crab, "and what does the story mean?"

"Oh, poor fellow, have I not told you? The so-called land friend, the snake—may the sea spit out his kind forever—tries to make friends only with those he can overpower. Perhaps it is his nature."

"Let us return to the sea!" All the crabs, fish, and shrimp scrambled back to the water. A huge wave sucked them under and swept them out into the deeps. But one lone stingaree stayed just at the edge of the beach looking for a friend.

In the dream, Marte also walked away from the stingaree.

The dream fused with Julia's shrill words about her mother. Marte had a vague idea that there was something she must do, that the dream could have some purpose, that she could learn something important from it if she tried hard enough. But if so, what was it that she must do? And could she do it?

Mother came and stood close beside her. Marte continued to stare into Fish River.

"Marte, why are you so quiet?"

"I don't know."

But she did. Julia was *their daughter* now, father had said this morning. It sounded so forever-ish.

"I don't care what Uncle Curtis says, I think he's out to get my money. Why else was he so eager to take care of me?"

Why else indeed? Marte thought. *It surely isn't because you're so sweet and lovable and trusting.* . . . Marte was sitting on the windowseat working on a wall plaque mother had given her from her craft supplies and priding herself on not avoiding

Julia. Julia was looking at her through slitted eyes, pretending to straighten her dresser top. It didn't need straightening. She kept everything of hers in perfect order. Marte was not going to be angered by that remark and drawn into a defense of her father. He needed no defense.

"This is the most boring place I can imagine. In St. Louis I'd be practicing every day for the Muni Opera production." Julia twirled on her toes and glared accusingly at Marte. "Did you know I was the only one in my class selected to dance with the Muni Opera this summer?"

"Congratulations!"

"For what? For being hauled off to this God-forsaken place?"

"This isn't a God-forsaken place! Grandfather was pastor here too long to call it that!" Marte flushed with hot resentment. "Julia, this has been a nice day" (except for Julia's accusations of Father), "so let's keep it that way."

"Miss Perfection! Marte never gets mad, does she?"

Marte rubbed the scratchy barnacle—her Distinguished Conduct Medal from Brad—which she had just glued to the pine plaque along with a shell she and Fran had found on the beach this afternoon. That was just what Julia wanted—for her to get rip-snorting mad. She decided she had better talk to Stephanie.

How can she topple me off a pedestal I've never

been on, Steph? Talk about Perfection—she's it with a capital P.

'It's all how you look at it,' Steph answered. 'Now, if you want *my* opinion of you . . .'

Never mind!

Julia stomped her foot. "What're you staring at?"

"I guess I'll finish this plaque tomorrow. Yep, I can get pretty mad, Julia, but I choose what I get mad about." Boy! Did that sound self-righteous, but she kept right on talking. "And tonight I'm sitting on this windowseat, and nobody is going to spoil the evening!" Actually, it was all she could do to stay in the room.

Julia merely sniffed haughtily, then stooped to remove her slippers and fold them neatly away in a drawer. She probably couldn't sleep with one thing out of place. Marte forced herself to control her thoughts and not feel Julia's prickly presence. She would not allow Julia to dispel her happy memories of the trip to Marlow. And of Fran . . .

. . . Her walk with Fran that afternoon along the foggy beach all the way to the public wharf a mile away had been special. Fran, her brown hair bouncing on her shoulders, talked nonstop, as if she must tell Marte everything about Bay City, the high school, her boyfriend Winston, and her family all in one outing. They chased sandpipers along the beach, walked logs washed up on shore, and tried to wipe away the fog.

Once at the wharf, she hunted out Hank Jones B, an old-timer who fishes, she told Marte, eleven days in every week. Hank repeated the names of the fish in his tub, accusing Marte jokingly of being a newcomer. Marte surprised herself by saying she wasn't a newcomer—that Drakes had lived here before.

"Drake—Drake?"

"My grandparents."

"Curtis Drake? Well, if that don't take the huckleberry off of my satsuma! Little lady, I sure knew your grandpappy!"

Marte glowed with pride. "Tell me about him."

Hank Jones B told her how he had joined the church when grandfather was here. "And I carried the Testament he give me in my shirt pocket all them terrible war years. It's still by my bedside too. I read it every night."

They stayed as long as he allowed them, and then he shooed them off, saying their chattering kept the fish from biting.

"How does he spell his name?" Marte asked Fran as they walked down the pier.

Fran grinned. "With a capital B after Jones. It seems his great-grandfather got tired of the name Jones—too common, he said. So he went to court and had a distinguishing B added. It works! We never think of him as Jones—he's Jonesbee!"

On their return home, with Fran bobbing two feet in front of her, somehow it seemed quite natural and ordinary for Marte to tell her about the stingaree and the frightening water—but not about the motorboat accident.

Fran came back and walked beside her. "You're not really afraid." It was a statement, not a question.

"If you knew everything, you wouldn't say that."

"But you can't be! You don't act like it!"

"I *feel* like it!"

"But, Marte, you're not the kind!" Fran stopped and faced her. "You know what? If I were you, I'd stay out of the water for another reason. You can't swim with that leg, can you?"

"It wouldn't be exactly good for her."

"Her?"

"Stephanie—that's her name."

"Oh, how cute! But, anyway, I'd hate to have to fiddle with it—uh, her—you know, taking it off, hopping around, drawing attention. I mean, that would be ghastly—for me. At least at first. I'd get over it; you will too. So you can call it being afraid of the water if you wish, but I don't believe it."

A million pieces were breaking up inside Marte. "I'll have to think about that."

Fran suddenly turned, picked up a broken bottle and headed for a trash can in the park. "Honestly! You'd think people could take better care of the public beaches."

66

"Fran, I like you," Marte said when Fran rejoined her by the water's edge.

"Same here! Oh—I forgot to ask Jonesbee if he's seen any signs of a jubilee coming."

Now Marte looked out at the foggy night. "A jubilee coming!" Maybe she really wasn't afraid as much as she thought. . . . And Fran liked her—enough to understand about Stephanie.

Marte turned from the window and smiled at Julia.

5

THEY TREKKED THE SHORELINE north until the beach gave way to the high cliffs, then climbed a private pier ladder to continue along the ridge. The forest of pines and oaks hid them from the sun, until finally a thin strip of beach below drew them down again to follow the water's edge. They drank from a clear spring that trickled toward the bay.

When they reached Fly Creek, Marte thought it looked no different from any other creek except it was as wide as some rivers. It was a desolate place. She scanned the ridges on each side of the creek and saw no houses in the thick forest. *I bet we're the only people for miles around,* she thought, and shivered.

Brad and Winston and Fran led the way as they turned from the bay and hiked along the edge of Fly Creek. Where the mouth of the creek narrowed, Marte glanced far ahead and saw a small pier. She stumbled. Her foot kept getting caught in vines.

"Shhhhh! We're getting close to the Devil's Hole!" whispered Fran.

Suddenly Marte could not see the pier. She blinked, trying to adjust from the bright sunlight on the beach to the shadows under the trees. Brad and Winston walked faster, and Marte concentrated on staying free of the tangled growth in the path.

When they reached the pier, Brad whispered, "We're here!"

"I don't see anything," said Marte.

They walked the narrow planks to the end of the too-small pier and sat, dangling their legs over the side. Brad's arm made a circular motion pointing out a large area of the creek water that was black as midnight.

"That's the Devil's Hole!"

Marte blinked again, then leaned over the edge of the pier and looked beneath her. The tan sandy bottom of Fly Creek lay several feet below. Clear water! But *there*—at the hole—all was black. Brad and Fran and Winston were staring also into the dark depths of the hole. They contemplated how bottomless was bottomless.

It was an abysmal pit, Marte decided, there in the center of Fly Creek. None of the stories she'd heard about it ever mentioned sunken treasure, or happiness recaptured, or seamaids of unmatched beauty luring the brave to plumb its depths. Instead, if you dared dive into the hole's center, its unknown spirit would drag you to painful beds of nettles, or to caverns where crab claws loomed as large as whales to devour you, or to underground chambers where monsters of a million limbs tore you to bits so tiny they could go through the eye of a needle.

Marte shivered. Her Whirling Whimpus story sounded downright friendly.

When Winston, swimming tentatively around the hole's edges, got too near dead center, Fran let out a scream that echoed up the bluff. Marte was sure it vibrated the vines that clung to the thick forest.

Winston reversed course and returned to the pier.

Brad was watching Marte solemnly. "You aren't scared, are you?"

She shook her head. "Just spellstruck!"

"Winston, if you do that anymore, I'm going home and never—I mean, *never*–speak to you again!"

"Keep going, Winston," yelled Brad.

"Aw, c'mon, Fran, I wasn't going in any farther."

"How did I know? You can't see worth two cents without your glasses."

"But I could *feel*–"

"How?" asked Marte.

70

"WINSTON . . . !"

"The water gets cold like ice at the hole. This shallow stuff is warm."

The clear water beneath them did not look warm. Marte lay back on the uneven boards, thinking that her mountain streams were cold everywhere. She gazed at the sky—well, at the forest. Its huge cypresses and elms and oaks hovered over the creek so that only one tiny patch of blue was visible.

"I can't see the sky."

Fran's laugh was gay and twinkling. "We just come here to try to see the bottom."

"Heresy! There's no bottom."

"Oh, hush! You know what I mean!"

"But we *can* see the sky," Brad said. "At night the stars shine through."

"Do you brave it out here at night?" Marte asked.

"Of course. Then you can also see, if you look that way, the moon's midnight path on the bay."

The rough pier boards pinched her back, but Marte lay still and kept the blue patch of sky in view. Eventually she said, "Dad says that they followed the moonlit path across the bay till the moon was within their reach—that it was his generation that landed on the moon."

"Was he saying there's a connection between dreaming on the pier at the Devil's Hole and the national space program?" asked Winston.

"Who knows? One of his friends is an astronaut.

72

But, no. Dreams don't need to have results you can measure, but they do sometimes come true—even through others, he says."

"What do *you* say, Marte Drake?" Brad quizzed.

Marte was silent. The forest, their bottomless realm in Fly Creek, and at night the stars overhead and the moonlight on the bay—no wonder father had wanted to return to the eastern shore. Marte had not felt so much at home since leaving her mountains. She answered Brad slowly, not caring if she betrayed her feelings:

"Who hasn't dreamed of going to another planet, to the moon, of finding a star to call your own?" She wondered if one could find a star from the close-hovering woods, the isolation, and the black mystery of the Devil's Hole.

"I don't know why we didn't go back the way we came—by the shore. Honestly, Brudder Brad, if I have to go up another side of a gulley, you'll have to carry me out."

"Just move, Fran."

"Can't we walk down the gulley to the bay and go the rest of the way along the beach?"

Fran and Marte plopped down on the hot sand. Brad's steely blue eyes dared them to back out on the trail.

"The fact is," he said, "that you don't feel how remote the Devil's Hole is unless you take the

73

forest trail either going or coming."

"Oh, you and your endurance tests!"

Brad and Winston rested too. Fran took off her sandals and wiggled her toes under the sand, hunting coolness.

"I feel nine years older than God," said Marte.

"This isn't a bad trail. Lots of shady woods." Winston wiped his glasses on his shirttail.

"Loose sand isn't the easiest thing to walk on, but when it's going up and down the sides of these gulleys—I never saw such deep gulleys in my life!" Marte laid back to rest.

"Is Stephanie balking?" Fran asked.

"Of course not!"

Liar. Stephanie had gotten quickly out of hiking shape, but she had something to say about that. 'You never prepared me for deep sand gulleys,' she suddenly bellowed.

We've only gone across two. . .

'Two too many!'

Stutterer!

Brad said, "This is the last one—I promise. Then we'll be on the bluff all the way."

"When we get up there in the woods, let's rest again," Marte said. Brad gave her a knowing look as if he figured Stephanie really was hurting her.

Fran shook the sand out of her sandals and put them on. "Deliver me from this trail. I'll lead the way."

They had bushes and kudzu vines and now and

then a pine to clutch on their trek up the sand embankment. Once Stephanie slipped and Marte slid down against Brad. He moved ahead, holding her hand to give support.

"I can make it by myself."

"Sure you can, but you don't need to."

"Maybe I do."

"Your pride may need it, but *you* don't."

After that remark she could not free her hand, but she tried not to depend on his to get her up the bank. When they reached the top, he pushed a damp curl back from her hot forehead.

"You're quite a challenge!"

A challenge, was she? She had already warned him she wasn't a lab specimen for him to analyze. She lowered her eyes from his "I'm in charge of everything I see" grin. *Don't ruin a perfect day, Brad,* she thought.

Back at home there was no one Marte could tell about the Devil's Hole. Father was nowhere in sight; mother and Julia were engaged in a deep conversation in the den. They did not even look up to acknowledge her presence, so they obviously did not want her to join them.

She moved toward the delicious smell in the kitchen. Crab gumbo! Father had caught enough crabs at last. She gave the pot a stir with a big wooden spoon, then fixed herself some lemonade as quietly as possible and rubbed an ice cube over her face and arms. If she could not talk with anyone, she might as well go to the pier and hope for a cool breeze. On her way through the living room she could not resist saying, "I'm going to the beach," but she got no answer.

Her mother might as well not be home. Marte hated that. All her life in Buena Vista she would slam the front door calling, "Mom!" when she came home. If there were no answer, she would hunt through the house and mother's art studio before putting down her schoolbooks. She might not want to talk with mother right then; it was often enough just to know that she was home. Today she wanted to share the Devil's Hole with her but couldn't because of Julia.

Marte wrinkled her nose and blinked her eyes. "Stephanie, I'm getting rid of you," she said in exasperation, taking her irritation out on her. Stephanie felt like deadwood after the ordeal of two sand gulleys. Either the long hike had heated her up or else the open pier felt hotter than usual—like a sizzling skillet, in fact. But once inside the screened enclosure at the end of the pier, the shade from the bonnet roof and a slight stirring of air welcomed her.

Marte placed the lemonade pitcher and glass on a table and removed Stephanie. What a relief! She was too restless, though, to settle on the chaise lounge for long. What were Mother and Julia talking about as if they were the only two people on earth?

She hopped over to the small closet built in a corner of the pier porch and changed into her bathing suit. It was new and unused. After looking up and down the beach to be sure no one was nearby, she climbed down the ladder to the boat dock platform at water level. She peered over the side; the water did not look so muddy. In fact, it looked almost clear, but she still could not see the sandy bottom.

Did she dare go into the water? It had been three years since the accident. . . . Some day she *must* try. But right now she lay on her stomach and dangled her hand over the side, then patted water on her hot cheeks. It tasted salty; she thought the bay was fresh water. No, now she remembered that Brad had said it had a balance of salt and fresh water, that an imbalance in it might be the cause of jubilees. She examined the pilings for soft-shell crabs but saw none. When she tried to remove one of the barnacles lodged there instead, she cut her finger.

"Marte! Marte!"

She jerked around to see Fran and Brad not more than fifty feet away swimming toward her. What could she do? Stephanie was on the upper level, and here she lay in her bathing suit. How would Fran and Brad feel if they saw her left leg cut off at mid-thigh?

Marte didn't wait to find out. She tumbled over the side into the water, thankful suddenly that the bay was not as clear as her mountain streams.

"Hey! Hey!" Brad shouted.

Marte dog-paddled away from the platform to keep from putting her foot down.

"It's not deep." Fran stood when she reached Marte; the water came just above her waist.

"Is this your first time in the bay?" Brad demanded.

"Y—yes."

"Bravo!"

"I guess it's better to plunge in without thinking," she said, trying to relax. She stopped dog-paddling and put her foot down, feeling only the rippled sand underneath.

"Where are you headed?" She hoped she sounded calm and relaxed, but it took all her will power to stay in the water. For the moment her embarrassment about her leg was stronger than her fear of the water.

"We're headed here. We saw you and decided we could swim this far. After a six-mile hike, this is about my limit," said Fran as she pulled herself up on the platform.

Marte would have to stay in the water until they left. She could stand the water better than their reactions to her stump of a left leg. She adjusted to the bay's slight rhythm, almost as smooth as glass, and tried to float. But her tense body began to go under. She put her foot down to brace herself; it sank into a shallow hole.

She yelped and thrashed the water wildly.

"Marte, are you afraid?" Brad swam over, put his arm around her waist, and picked her up.

"I stepped on something in a hole!" she exclaimed.

"Was it sharp?"

"No—smooth. Smooth and slimy!"

"Did it move?"

"Yes—yes."

"I bet it was a flounder!"

"Come up here by me," said Fran, "before Brad dumps you. I know *him*–he wants to find that hole."

"I'm okay," Marte said, sounding better than she felt. She tried to free herself, but Brad carried her to the platform ladder.

"Thanks," she said, her hands gripping the ladder.

Brad grinned. "I'd like to keep on holding you, but that hole is calling me." He swam back to hunt for it.

"You see, if it's a flounder," Fran explained, "that's one of the jubilee signs."

"How do you mean?"

"Sometimes flounders tuck themselves into holes close to shore—but only if a jubilee is brewing. That's what I say anyway. Brad says they often do it, but the way he's hunting—I think I've convinced him. And we've had an east wind for days—"

79

"It's still not right," Brad called. "It's got to be an east-northeast wind, and this is an east-southeast one."

"And I don't see any soft-shell crabs on the wharf posts," Marte said.

"So what? There're other signs. The water is saltier—that's a good sign. Marte, are you coming up here with me or not?" Fran demanded.

Marte glanced over at Brad, then back to Fran. Finally Fran asked, "Where's Stephanie?"

"Upstairs."

"Do you want me to go get her? You can't stay in this water forever, you know."

Marte winced. "Fran, do you remember our talk the day we saw Hank Jones B?"

"Sure. Why?"

"You said you'd stay out of the water because you'd draw attention to yourself if you had a Stephanie to put on and off."

"Yes, but you're in there now, so all that's over. What difference does it make?"

It made a lot of difference when it caused this much misery. She glanced again at Brad. If he just wouldn't look at her.

Fran jumped up to give Marte a hand. "Will you forget about Brad? He's got his mind on finding that hole, and he's as lost in it as Alice was down the rabbit hole. He's probably got a race on with Hank Jonesbee to see who can find the most signs. Now, c'mon!"

Marte wasn't convinced, but she gave Fran her hand. Fran pulled her out of the water.

"Marte!" someone shouted in rage.

Fran let go of Marte's hand and, caught off balance, Marte fell backwards into the bay. She surfaced sputtering. Fran was giggling like a gull.

But Julia from the upper pier was glowering at them.

BEFORE MARTE COULD GET the water out of her eyes, strong hands grasped her waist and lifted her up to the platform. Brad gave her his cocky grin as if he were taking credit for her first plunge; then he dived backwards to hunt the flounder hole, not glancing once at her legs.

"Be a sport, Julia," Fran called, "and bring Marte's leg down here. It's inside the porch."

Oh, no! Marte cringed. If Fran only knew how Julia felt about Steph, she wouldn't say that.

"I will not!" Julia shouted.

"Then throw it down to us."

"Never! I won't touch it!"

Fran headed for the upper ladder. "Do I have to go up there myself? Come on, Julia, hand it to me."

Julia defiantly stood her ground.

The sound of a nearby motorboat suddenly caught Marte's attention. In a panic she scrambled up and hopped to the ladder. "Move over, Fran. I'll go up." She was trembling with fright.

"What's the matter?"

"Nothing!" Marte for the moment didn't care who saw her without Stephanie attached. The important thing was to pull herself up the ladder as far away from the boat as possible. Her heart was racing and sweat popped out on her forehead. As soon as she reached the pier, Julia bounded toward her and followed her into the porch.

"I came out here to sunbathe," Julia snapped in fury, "and look at you! I'm so ashamed of you I could die!"

"Whatever for?"

"Your leg, what else? How dare you take it off in front of these strangers?"

It wasn't easy. And that was the understatement of the year. "It's my life, Julia," she said. "I—"

"Marte! Julia! It's Coach Calhoun. Hey, coach! Give us a ride!"

Coach shut off the motor and docked the boat. "Not on your life, Fran. Where's your father? Where's Drake? We have to do something! Where are they?"

Brad and Fran followed coach up the ladder.

"We've got our work cut out for us," he was muttering to himself.

"I don't know where dad is," Marte called from the porch and hoped they didn't come inside.

"Take it easy, coach. I'll get them," Brad said as he headed for shore.

Coach raked his fingers through his hair. "I've

been saying for years—you know I have, Fran—
that we need an environmental committee to
check on these confounded realtors—haven't I said
that?"

"Loudly! You forget daddy is a realtor."

"Exactly—he's different. And now do you know
what that Biglow scoundrel has done? He's bought
one hundred acres on both sides of Fly Creek. Can
you imagine bulldozers tearing up that forest just
to add another subdivision?"

Marte's lips stiffened in disbelief. "What will
happen to the Devil's Hole?"

"What do you think?" coach exploded. "Where is
that boy? Where is everybody? Can you tell me
that?"

Before they could attempt an answer, he was
prancing down the pier toward the Drake house.
Fran joined Marte and Julia inside the porch.

"Let's follow coach. We've got to hear this,"
Marte urged. Brad's parents and Marte's had con-
verged on the Drake lawn.

"Julia! Catch!" Fran picked up Stephanie and
threw the leg to her.

Julia recoiled as if Stephanie were a snake and
let her clatter to the floor. Fran marched over and
picked up the leg, handing it to Marte. "Do you
want us 'strangers' to leave so you can attach her?"

"No." Marte surprised herself at her response.
She put Stephanie on quickly, realizing that Brad
and Coach Calhoun had not even noticed her when

they came up on the pier. She sighed with relief. "She's easy to get on now, Fran. At first Stephanie had to be held on by a body strap, but thank goodness we graduated from that."

"Now, Julia," Fran said in an infuriated tone, "I think you ought to apologize—"

"Wait!" Marte interrupted. Julia didn't need a lecture. She went over to Julia and took her by the hand. "We need you to go with us—you've got to find out about the Devil's Hole," she urged. She wanted Julia to understand almost as much as she wanted to change the subject.

Julia pulled her hand away and flipped back her long golden hair. "I think I'll stay here. I don't care about some hole in a creek."

Marte shrugged, anger swelling in her. "Suit yourself." She grabbed her beach coat from its peg in the closet and put it on.

Fran followed her off the pier. "Is she a thunderblast all the time?"

Marte didn't answer as she stomped off the pier toward the circle that included their parents, Coach Calhoun, and Brad. She passed them by.

"Where're you going?" Fran demanded.

"To get some fresh air—I think I'll try the formaldehyde in Brad's lab," she retorted and headed around the side of the house alone. Stephanie almost kicked out at the flying anthill at the corner of the porch but thought better of it. No matter what they said about the Devil's Hole, what could

85

Marte do about it? She would hear all the details when her parents thrashed them over at supper.

Meanwhile, if she did not take time to talk to Stephanie, she would likely explode. *Mudhole, indeed! I try to save Julia the embarrassment of having to apologize, and she treats me like dirt. Then she expects me to share mother and father as if that were some minor effort like waving to the shrimp fleet.*

"Steph, even when I *try* to be nice, she turns it all around and ends up blaming me," Marte complained as she sank down on the back steps.

'Patience isn't one of your virtues,' she thought she heard Stephanie say. 'After all, what's a leg compared to no mother or father—especially a live mother who abandoned her? That's what I call unloved.'

"Does that give her the right to be so dreadful?"

'No, but she doesn't know that.'

"So I'm to turn the other cheek, huh?" Marte asked, feeling bitter.

'It has been done—even by ordinary people like you. Besides, nothing else you could do would help the situation.'

"Thanks! You're so generous-minded."

'Any time.'

"Stephanie Drake, I can't even win in a conversation with you! You're blaming *me* for impatience, not understanding, and all sorts of nasty things!"

'Well, there's another thing, while I'm at it, Marte. I'd appreciate it if your friends kept their hands off me. I do not like to be tossed around—tell that to Fran, will you?'

"What're you doing here?" Marte blurted out as Brad joined her.

He grinned. "Just meddling—sort of slapping my oar in everybody's boat. Yours at the moment. So what are *you* doing here?"

Marte cleared her throat of the elephant inside it. "Talking to myself, and it isn't doing a bit of good."

"C'mon, then. I'd like to show you my lab."

"And miss Coach Calhoun's tirade?"

"They'll get it settled. I thought Biglow was up to no good when I saw him at Fly Creek the other day. Coach wants to stop him from selling lots and transforming that area into a housing development."

"Can he?"

"Not alone. But they're airing all the problems now. In fact, your father invited us all to join you for a supper of crab gumbo so they can continue their discussion."

Marte laughed despite herself. "Dad must have made the gumbo. But I don't understand why you left them."

Brad gave her a searching look. "I told you. I

want to show you my lab." They stooped to walk under the mimosa tree in his yard. "We built this shed as far from the house as possible; the odors are sometimes overwhelming."

"I'll bet!" Marte said, her nose detecting the unmistakable smell of formaldehyde. She did not remember much from her dissection of a frog (required, of course) in ninth-grade biology, but the odor of formaldehyde would stay with her forever.

They stepped inside the shed. It was another world. Cages in one corner contained several mice and two chickens. The four walls were lined with cabinets and work space. On an operating table in the center of the floor sat microscopes and slides. Bottles and specimens and bones, carefully labeled, covered the shelves. Tanks contained all sorts of crabs—mole, hermit, and fiddler.

"You'll have to tell me all about them sometime," Marte said.

"Sure. I'll show you how to hunt some of them out on the beach."

"Those look like armored tanks."

"They're horseshoe crabs. I have too many different kinds. What I ought to do is concentrate on one type of crab at a time, but their various habits are so fascinating. I caught these horseshoes swimming in upside down near the surface. They actually aren't crabs, you know."

"I didn't know."

"They're in the spider family. And after millions of years, they're still very much like their ancient ancestors."

Marte was intrigued by their eyes on the outer shells, protected by spiny ridges.

"There's so much I want to do," Brad said intently.

"Alone?"

"That's what makes it frustrating. I do get down to the marine lab on the island pretty often but not often enough."

"Yours is mighty impressive."

Brad shook his head. "You should see a *real* lab. Next summer I'll probably work in the one on the island, but this year I wanted to do my own experiments—partly to prove to myself I could. Anyway, land animals fascinate me too. Tomorrow I'm going to try a skin graft on these chicks," Brad added casually.

Marte stared at him. "In this place, I feel I don't know you at all."

"It's just a side of me you haven't seen yet. But you'll get acquainted, especially if we're in a science class together next year."

"I'm not sure I want to be in a science class with you!"

Brad poked a finger into the cage for a white mouse to nibble. "Who knows?" he asked. "You may do well enough to qualify as my assistant."

Marte wrinkled her nose. "I think I'd better sign

up for coach's debate team in self-protection."

As they left, Brad asked, "Have you noticed that I haven't asked you a single question about everything that happened to you down at the pier?"

"Now that you mention it, yes."

"How do you like that? I try to practice the moderation you were insisting on, and it goes completely unnoticed." He turned her to face him. "Are you still afraid of the water?"

She nodded. She wished she could talk with him, especially about her feelings toward Julia. Instead she said, "Thanks for showing me your lab. When you came, I felt like sand crabs were stirring around inside me, but I don't feel that way anymore."

When their guests began asking about what all he had added to his crab gumbo recipe, Curtis Drake kept them guessing.

"I have all the regular things isolated," Irene Baker said, "such as bell peppers, celery, okra, onions, tomatoes."

"Did you find crab meat?" father asked.

"Since when do we have crab gumbo without crab?"

"It's there. I taste it."

"I have it!" Coach Calhoun put his spoon down triumphantly. "I haven't cooked for myself these years for nothing. Curtis, you have added a creole gumbo recipe to this. I taste shrimp and oysters. Am I right?"

Mother nodded. "You're right."

"It looks like everything but the kitchen sink is included. How did you figure it all out?" Marte asked.

"I don't disclose my secrets," coach said smugly "Chalk it up to my superior taste."

Over dessert of apples and cheese on the front porch, the topic of the Fly Creek property sale to Biglow came up again for discussion. Bulldozers would level the land and dump soil and underbrush into the creek, Mr. Baker said. Half the forest would be lost, and the Devil's Hole would be filled up.

"It can't disappear just when I'm getting acquainted with it," Marte said. Julia looked disgusted at her comment.

Brad said, "Don't worry. Not even Biglow can fill up a bottomless hole."

"If you think that, you're just a barnacle with your head fastened to a post," retorted Fran.

"Even if it doesn't disappear, why go there just to sit on top of suburbia?" Marte asked.

"It'll disappear right along with all the forest," said Mr. Baker.

"If we could only form a corporation and make an offer Biglow couldn't refuse, perhaps we could buy the land back and save it," coach said.

"It might be worth a try," Mr. Baker said. "We

could work through my agency."

"We can do it if we put our minds to it," father said. "I remember that my father raised two thousand dollars in this town in one day to pay off the mortgage note coming due on the new church property. The board sat back and said he couldn't do it, that they would have to go back to the tiny church they were too large for and be satisfied with that. Dad wasn't interested in saving a new building dream; he was saving a congregation. And that was back when two thousand dollars was a heap of money. Now we need to raise several thousand to save our land."

The families began writing down suggestions as they talked. Marte slipped away into the living room and looked through a stack of stereo albums; she couldn't bear to think what the future of the Devil's Hole might be. The cuckoo clock sounded eight times, followed by a German folktune that played only the first notes. She went over and pulled up the third chain. When the hammerhead reached the top, she released the chain and the music continued. She wished it wouldn't end. When it did, she went back to the stack of records. But all the titles—even her favorites—seemed dull and gloomy.

Fran and Brad and Julia joined her in the living room.

"What do you suggest, Marte? Put on something that will liven this crowd up," Fran said. "Come here, Brad. I want to show you this silly hammerhead on the cuckoo clock."

Marte was surprised Julia was staying with them. *Don't let me do anything to upset her,* she prayed. She flipped the albums over. *The Nutcracker Suite* caught her eye. She wondered if Julia . . . well, it was worth a try. She joined her where she was gazing out the window at the lavender and pink sunset, which colored the entire sky.

"Julia, let's surprise them. If I put on one of the *Nutcracker* records, would you get your slippers and dance for us?"

Julia hesitated a moment. "Do you think I should?"

"Sure! We'd love it—at least, *I* would. I haven't seen you dance, remember?"

"You won't laugh at me?"

"Of course not. Why do you ask that?"

"My mother always laughed. She said I looked like an ugly duckling on tiptoe."

Marte's lip trembled. She would take Stephanie any day rather than Julia's handicap. "Listen, Julia," she said, "anybody invited to perform with the Muni Opera deserves an audience."

"I guess I'll do it," she said halfheartedly and went upstairs.

Would Julia return? While Marte dusted the first record, Fran requested that she tell Brad the history of the cuckoo clock. When she finished, it seemed that there had been more than enough time for Julia to get her ballet slippers. She put the record on the stereo and adjusted the volume control.

"Brad, you and Fran sit here on the couch."

"What gives?"

"Julia and I have a surprise for you."

The Nutcracker Suite filled the room, and Marte held her breath when she heard a noise on the stairs. Julia was gliding down in full costume— black leotards, short lacy pink skirt, and pink ballet slippers. Her gold hair shone against the black top. As she danced, they kept their eyes riveted on her but periodically shoved furniture toward the walls to give her more room.

She's fantastic! Marte thought. *Mother will have to get her to a ballet school in Mobile.*

At the end, their applause, including the adults on the porch who were sitting in the screened windows, deepened the pink in Julia's cheeks. She bowed low in response.

Marte went up and hugged her. "Julia, you're great. Will you do it again?"

Father was still clapping. "Give her time to rest, Marte."

Everyone on the porch came inside and gathered around Julia. Marte had never seen her so happy.

"Now I can understand how disappointed she was to miss the Muni Opera," Marte said softly to her mother.

"It's important for us to help her into happy experiences," mother said, "so that her grief won't continue to overwhelm her." She sighed, and her questioning glance made Marte feel she needed reassurance. Marte put her arm around her mother and wished what she had said were as easy as it sounded. Julia was so moody, sometimes almost friendly when with a group—other times devastating in her hostility. Marte never seemed to be prepared for whatever mood had struck her.

When Marte and her mother served lemonade to everyone, Julia slipped away upstairs. She did not return before the guests left. Marte helped her mother and father clean up the kitchen, remembering how Brad had whispered to her just before he left, "I think we'll have a jubilee soon. One can come without any signs at all, but the bay is glassy still and the wind is shifting. There'll be more signs soon."

"Oh, I hope so!"

"I promise it—just for you, Marte."

Marte went off to bed remembering the warm texture of his voice and the glow in his eyes.

Julia was asleep. When Marte turned back the covers of her bed, she found a note pinned to her pillow. The bed swung her gently on its chains as she read the scrawly handwriting:

"Thanks for *The Nutcracker*. I loved it. And thanks for not laughing. Your sister (doesn't that sound odd?), Julia."

7

THE NEXT MORNING Marte couldn't have felt happier or more generous. She taught Julia the Johnny Appleseed blessing at breakfast and discovered that she had a pretty nice voice.

> Oh, the Lord is good to me.
> And so I thank the Lord
> For giving me the things I need:
> The sun and the rain
> And the appleseed.
> The Lord is good to me!

Marte hummed the tune all morning. It expressed her feelings beautifully, and once, while the family worked around the house, she was able to say to Julia, "Thanks for the note."

Julia nodded. "Except I'm not *really* your sister."

They were sitting on the living room floor sorting books from packing boxes and arranging them in three large bookcases. Father was building additional book shelves in the den, and mother was rearranging the furniture from last night's party.

Marte struggled for a way to answer Julia that

would not exclude her from the family circle.

"By blood kin we're cousins. But I had friends in Buena Vista who were adopted, and I remember once when one of them got angry and said she wasn't her brother's sister."

"And really she wasn't."

"Yes, but blood kin isn't that important. Barbara's mother told her, 'You're brother and sister because you have the same parents.' And that's true. Their parents are the ones who have loved them and taken care of them. They'd be different personalities if they had lived with someone else. They're more brother and sister than some biological ones are."

Marte laid aside a couple of books to take to her room.

"Are you saying we're sisters because we now have the same parents?"

Marte ached as she said, "That's what I mean."

"But what if I don't accept your parents as mine?" Julia asked quietly as she shelved *The Complete Poetry and Selected Prose of John Donne.*

"I guess they are anyway—whether you accept them or not," Marte said and wished this painful conversation had never begun. It was one thing to say all that. It was another feeling altogether to realize how much she missed the warm sharing and quiet togetherness she'd had with her mother and father that changed when Julia arrived. Julia said nothing and the subject was dropped.

Marte held a tattered copy of *Daddy Long Legs*, which had belonged to her mother when she was a child. She remembered the fun they had had packing these books in Buena Vista. They could not resist reading favorite passages to one another, and once mother had threatened to fire father if he did not get more books into boxes; then she had stopped to read them the opening paragraphs of Kazantzakis' *The Fratricides*. "One page," she had said, "and you know *exactly* what that village is like. You can see it and feel it and taste it!"

That afternoon a heavy thunderstorm came up. Pines and the tip-tops of giant oaks swayed in the wind, and the mimosa limbs danced in a wild frenzy. Lightning seared the blackened sky, and Marte could not tell where the rain stopped and the bay began. She sat in a swing on the porch, resting from helping father with the bookshelves. She watched the storm and read. Occasionally a change of wind would spray her with a fine mist, and she shivered in its coolness.

Soon the storm disappeared almost as quickly as it had begun. Tree trunks looked like black pathways through the new-washed green. Clouds hung low and the bay looked as if a squall might come up again. Whitecaps rode the waves.

Mother and Julia returned from the grocery store drenched from head to foot. Fran and Brad followed them through the back door.

"Where's Marte?" Fran asked.

"Front porch," Marte heard her father answer.

"These groceries okay right here?" Brad asked.

"Yes, thanks for helping," mother said. "Please excuse us while we get on dry clothes."

"We'll wait for you, Julia," Brad said on his way through the house. "We're going hunting along the beach."

"Hunting for what?" Marte asked when they joined her.

"Signs! What else? If we don't have a jubilee soon this season, Brad will go stark raving mad!" Fran rolled her eyes.

"What happens after this rainstorm is important," Brad said, excitement in his voice. "Besides, I want to show Marte a kingfisher's nest. That's the reason for this flashlight." One was hanging from his belt.

Fran ran back to the spiral staircase and called to Julia. "Wear your grubbies for cliff climbing."

Marte asked Brad, "What about your chickens? Did you try the skin graft?"

"Yep, early this morning. The chick's been living five hours now. Mother is keeping an eye on it while we're away."

"Wow! Why didn't you call me?"

"Didn't think about it."

"When he gets in that lab," Fran added, "he forgets everything—including food."

Brad took them to the kingfisher's nest, claiming that they might not get there if they hunted for jubilee signs first. But as they walked the beach, he asked, "Seen any signs?" to anyone who happened along. A fisherman had noticed a few small crabs swimming on top of the water.

When Brad pointed to the cliff they must scale to reach the kingfisher's nest, Marte was sure they would not make it. But they did. They helped one another, clung to a bush here and there, dug their heels and fingers into clay, and finally reached a pine growing horizontally out of the side of the cliff.

They sat in a row on the trunk like four vultures looking down at their muddy zigzagged path up the cliff from the beach. They wiped the wet clay from their hands onto the tree trunk. Fran said Brad's brain must have melted away in the rain to bring them up a clay cliff right after a storm.

"I made it!" Marte said excitedly.

"I don't know why I'm here. I've never done anything like this in my life," Julia said, holding onto a limb with one hand and wiping her face against her shirt sleeve.

"Look at the hole just over our heads," Brad said at last.

"Is that all we came to see?" Fran asked in disgust.

"We can take turns with the flashlight. That little hole is the opening to a small tunnel. The tunnel leads to a sort of den that's the nest."

Brad handed Marte the flashlight first. She pulled herself up by a smaller limb and edged along the larger one until she reached the side of the bank. "I see a bigger section—is that the nest?—at the end of the tunnel, but I don't see any birds."

"The babies are out of the den now, but in the spring I saw them. They sat in a circle."

As each one took a turn peeking through the hole, Brad continued, "They know the mother has arrived when the light through the tunnel disappears. The mother brings a minnow, and the babies move one place to the right in the circle."

"What for?"

"So that each one has a turn for the food as the mother comes back and forth with the minnows. The circle of babies is always moving."

"How did you see that?" Fran asked, disbelieving.

"I didn't, but that's the way it is. I'm going to experiment with a tube and mirrors, and if I can figure out how to bore into this cliff without disturbing the birds, I'll have a mirror in that nest next spring." Brad looked at Marte and then added quickly, "Marte, I won't do anything to upset the kingfishers. They worked too hard for this den."

"Okay." Marte felt better. She glanced down the tall cliff they had climbed. "It was worth it all," she said, "even to see an empty nest."

"Hank, this is Julia, Uncle Ben's daughter."

"I guess you found it by seeing a kingfisher flying in and out," Julia said.

"You're right! I stood here for an hour one day watching. That mother must have flown in and out fifteen times with minnows."

On the way back they stopped off at the public wharf and hunted up Hank Jones B, who was cast net fishing for mullet.

Marte said, "Hank, this is Julia Drake—Uncle Ben's daughter. Any signs of a jubilee?"

Hank tipped his gray felt hat, which held at least fifty years of dirt and fish stains. His eyes crinkled with pleasure. "My, My! How I remember your pa! I used to sit by him in church to keep him still while your grandma sang in the choir. I give him a piece of bubble gum once for sitting still for ten minutes, and do you know what that little rascal did? He popped it in his mouth, and before I knew it he had a bubble as big as his head."

"I bet it popped all over his face right in the middle of the sermon," Marte said, laughing.

"You is dead right. I learned quick to save my rewards."

Julia turned away. "Do you mind if I go back to the house?"

"I'll come with you," Marte said.

"No! I want to go alone."

Marte watched Julia walk down the pier as long as she could stand it. She wanted to run after her but turned back to Hank instead.

"Did I say something wrong?"

Marte shook her head. "No, but Uncle Ben died less than a month ago—heart attack. Julia still won't talk about it. He was both mother and father to her."

Hank took his hat off and put it against his chest. "He was a special one—even if he did squirm in the house of the Almighty. I'll remember Miss Julia. I have something at home she might like to have." Just a hint of a tear appeared in Hank's eye. Then the conversation turned to the possibilities of a jubilee.

"I've told you all the signs I've found," Brad said accusingly, "and now the whitecaps have left and the bay is getting still again. Don't tell me, Jonesbee, that you haven't seen anything in the last two days."

Hank winked big at Fran. "I've done seen so many signs that I slept on my pier last night."

"Some friend! Why didn't you tell us?"

"Well, now, don't get so het up. If I had, it would of been a false alarm." Hank was gathering up the sides of his net to throw it out again into the water. "But you better sleep out tonight after that thunderstorm this afternoon. We got a heap more signs now. Just look down there!"

"Eels!" Fran exclaimed. "A whole school swimming in to shore!"

"Yup!" Hank Jones B agreed.

"There's blue crabs on top of the water too!"

104

"And what about the wind?"

"East-northeast," Hank admitted with concealed excitement.

"Hot diggedy dog!" Brad exploded. "Let's go—we've got to get ready!"

"Stay cautious," Hank warned. "The old bay sure do play tricks on us more often than not."

Julia was coming down the stairs, ballet slippers in hand, when Marte dashed in the door to tell them what Hank Jones B had said. "After supper, Julia, will you help us get all the stuff to the beach?"

"Why should I?" Julia marched over to the stereo and thumbed through the albums. When she found *The Nutcracker Suite,* she slipped one of the records out of the case. Marte watched her, deciding Julia was acting dreadful again, and wondered where mother and father had gone.

Marte shrugged. She ought to ignore the question, but instead she asked, "Why shouldn't you?"

"Because you laughed."

"Laughed? When did I dare do such a thing?" she retorted, but Julia wasn't in the mood for jokes.

"You laughed at my father."

If she had to weigh everything before she spoke, Marte didn't want a sister. "Julia, I thought it was a cute story. Can't you just see Uncle Ben wiggling around—sort of like that first-grader sitting in the front pew last Sunday?"

"But you didn't have to laugh."

"You didn't have to get your feelings hurt either. I'm beginning to think one of the most fun parts about living here is the things we're finding out about our parents and grandparents. It's making me not miss my mountains so much anymore. All these stories add to our parents—and to us—I mean, they aren't just parents but humans who do funny things, good and bad things, and have the same kinds of feelings we do." Marte took a deep breath from such a long-winded speech. "Don't you think so?"

Julia sulkily flipped her hair over her shoulders. "You want to know what I really think? I think you're blaming me everytime I say a word, everytime I don't do everything just the way you do it. 'Don't complain—Marte doesn't. Don't get mad—Marte doesn't. Why aren't you perfect like Marte?' " Julia tied on her slippers in fury. "Well, my mother couldn't change me to be you, and you can't either! I'm me—Julia Drake—so leave me alone!"

The Nutcracker Suite blared out all over the room. Julia began the dance, ignoring Marte. Marte was so furious it took all she could do to keep Stephanie from stomping.

She marched right up to Julia so that she had to stop dancing to keep from hitting her. "I have just one question," she seethed. "How do you figure

106

somebody who's so perfect can blame you for everything you say? I wouldn't call that perfection. So you figure out how you really feel about me, Julia Drake, and leave your mother out of it."

Marte turned and marched up the stairs to find her parents. A jubilee is coming. *So what?* she thought bitterly. It wouldn't change a thing.

Marte left the campfire on the beach and climbed the tall ladder to the pier. On her way out to the pier porch, she pulled up each cord along both sides and checked the baskets for crabs. Father must doubt the signs enough to keep these baskets in the water. He surely would not need them if a jubilee came.

She settled down on the chaise lounge, her back to the warm fire on the beach, and gazed out over the black sea hunting for a star. She had to get away to herself. She had avoided Julia all evening; luckily she could do that fairly well, with all the excitement and activity in preparation for the vigil on the beach and all the neighbors coming and going and exchanging rumors about weather conditions. Also, Julia had spent a couple of hours with mother up in her room.

Everything was fun around the campfire until Julia came over and sat by Marte. Right away she whispered, "I'm sorry, Marte, for what I said."

107

Marte's head began to roar like breakers on the surf. She kept her gaze on the red and purple flames in the fire, acting as if she had not heard. A minute later she escaped to the pier.

Lights from distant ships twinkled in the bay's blackness. It was still and calm on this moonless night. What monstrous conditions could lie under that calmness to make the sea life fight frantically for shore?

Marte was beginning to wonder if there really was such a thing as a jubilee when she heard the screen door close softly behind her.

It was her mother. Without a word she curled up comfortably in a wicker chair.

After a long while mother said, "This is a nice place to be after such a busy evening. I feel like I haven't seen you lately, Marte."

"Things are different all right."

"I've been trying so hard to help Julia with her grief that I've neglected your loneliness over moving from Buena Vista and being forced to share your parents."

Marte squirmed. "I guess you overheard the argument Julia and I had."

"I'll not talk with you about that. Julia's trying to sort out all her feelings about both her mother and father. She's really working hard, Marte, to separate you from all the things her mother screamed at her about you long ago. But I am confident you and Julia can work things out."

Marte wished she shared her mother's confidence.

"There is something else I would like to share, though," mother continued. "I have never told you that several years ago we lost a couple of babies by miscarriage."

"No, you didn't tell me." Marte could think of nothing else to say.

"I remember that each time we prepared for the coming of a new baby into our family, we thought about what this event would mean in our relationship to you—our only child. We loved you, enjoyed every moment with you . . . almost," mother laughed as she qualified her statement. "But we knew another child would change our life with you. We would enter into a new relationship together."

"I can't imagine your being happy about losing the babies."

"We were crushed over it." Mother's voice trembled. "We knew we wouldn't love you less—"

"But it would be different," Marte added. "Sort of like now with Julia?"

Her mother answered softly, "Yes. Our love can surround Julia without taking away from you, but right now I miss having you to ourselves."

Parents have the same kinds of feelings we do, Marte had told Julia that afternoon. The bay was blurry in front of her. "I knew our family never would be the same after she came," Marte said. "I

109

just thought nobody cared but me."

"No, it won't be the same, Marte. But I feel God had something to do with this decision. And I believe that there's the possibility that our family could be richer in love because of these struggles."

I'll wait and see, Marte thought. *It surely can't get much worse.*

8

MARTE SAT QUIETLY and listened to the tall tales around the campfire. The conflict with Julia gave her an empty feeling. She glanced at her sitting across the fire with father and drew in a breath of the faint east-northeast wind. She really ought to resent Julia for taking away the excitement she had felt the first night they had waited up for a jubilee.

But she did not. She felt only emptiness.

The campfire. The same ones were back keeping vigil together. No—Coach Calhoun and Mr. Baker were missing. Probably negotiating with Biglow for the land up at Fly Creek. Father had said it might take weeks; how could they wait that long? Marte's gaze continued to circle the campfire, and she discovered that Hank Jonesbee had joined the group while she and mother were out on the pier.

111

Marte looked out over the reach of sand and waited. . . .

It was a waiting time. Nothing they could do would bring the sea creatures to shore.

She lay back on the sand still damp from the afternoon thunderstorm. A lone star twinkled at her through the cloudiness. What if she had not looked up? The moon and the tides, the star and the sea life, she and Julia and all the rest of the human race. Somehow they all seemed joined. Other than being God's creation, how? Marte wondered. . . . Her mind wandered back to Julia. I hope she doesn't like all this fighting between us. I hope we can do something about it. And I hope God knows what he's doing by bringing all of this together. . . . This is not only a waiting time, she thought, it is a waiting place.

Brad was sharing another theory about jubilees—a marine biologist's view, he said. Logs and leaves and debris from the nine rivers flow into the bay, and where they settle and rot, they use up the oxygen from the surrounding water as they oxidize. Then as the currents and winds change, he explained, sea life caught in that stagnation flee from the water for oxygen.

"That may explain why some jubilees bring only crabs, or flounders. Sometimes that's all that swims through that pocket of water."

112

"It's still just a theory, ain't it?"

Brad nodded.

"Then I ain't believing it neither."

"Someday scientists may find out conclusively what causes them," father said, "but that still won't take all the mystery away."

Hank scratched his ragged beard. "Well, I wanta git away from this here theory and git to truth. Now I got a *real* sure 'nuff story. Everybody ready?"

They all nodded.

"Two years ago I think it wuz, the mosquitoes got jealous. Everytime a jubilee come along, they outdone themselves. I mean, them skeeters was the biggest I ever seen, and so thick we couldn't kill 'em fast enough."

"Did they run you off?" Marte asked.

"On a jubilee night? Shoot, naw!" Jonesbee spat in disgust. "Once I crawled under a iron syrup kettle. But them skeeters stuck their snouts through the kettle and I pounded each one to the side with my hammer. Yeah, you know what happened? Them skeeters was so big and so many, they all started buzzing together and flew away with the kettle."

Marte glanced over at Julia during the good-natured groans from the crowd. At least she was not flipping her hair and scoffing, "Just a bunch of kids' myths!" She looked this time as if she were really listening.

113

Hank moved over and squeezed himself in between father and Julia. "Little lady, I got something for you." He pulled out a photograph from his shirt pocket. "It's a picture of your daddy when he wasn't knee-high to a skeeter hisself."

Marte held her breath. How would Julia react?

Julia stared at the picture in her hand. "What's he holding?" She bent toward the firelight.

"Beats me. Some fool contraption he was always building."

"He looks mischievous."

"You don't know the half of it," Jonesbee said. "Many is the time I give him thunder and lightning stewed down to a strong poison for all his shenanigans."

Julia laughed. "Thank you—oh, thank you," she said with joy. "It's the only photo I have of daddy when he was little."

"We'll have to add to your collection," father said.

Julia looked for a long time at the photo, then tucked it into the pocket of her shirt.

Marte breathed a sigh of relief.

Brad was restless. He and Winston decided to take the outboard motor and check the water away from shore. "We'll yell if we see any life," they said.

Mother started singing, "I wish I had a nickel, I wish I had a dime, I wish I had a pretty little girl to love me all the time." Everyone joined in on the chorus of *Getalong Home, Cindy, Cindy*. When

114

they were on the 23rd verse, Marte left for the house to get more grahams, chocolate bars, and marshmallows for Sa'Mores.

Brad and Winston were standing up in the idled motorboat, waving their arms. "We're coming in on a wave of hardshells!" they yelled.

"Jubilee!"

"Jubilee! Jubilee!"

The quiet of the early morning exploded into activity. Everyone scrambled for gigs and nets and lanterns. It was not yet dawn.

"Jubilee!"

"Jubilee!" Shouts split the air all along the beach and echoed up the bluff. People ran from their beach homes. Others ran down the streets, their feet thudding against the pavement.

"Jubilee!" Marte could hear it passed on up the nill through the village. *Like an old-time town crier,* she thought. *I can't believe it's really here!* She grabbed a lantern and turned it out to sea. The first waves of hardshell crabs were coming to shore.

They spread out into the shallow water—everyone but Marte. Even Julia was swinging a scoop net, dumping her catch into a nearby barrel.

Fran slapped a scoop net into Marte's hand. "Join the fun!"

Marte had on knee-high boots to protect

"JUBILEE!"

Stephanie from the water, but she was not about to wade out into it as the others were doing. She stared at the edge, and when she saw no sting-arees, she set the flounder lantern down and scooped up a net full of clawing blue crabs.

"Ho! Ho! Got me a mess of flounders!" Hank Jonesbee shouted.

"Jumbo shrimp for me!"

"A stingaree! Do you want it?" father called to Brad in the boat.

"Yes!"

Father gigged the ray and put it in a tub marked "Brad's Critters."

Marte shivered, and Stephanie started scolding her, 'I'll flip you flat in a mess of eels if you don't quit being afraid.'

"I'll concentrate on how shy the stingaree is," Marte answered, but it wasn't too reassuring.

"Marte, meet me at the dock! I have something to show you!" Brad called.

By the time Marte had climbed the ladder, jogged down the pier, and descended the ladder to the dock, the beach was jammed with people. Some were in pajamas, and a barefooted priest was wielding a scoop net.

Winston had crawled out of the boat in shallow water and waded to shore. "Get in the boat!" Brad directed when Marte reached the dock.

Marte swallowed hard and felt dismal. If only she weren't so afraid. Brad held out his hand, his

117

cocky grin daring her to join him.

"But I haven't—"

"I know. You haven't gotten in a motorboat since the accident. It'll be okay, Marte. This is just a little putt-putt. And it'll be worth the trip."

She swallowed again. The others were so preoccupied with their own activity and shouting back and forth that only she and Brad would know if she refused to go. Her breath exploded in a gasp. "Okay," she said and felt the world caving in on her.

"Atta girl!" Brad held her hand steady until she was securely on the middle seat. "That's the first step, Marte. It's the hardest one of all."

His warm voice reassured her as she gripped the seat so tightly that her hands ached.

"Now, keep the flounder light shining on the water as we move out."

Brad started the motor and moved away from the dock. Marte was trembling like a shutter loose on its hinges.

"I—I—I can't!" she whispered.

"You can, Marte! You will! You don't want to be crippled all your life with an unreasonable fear of boats and the water."

"Unreasonable!" she shouted in protest.

"Yes!" Brad argued. "It's explainable—but still unreasonable! And what better time than now to throw it overboard?"

Marte was furious. "Big brother, Brad. You

won't let me do anything in my own good time, will you?"

"Nope!" Brad said confidently. "I gave you till the first jubilee. But I decided you couldn't miss this experience just because of a stupid fear. Now, flash your lantern out over the water."

She did. Hundreds of fish and crabs, shrimp and lobsters, struggled on the shallow bay floor. Brad shut off the motor. The boat was perfectly still, except for the gentle rhythm of the water, but beneath them was a turbulent chaos of sea life rushing headlong to shore. Marte shone the light out far beyond the piers.

"Look at the cats!"

A sea of black heads had reared out of the water, catfish seemingly gasping for breath.

Deep joy such as she had never known suddenly flooded Marte. It was as if God's Spirit had moved across the waters. She did not know why God chose this shoreline for one of his natural splendors. But she did know that having participated in it, she would never be the same again.

Marte's breathing seemed to be in tune with the tide as she and Brad rode back to shore. And she was not afraid! In fact, she wasn't thinking about the boat and possible or imagined dangers that the water brought. She was part of it in some unexplainable fashion that was larger than

119

anything she had experienced, larger even than the bay and its teeming life.

Brad was watching her intently.

"It's all so big and so wonderful—I can't express how I feel," Marte whispered finally.

"You don't need to. I know," Brad said softly, almost as if he wanted to kiss her.

In all the turmoil of the bay life and the mobs of people up and down the beach, she and Brad seemed to be a quiet island to themselves, a special blessing of this predawn morning.

Brad shut off the motor and pulled it up so it would not drag in the shallow water. "I'm bringing you back to solid ground, Marte. How did you like it?"

How could she tell him what this had meant? To know that forever she could turn her back on the past she wanted to put behind her. Finally she gave him a trembling smile and said, "It was great!" How inadequate words were. "Next time I'll go out on your sailboat with you." The prospect did not frighten her at all now.

Brad jumped to his feet. "Jubilee!" he shouted.

She did not yell at him for rocking the boat.

They were nearly at the shoreline.

"Watch it with that gig!" Brad yelled to Fran. "You nearly got me!"

Marte shone the lantern toward the pier. "Look!"

Crabs were climbing the pier posts.

"What makes them do it? Someday, Brad, I hope some scientist like you will discover the secret."

"I do too. It's quite a run they make."

"Sad too. They seem to be fleeing for their lives, but they're actually coming to their deaths. There has to be some purpose in it."

"Beyond filling our nets and stomachs! I know what you mean. . . . If we can save the Devil's Hole, perhaps we can save the bay. Ecologically, I believe there's a connection between Devil's Hole and the jubilee."

"Perhaps spiritually, too," Marte added.

"Watch it, Julia!" Brad called. "Don't let our boat hit you."

"Okay!" she answered happily.

Marte responded to her warm tone. "Julia, let Brad take you out in the boat. It's unbelievable!"

"I'm having too much fun here," Julia answered as she swooped up a fresh catch.

"That sea of catfish will be close to shore pretty soon—you'll see," Brad said.

"Let's abandon ship, Brad." Marte reached over in the water and scooped up jumbo shrimp with a scoop net Julia handed her. "I'll add these to your critter barrel."

Brad steadied the boat with the oar as Marte stood. She slung Stephanie over the side into the shallow water, then crawled out of the boat.

"Be careful, Marte," insisted Brad.

"I will—I will! I have to dump these shrimp."

"Don't forget your lantern."

"I can't hold it—here, Winston!" She handed the net to him.

Julia was back with no light, dragging a croaker sack. She gigged a fish and added it to the sack. Mullet began to hit the back of Marte's legs.

She swung out her lantern. "A school of mullet!" Fran cried.

The lethargy of the fish was unbelievable. They did not fight being caught. Marte stepped lightly toward Julia, the lantern directing her path. She stepped on a mullet and lost her balance.

'Steady!' Stephanie urged and straightened her up again.

Julia stopped gigging and looked at her. "You all right?"

"Yep!"

"Aren't you scared?"

"Only a little."

"Me too—when I stop long enough to think about it." Julia turned and took a step away.

Marte flashed the lantern at Julia's feet. The light picked up a swift movement. She stared at a long whiplike tail—Julia had struck a stingaree and didn't know it.

Disaster was coming. Marte's heart pounded like a drum. Her hands were icicles. Her blood vessels wanted to explode. In an instant, a stream of thoughts raced through her mind. She remembered Julia saying "I'm sorry" to her at the campfire and the stingaree Marte had almost stepped on the year she was eight and how father swooped her up in his arms to protect her and mother saying they could have two daughters and not love her any less and Julia screaming at her about how perfect she was. Perfect indeed! If Julia hated her so, leave her alone. Nobody knew she saw the stingaree. Don't do anything. Let it strike. Let her find out how it feels to have a wooden leg.

"Stephanie!" Marte shouted but her lips were clamped shut.

She couldn't put it off. Disaster was coming now. She could not let it happen. Ballet was Julia's whole life. She couldn't take it away—not from Julia. The jagged sawteeth that ripped flesh, and the poison. She must move. Help her!

It seemed forever had passed in a second.

Marte kicked Stephanie out and knocked Julia sideways.

The instant her artificial leg came back to the water, the swift tail of the stingaree lashed it instead of Julia.

Someone screamed. Marte felt a jar. The jagged teeth in the tail's center slammed into Stephanie.

Julia stared at the leg as if in a trance. Someone gigged the stingaree's flat body. It was Brad.

"Marte, are you all right?"

"Catch Julia! She's passing out!"

Marte did not move. She heard the voices faintly, as if coming out of a thick fog—mother's, father's, Brad's. They were there somewhere.

So was Stephanie. "I'm sorry, Steph," she whispered.

'It didn't hurt me.'

Suddenly it seemed everyone was crowding around talking at once.

"Thank God it only hit Stephanie."

"What quick thinking!"

"Brave Marte!"

As father carried Julia to shore, Marte staggered along behind wanting to cry in panic. Only she knew how near she had come to doing nothing.

9

THE JUBILEE WAS OVER.

It was one of the largest anyone could remember, lasting well into the morning. . . . The Drakes had more seafood than they could eat in a year. All day was a fisherman's picnic—cooking and eating, swapping recipes, sharing their bounty with friends and passersby, preparing the rest for the freezer that was now stuffed "to the gills," as father said.

Marte did not have time to think about the stingaree; for that she was thankful. Stephanie had come through the ordeal with minor damage, but her boot was ruined. No one had made a great fuss over the accident. After it was clear Julia and Marte were unharmed, everyone got back to their nets to enjoy the jubilee, except mother, who stayed with them on the pier until they had gotten over the fright.

The cuckoo clock in the den struck five. As the German folk tune played, Marte thought, *This is one of the most important days in my life.* She glanced at her family—mother and father teasing each other in the kitchen as they dug meat out of blue crab shells while Julia curled up in a lounge chair next to her. Julia was watching them tease each other, and Marte remembered how usually she had turned her back on them or gone to her room. They were so different from Julia's parents that it was hard for Julia to accept the change, mother had once told Marte. At least this afternoon she wasn't running away from it.

Julia had been pretty decent all day. She had spunk too; she finally got back into the midst of the jubilee fun as if the accident had never happened.

"Are you asleep?" Marte asked hesitantly to try to open conversation.

"Nope! Just thinking that it's going to be a long time before I want to peel any more shrimp."

Marte agreed. She said, "A jubilee is different from anything I expected."

"Why?"

"I always thought what fun and excitement a jubilee must be. But it's sad too—look where all that sea life lands—in somebody's cooking pot! For all that effort to escape whatever they're fleeing, they should live. I never thought I'd feel this way."

"I'm glad you do," her mother responded from the kitchen. "I call it a reverence for life."

"Aunt Jo, you have ears ten feet long," Julia said.

"Will you stop exaggerating? You've been around your Uncle Curtis too long!"

Julia laughed. Marte was pleasantly startled; it was the first time Julia had accepted any teasing directed to her.

Marte couldn't shake her sadness. . . . It clung for another reason too. She didn't want to think about it, but the stubborn thought came back again and again to torment her. She grew tense as she relived it—seeing the stingaree's tail, remembering how she'd almost pretended she hadn't seen it and let it strike Julia. The memory made her feel ill.

She looked at Julia, now joking with mother. Marte wanted to keep in mind only the thought that she had not acted on that impulse, but had moved to protect Julia. She really had not seriously considered such a horrible idea. Not to Julia. Not to anyone. Her chest tightened, gripped in fear again. She must quit thinking about what could have happened.

"Julia, will you go to the Devil's Hole with me?" she asked.

"I don't want anything to do with that stinking Devil's Hole!"

"Why not?"

"It's hot—and I'm tired—and I don't like much of anything right now."

"You liked the jubilee."

"But look what happened!" Julia shuddered and stroked one of her ballet slippers. "I heard somebody say this morning that a friend of his got struck by a stingaree once and they had to amputate his leg. That stingaree almost got me."

"Almost—but it didn't!" *Remember that yourself, Marte,* she thought fiercely.

"I know. My mama would say I was saved by brave Marte." Julia's voice did not have the shrill mimic of her mother in it, only a calm statement of fact.

"I *was* brave!" Marte said hotly. She knew it was no boast. "But I was also scared to death. And it was partly a simple reflex action. I saw the tail and reacted almost instantly. If you had been in my place, you would have flung out a gig or something. I just happened to have Stephanie handy."

"Do you really believe that—what you just said about me?"

"Yes, I believe that."

Julia sighed. "I don't."

"You might change your mind if you come with me to the Devil's Hole. Your dad and mine spent part of their childhood there too."

"Heritage and all that stuff. How about just letting me go my own way, Marte?"

Marte was taken aback. The accident hadn't changed anything. Julia had been pleasant all day, and now the longer they talked the more she sounded like the same old Julia. Maybe the conversation should stop while they were ahead. Marte could hear Stephanie talking to her, though, in her head—demanding to know why she thought Julia would change in an instant.

'You weren't *that* much of a heroine!' Steph retorted. 'Besides, there'll still be days too when you'll wish she weren't your sister. What did you expect? Anyway, are you just going to react all the time to everything she says?'

Hush—so I can think, Marte answered.

Steph might be right. Julia had her ballet— knew what she wanted to do with her talent. Marte had the Devil's Hole and made friends easily and still must discover what she wanted to do with her talent. They were different people and would respond to life in different ways. And Marte had wanted—and expected—Julia to respond the same way she did! A terrible sense of insight overcame Marte—perhaps *she* was part of Julia's problem.

"Okay, Julia. I won't push you."

"Thanks. I'm glad you want me to go, I really am. And I will—but not yet. I'm not ready to go yet."

Marte didn't know what she meant but responded, "Okay."

The back door slammed.

"Where's Marte?" Brad asked.

"In the den."

"Thanks." Brad squeezed around the end of the bookcase from the kitchen.

"Come on, Marte, I've got something to show you at the lab."

"Sounds exciting!"

"You want to come, Julia?"

Julia yawned. "I'm asleep! And besides, I think my sister doesn't want anybody else tagging along."

Marte blushed.

Brad gave her his "I'm in control" grin and took her hand as they started out the door. "How's it been this afternoon?"

"Okay. But I'm glad you came when you did. Where's Fran?"

"Asleep! She passed out three hours ago."

Inside the lab Brad guided her over to a large tank. Blue crabs swam in the water, but he pointed out the stingaree nestled on the sandy bottom.

"It's horrible!"

Brad grabbed her hand again. "Don't leave. Look at it! It's really beautiful in its own way."

She looked. Seeing it breathe through gills on the top of its cinnamon body, she was reminded of the rhythmic pulse of the ocean she had felt the day she and Brad took the rowboat out in the bay. She could tune herself to that rhythm. But when she looked at the deadly tail, it brought back the nightmare of the early morning.

She turned away.

Brad took her lightly by the shoulders and turned her back. "You have to see it, Marte."

130

"You can't make me like it."

"Yes, I can. It's most special for lots of reasons. First, it brought out the best in you—"

"No!"

"Yes!"

"I was dreadful—I almost didn't do a thing, Brad. I almost left it alone." What a burden was lifting to tell that to someone.

"Who wouldn't! Most people would be scared to death with a stingaree at their feet!"

"No, you don't understand!" Marte was sobbing. "For a second I wanted it to strike Julia—let her see what it's like to lose a leg. I did. And I hate myself for it." Tears were streaming down her face.

"But you didn't do that, Marte. You were stronger than those feelings. God knew that you had Stephanie, and he just helped you do what you were strong enough to do."

"Maybe so."

"I know so."

"I haven't heard you talk this way before."

Brad laughed. "I think he's been working on me too."

"How?"

"I'll show you. Look at the stingaree."

"I'll try."

"Now—see his eyes? I've been studying them today—mostly to get over my fright at seeing him strike you."

Marte trembled.

"Stingarees are vertebrates just like humans. Things without bones, like squid and octopus, are called cephalopods. And, Marte, the eyes of all four are almost identical, although we're not related."

"How do you mean?"

"It's a camera-like eye. Each one has a cornea to let in light with an iris to regulate it. They all have fluid to keep the spherical shape. And a lens. Name me one thing that's greater than the eye in the world—and here we have it in two totally different animal groups."

"I see."

"Do you? Seeing how much that eye of the stingaree is like mine made me realize something today. It's sea life I really want to devote my life to—no more transplants and skin grafting on chicks and all that stuff. I know I can get into the sea lab on the island for weekends and summers during high school. I'll turn my lab here over to sea life study too."

Marte took a deep breath. "When you talk about the eyes like that, I see the stingaree's beauty. And it really is shy, isn't it? Brad, such a long time ago I had a dream—like a fable actually. I must tell you about the snake and the Old Venerable Crab and the stingaree."

As she told the story and repeated the words of the Venerable Crab at the end, her voice shook with new understanding. "The snake tries to make friends only with those he can overpower." She would never be able to love Julia as long as she demanded that Julia live up to her expectations.

'Yeah, stop trying to make her over into your image,' Steph muttered. Steph always had to have the last word.

"Brad—" he had to bend his head close to hear. "The stingaree is waiting in the shallows for a friend."

"What do you mean?"

"I think the Lord's been moving through a dream, saying I must accept someone from inside myself rather than basing my feelings on what she says and does."

"You can do it."

She gave Brad a brilliant smile. "I think I can. Now we need to go find Julia."

"Shall we get the whole gang and hunt out Jonesbee at the big wharf?"

"Don't tell me another jubilee is coming so soon."

"There's always another jubilee coming!"

They left the shy stingaree bedded down on the sandy bottom and closed the lab door behind them.

Ahead, ducking her shining head under the mimosa branches, was Julia. She was running to meet them.

THE OTHER SIDE OF THE TELL

Bettie Wilson Story

Illustrated by Seymour Fleishman

1

The Tell

IT WAS LATE AFTERNOON in early July. The desert sun zeroed in on us so strong that I sometimes felt we were trapped in an oven. Finally our rented car turned off a highway in Israel. The trip through the mountains from Jerusalem was behind us and we bumped up and down on a dirt road in the foothills. I pointed to a deep blue band beyond the plains below us.

"Is that the Mediterranean Sea or just the sky?"

Mom and Dad answered at the same time. "It's the Mediterranean."

"I see the tell! I see the tell!" Jennifer screamed.

Dad pressed his ear and apologized to the driver.

"It's just another hill—not the tell," Mom explained.

"Jennifer, if you don't stop bouncing on this seat, I'm going to . . ."

"Now, Jeff," Dad said, "we celebrated your 12th birthday yesterday, so grow up a little."

My parched tongue stuck to my teeth like skin to dry ice. I rubbed the dust on my arm up into little dirt balls. Why didn't Dad stop Jennifer when she yelled at me? Besides, I *was* growing up, and I was excited, too. Sometimes my chest tightened up so much I could hardly breathe, but I wasn't ruining the springs in the car seat or bursting eardrums.

When we passed through a tiny farm village, the driver pushed back his cap and pointed ahead. Just on the edge of the plains lay the tell.

"It looks like a long hill with a flat top." Jennifer sounded disappointed.

"But it's not a natural hill," Dad said in his teacher voice. "It's a mound made of the ruins of many cities over several centuries. It's like a layer cake that must be lifted off layer by layer."

"Why?"

"To discover, Jen, all we can about the ancient peoples who lived here. Each layer represents a period of years—perhaps even centuries."

Our dad and mom taught at a university in Illinois during the school year, but here they were going to be plain old volunteers for a month on an archaeological dig.

The road wound along the length of the tell. I

gazed up its slope, licking my cracked lips. This time I nearly jumped on the seat myself.

"There's a cave!" I shouted.

"Where? Where?"

"In the side of the hill!"

The driver eased the car over the bumps and rocks in the road.

"Can I get out, Dad? Please?"

"Jeff, you can't go in the cave alone so you may as well stay in the car."

Mom's lips and forehead puckered up into a frown. "Mr. McDowell wasn't sure such young kids ought to come, and here you want to run off alone before we—"

"Don't you trust me, Mom?"

The car stopped.

Before Mom could answer—I knew what she would say anyway—I opened the door and ran to move two huge stones that blocked the road. My chest tightened. I wanted to dash up just to look at that cave so bad I could taste it.

I straightened up and called, "I'll meet you at the top!"

I sprinted out across the rocky ground toward the cave before Dad could call me back. I turned once and waved as the car followed the road slowly toward the other end of the tell. Good old driver! He kept right on going. My parents did not look happy, but Jennifer was sitting there waving her hand off.

When I crawled up to the cave which was several yards from the top, a boy—he scared me silly just standing there—faced me just inside the dark entrance. I couldn't understand a word he said, but he motioned for me to move away. That was funny.

"Why can't I go inside?" I wasn't really planning on it after what Dad had said, but when this strange boy blocked the entrance, I was tempted.

"You can go in with me," I begged. With him I wouldn't be alone.

He didn't understand. I pointed stupidly and tried to see inside the cave. No sunlight invaded it. I saw nothing.

The boy said nothing. He was about my height, but thinner. His black eyes stayed glued to my face.

"What is your name?"

His eyes flickered once. "Kerim," he said.

So! He understood.

"I want to know why I can't go inside."

Again he said nothing. We stared at each other.

"Jeff! There you are!" Jennifer slid partway down the hill.

"Jennifer, will you leave me alone?"

"Dad wants you. The tents are way at the other end, and he needs you to help get our stuff unpacked."

"I told him I'd meet you at the top."

"But he thought—"

140

"I know, I know. He thought I went in the cave alone, didn't he?"

"He didn't say so."

"He doesn't need to."

Jennifer edged back up the distance she had come down from the top, taking two steps and sliding back one. "And, anyway, I was curious about the cave, too."

That strange Kerim still stared at me. I wasn't the kind to fight to get inside, but I sure did want to know why he was guarding it.

He stood in the shade of the cave entrance while the sun beat down on me. I was dying of thirst. Finally I gave up and scuffed up the hill to join Jennifer.

"You stick your nose in everything I do," I grumbled. "If you hadn't come along, I bet I could have had at least a look inside."

I gazed out over the flat surface of the mound. This end, probably two or more city blocks long, was covered with trenches where the archaeological team was digging. At the other end were the living tents, a water tower, and a bunch of sheds covered with tin roofs. There was not one single shade tree on this whole desert tell.

2

Ibriks and Sherds

A STRANGE THING HAPPENED the next morning. Somebody in the family woke up before me. It was Jennifer.

I did not even hear the artillery-shell gong sound at four a.m. Jennifer shook me awake. "Get up, lazy!"

I lunged out in the dark to push her away.

"Miss me—miss me! Now you got to kiss me!"

"Oh, Jen, stop that baby stuff," I answered, pushing back up on my bunk.

"All right, Jeff," Dad said. "It's only four o'clock in the morning. You have 20 minutes till breakfast."

Ugh! How could I eat at that time of day? Work started early and ended at noon because the sun's heat was supposed to be unbearable most of the afternoon. I lay still, hugging to myself the last warm quiet second in my sleeping bag, then wiggled out of it and into my clothes. Jennifer was already dressed.

There were four long rows of sleeping tents; ours was at the end nearest the dining shed. We didn't have far to walk for our breakfast—three peanut butter sandwiches.

"I'll get up early every morning for these," I said to no one in particular, and discovered that most of the 125 others were too sleepy to talk.

"Where are most of them from?" I asked Mom.

"Most of them are Americans, Jeff, both Christian and Jewish volunteers from universities and churches all over the country. There are also a lot of Jewish people from right here in Israel, and Arab Bedouin who live here too."

I looked up and down the long table. "I met a boy, Kerim, at the cave yesterday. I don't see him now."

Hank, a college student from Colorado who looked as if he considered it worth a trophy that he had gotten out of bed so early, gazed at me with his baggy eyes.

He said, "Kerim lives out on the plain. He's one of the Bedouin tribe. He can disappear and reappear the quickest of anybody I know, but he'll be around here somewhere. You kids ought to get together and find something to do."

Kids! Everywhere I turned on this tell somebody was reminding me of how young I was, as if I was a puny third-grader like Jennifer. I concentrated on eating my sandwiches.

By five o'clock everyone had passed through the gates to the unfenced area of the tell where they all went to work in the trenches that had been assigned to them the afternoon before.

Mom suggested that Jennifer go back to our tent and sleep.

"No! I'm too excited," she said. "I don't want to go to bed."

Mom glanced at me. I didn't want to look after Jennifer, so I said, "I gotta find Dad," and headed toward the cave where he was going to work.

When I saw Kerim standing at the entrance, I stopped, remembering that Dad said I could not go in alone. Since Kerim didn't seem to speak English, I couldn't talk him into going inside with me. All the cave workers must have already entered. I glanced up at the rim of the mound and saw Hank.

"You better get your *ibrik!*" he yelled. "You'll need it pretty soon."

"Are you coming down here?" Maybe he would go in the cave with me.

"Nope, I work on the top."

Just my luck! There was nobody I could follow into the cave. Kerim ignored me.

"Your *ibrik!*" Hank shouted again before leaving the edge of the tell.

The leaders said last night that we had to drink

144

lots of water to keep from being dehydrated, so I took the long trek back to the gates, inside the fenced-in living area, and to a shed for a jug.

I filled the clay jug. *Ibrik* was a nicer word than jug; it was also the first Arabic word I had learned. It worked like a desert bag, keeping the water inside as cool as if it had just come from a spring. Carrying it, I headed back again.

"What're you doing scratching through that mound of pottery?" I demanded of Jennifer as I passed her.

"That man said I could."

"Don't point!"

She went back to scratching.

I glanced at the man—Mr. McDowell, one of the professional archaeologists. His stern eyes, dark brown like cocoa, and his thick black beard reminded me again that Jennifer and I were the youngest ones there. Mr. Mac had probably let us come against his "better judgment" as Mom would say. Finally he spoke in a gravelly voice that made me pay attention.

"That's just the discard pile. She may have any of those sherds she wants."

"Sherds?"

"That's what we call pottery pieces. It really comes from the word 'potsherd' or 'the broken pieces of a pot.' "

"Oh!" Jennifer held up a triangular piece. "This one has designs. Don't you want to keep it?"

145

"What're you doing scratching through that pottery?" Jeff demanded.

Nosy Jen. If he wanted to keep it, would it be on the discard pile? It really was pretty. I wished I had found it myself.

Mr. McDowell said, "We have other pieces of that type which are even more distinctive."

"I can really keep it?"

"Of course, since it came from the discards. No one may keep anything that's found on the tell until we have had a chance to decide if we need it or not. If we don't need it, it goes on this discard pile, so take anything you like."

Jennifer rubbed the designed piece with her fingers. "I feel sorry for discards; nobody wants them," she said and started scratching in the pile again as if determined to save more of the broken pieces.

"Young fellow, you should get a cap or handkerchief on your head. That sun isn't merciful," Mr. Mac said.

For Pete's sake, it wasn't even seven o'clock yet. Miss Perfect patted the cap on her head and grinned at me. She was asking for it today.

"I'll get one," I muttered and headed for our tent.

"You look like Abraham Lincoln," I heard Jennifer say to Mr. McDowell. Brother! What would he say to that? To my surprise, he laughed.

"Does everyone with a black beard remind you of Lincoln?"

"Oh, no, Sir. Only you."

I walked out of hearing range so missed his answer, but Jennifer was laughing with him. I wished I did not keep remembering the sternness of his eyes.

Inside our tent I stuck my thumb into the handle of my *ibrik*, rested the base on my shoulder as I had seen others do, and drank from it. I rubbed the moisture collected on the outside onto my face. It felt cool and good.

After I found my cap I wandered around from area to area watching the volunteers. They were not finding anything much as far as I could tell. Walking to the rim of the mound, I noticed that Kerim was still guarding the cave entrance. I sat on the ground and threw pebbles down the slope and stared at the Bedouin camp on the plain at the base of our tell. I counted 18 black tents which Dad said were made of goatskin or woven from rough wool. Kerim lived there, so Hank had said, and I wondered if he lived inside or outside the area fenced in by cactus plants. Camels lounged inside the cactus enclosure, but some older children had taken the goats and sheep out to pasture in the foothills of the mountains.

I saw the women spinning and weaving and caring for the smaller children. From that camp the men left every morning for work—a few on the tell, others down in the rich farm valley. I wondered if the life of these Bedouin was different from the nomads I read about in the Bible. They looked as if they had lived this way thousands of years. If Kerim knew a little English, I could ask him.

By 8:30 a.m. when work stopped for our second breakfast of eggs, cheese, yogurt, tomatoes, and fruit, it was already getting hot. And I was beginning to wonder how long a month would be with 123 adults, Miss Perfect, and an Arab boy I could not understand.

3

Who Needs a Sister Around?

I WANTED TO HELP with the digging. Sure, I knew volunteers must be at least 18 years old, but since I was here I figured I could do the real work too. Mom, with a small hand trowel, was working with others in a limited square area, carefully measuring and recording each level as they dug. It looked simple enough.

"Why won't Mr. Mac let me be a dirt archaeologist and help dig, Mom? Maybe I could find something exciting—a whole pottery bowl, coins, or an old tool—or something."

Mom wiped her face on a blouse sleeve. "You're really too young, Jeff, but whether or not you can help may depend on how responsible you can prove to be."

I picked up a rock and flung it angrily off the

side of the tell. I did not want to have to prove myself to anybody. I was having a hard enough time trying to get my parents to trust me.

"Why don't you suggest to them that I can help?"

"I can't tell them. You must show them by being careful with chores, attending the evening lectures, and—"

"Then, I might as well give up."

"I didn't mean to discourage you, Jeff. There are lots of things you can do. How about getting a goofer bucket to collect discards for us? We have a lot of dirt and stones to move out of here."

On my way back to the sheds at the other end of the tell, I walked the rim and checked the cave entrance again. Kerim was not there! I ran down the hill. At the entrance I stopped and listened. No sounds reached me. I stepped inside to see if I could find Dad and the other workers. As I moved cautiously ahead, the cave curved suddenly and plunged me into darkness.

I stopped and listened again but could hear only my heart thudding against my chest. I drank from my *ibrik* and wiped the sweat off my face with my shirttail. Sliding my feet on the ground, I inched along perhaps three more steps. I could not see my hand two inches in front of my face. I thought about Carol, the blind girl in my school back home, and wondered if her blindness was as black as this cave. I turned around and trudged back to the entrance. The bright sunlight blinded me in a different way.

"Scaredy-cat!"

Jennifer stared down at me from the top of the tell.

"Quit following me around! Go back to the tents."

"I don't want to!"

If I made her go she would run crying to Mom and, as usual, Mom would think I should look out for her. Being a big brother sure is a pain—in more ways than one. I couldn't let her see that the dark cave really had scared me.

"Listen, Jenni-*fur*, have you been drinking water like you're supposed to?"

She straightened proudly. "Nope!"

"Didn't you hear what Mr. McDowell said last night?" I asked as I climbed the hill to her.

"What?"

"About how the sizzling sun dehydrates us and we have to keep an *ibrik* of water with us all the time and drink, drink, drink. Why aren't you doing it?"

"I dunno."

I handed her my *ibrik*. "Drink!"

She did, her big brown eyes wide and questioning. I better scare her plenty so she would remember what to do.

"If you let the sun shrink all the water out of you, you'll turn into a goofer!"

That made me remember Mom's request for a goofer bucket so I lit out for the gate and the supply sheds. Jennifer ran along right behind me.

"What do you mean, 'goofer'?"

"Just what I said."

"I don't want to be a goofer!" she wailed.

"You see this bucket? It's to pick up goofers!"

"How do you know?"

"I just know," I said, feeling important. "You ask Mom. She'll tell you this is a goofer bucket."

Jennifer grabbed my *ibrik* and drank to the bottom. "There!"

"Yeah, well, fill it up and bring it to me at Mom's square."

I ran down the length of the tell to deliver the bucket. I was relieved that Mom didn't say anything about the delay; she just pointed to the pile of debris that needed to be dumped in the nearby wheelbarrow. I started to work. Without my water supply it seemed that the sun was concentrating on me. Sweat dripped off my nose.

When I had filled the wheelbarrow, I pushed it to the dump pile. Since there was no shade tree, I plopped down on a big rock and gazed out over the plain toward Tel Aviv 15 miles away. I sniffed the air for a Mediterranean Sea breeze and snuffed up dusty heat instead. Off in the opposite direction were the mountains we had driven through yesterday.

I was beginning to like this land. It felt different, I guess, because people had lived here for so many thousands of years.

Dad told me that the month before we arrived, the archaeological team had discovered some 15th century B.C. burial mounds in the cave. That seemed like a long time ago, but groups of peoples had lived here as long as 2,800 years before the birth of Christ. That meant people had been right here where I was sitting almost 4,000 years ago. Fire or disease or hostile tribes might cause the people to leave; then maybe for 100 years or more no one would live here. Later the city would be rebuilt. I could hardly believe King Solomon had lived here about 950 years before Jesus lived in this land.

I wondered if the sun was this hot back in those days. Maybe that's why King David sang, "He leads me beside still waters." I supposed the *sun* hadn't changed much. It gave me a sort of funny feeling that I was living where once King Solomon had lived and in the land of David. It made them *real*!

Jennifer appeared, drank from my *ibrik* she was carrying, and handed it to me.

"Why don't you carry your own *ibrik*?" I asked as she sat on the ground beside me.

"You can share, Jeff. You want a goofer for a sister?"

I gulped down the water. "Sometimes I don't want a sister around," I said crossly.

154

Her brown eyes widened. So what? Sometimes I felt just like that. Why couldn't I say it?

"Here!"

She dropped into my hand a curved piece of pottery which fit exactly into my palm. It was a glazed piece painted red. The designs looked like stick figures with a round ball and spokes standing out from it. Could that be a sun? It was the prettiest piece I had seen yet and she was giving it to me.

"Is this another one you dug out of the discard pile?"

She nodded and reached over to rub it with her thumb. Her soft brown hair brushed my cheek and her arm felt cool against mine. I held the pottery carefully and mumbled, "Thanks, Jen."

She stuck her chin in the air. "I'm giving it to you, Jeff, even though you don't like me. And I don't like you a bit either for what you said."

She stamped off, her small body stiff and proud. I rubbed the pottery with my finger. It was a fantastic piece and I didn't deserve it. I tucked it carefully in my shirt pocket; tonight I would keep it under my pillow.

4

Kerim

I DID NOT WANT JENNIFER TO LEAVE after giving me this sherd so I called to her.

She stopped but didn't turn around.

"Come on back and sit beside me."

"OK." She hesitated, then bounced back as if she had forgotten all about our fuss. I hoped so.

A jet plane passed overhead, and she pointed to it. "*That* doesn't belong here!"

"It sure does," I said, eager to show off some of my knowledge. I tried to mock Dad's teacher voice. "Israel is just as modern as it is ancient. I bet Tel Aviv is as modern as Chicago."

"But look at the moabs down there!"

"Not moabs, Jen. Nomads! Bedouin. Can you say Bed-oh-in?"

"Yep. Bed-oh-in. What are Bed-oh-in?"

"They are people who move their families and

animals wherever they can find work and water. They don't live in one place all the time."

"Like the migrants that come to Illinois every summer?"

"Not exactly. Maybe like shepherds in the old days that were led to still waters." I was thinking about King David's song.

We sat and looked around us for a while. I finally said, "It's quiet here. Makes it hard to believe fighting is going on in other parts of Israel."

"Fighting? Is that why we saw soldiers in Jerusalem?"

"I guess so."

"Why are they fighting, Jeff?"

"I don't know exactly. Something about the Arabs living here for hundreds of years in this country they called Palestine. Then the United Nations gave Palestine to the Jewish people about 30 years ago and they call it Israel."

"My New Testament says the Jews lived here when Jesus did. He was a Jew."

"Sure, they lived here hundreds of years, too."

"Then what's the fuss?"

"Well, a lot of Arab guerrillas are trying to get their land back. And I guess the land really belongs to both sides."

"Gorillas? Real live gorillas? Like in a zoo?"

"For Pete's sake, Jen, these guerrillas are people. They fight other people."

"Are all Arabs gorillas?"

"Of course not, silly. Lots of Arabs live in Israel who aren't guerrillas. Kerim is an Arab."

"I don't understand. Nobody fights here. Everybody likes everybody."

"Yeah, we're all working together—the Bedouin Arabs, Jewish Israelis, and us Christians—and Jews—from other countries."

Jennifer pulled her cap down over her eyes. "Aren't the Arabs Christian?"

"Silly, they're Muslims." I was glad to get off the guerrilla subject because I had told her everything I knew.

"I'm not silly! We visited an Arab Lutheran hospital in Jerusalem. And Lutherans are Christians!"

I remembered that visit, but it was hard for me to give up my old idea that all Arabs were Muslims. I wondered if Kerim were a Muslim or a Christian. I surely was interested in him—partly because I wanted to figure out a way to talk with him—but mostly because he had kept me from entering the cave. I still wanted to know why.

"Jeff! Jennifer! Come here!" Mr. Nebergall, one of the field supervisors, was waving to us. We raced each other to the cooking shed.

"How about ringing everyone to dinner?"

"Oh, boy!" Jennifer grabbed a shovel leaning against the wall and swung at the long artillery shell which hung from the corner of the roof. She missed.

158

"I never saw a dinner gong like that!" she pouted.

"It's left over from the 1967 war," Mr. Nebergall said in a solemn tone. "Somehow I like its present use better—calling all of us from many countries to meals three times a day."

Jennifer did not miss the second time. The artillery shell bonged loud and clear all across the tell and probably over the plain and in and out of the mountains. The way she held that shovel you'd think she had just slain a giant.

I held my ears. "I'm deaf!"

"I want to do it again!"

Mr. Nebergall took the shovel. "There'll be other times. Thanks for helping."

"OK."

"Race you to the sinks!" Jennifer challenged me.

Kid games. She dashed off but I walked slowly toward the long row of metal lavatories to wash my hands. The tin roof over them gave little relief from the noon heat. Suddenly I realized it was smart to work in the early morning coolness and quit at noon before we fainted.

I wondered if I threw a handful of water into the air if it would evaporate before it could hit the ground. I wouldn't dare try it; our water supply was too precious. In fact, we were required to have a two weeks' supply of clothes so that instead of washing them here at the end of a week, our dirty clothes could be sent into Jerusalem to be washed. The water in our supply tanks was only for drinking and for washing ourselves and the pottery we unearthed. Nothing else— especially crazy experiments with heat.

I glanced into the tiny mirror when I finished washing and saw Kerim coming up from behind.

"Hi!" I said as he washed his hands next to me.

"Hello!"

I nearly fell off the tell. "Can you speak English?"

"I understand a little English," he said as if feeling out every word. His hair, in black wet waves, was plastered to his head. His dark eyes met mine in the mirror.

My words tumbled out. "Why didn't you talk to me at the cave? Why did you keep me out? Why—"

"I do not understand."

I drew a picture of the cave entrance in the air and repeated the same motions he had used when he signaled me to leave.

"Cave—" I said.

"Cave? The cave, you say, is there." He pointed toward the other side of the tell.

"I know—I know. But I want you to tell me—"

He shook his head violently. "I do not understand."

I decided he understood a lot more than he let on. During rest time after lunch, I meant to pump

*Kerim stuffed some bread and fruit inside his
shirt when he thought nobody was looking.*

all the information I could about the cave from Dad.

I hardly knew what I ate. After lunch I saw Kerim stuff some bread and fruit in his shirt when he thought nobody was looking.

When Dad herded us off to our tent after lunch, Kerim ran down the side of the tell in the direction of the cave. I wanted to run after him. Instead I stumbled into a wheelbarrow and fell sprawling.

Jennifer giggled. "Better watch where you're going!"

"Why didn't you warn me?"

"I don't like you. Remember?"

Nobody, not even Jen, forgot my faults.

She picked up the pottery sherd she had given me which had fallen out of my shirt pocket and handed it to me. I rubbed my thumb over it as she had done earlier.

"Race you to the tent!" she said.

I decided to let her beat me. After all, I would never get to be a dirt archaeologist if I ended up with a sunstroke my first day out.

5

The Cave

THE TENTS WERE ENORMOUS. I dreaded having to stay in ours for four hours. It was probably oven hot. I grabbed a towel and went for a cool shower. The shower stalls did not have any roofs—I wanted to glare at the sun. It was ruining my afternoon.

When I returned, a cool breeze off the Mediterranean Sea was sifting through the netting on the rolled-up sides of the tent.

"I bet the oak tree in our backyard would do wonders for this tell," I said as I plopped on my cot and gazed at the sky through the net patterns. The breeze felt as refreshing as the misty spray from Yosemite Falls when we had visited there once. I couldn't believe it could be so nice.

I scored zero with Dad when I asked him about the cave. They were working by lamplight deep inside, he said, to uncover more burial places *if* they existed. He had noticed nothing strange about the cave.

"That Arab boy acts like he's guarding it."

"You have an active imagination, Jeff, and I must remind you again that you may not venture alone inside the cave. If you want to, you may go with me tomorrow and see the excavations."

"OK." I'd settle for getting inside any way I could.

"What does Kerim do in the cave?" I asked.

There was no answer. Dad was breathing heavily, already disgustingly sound asleep. So was Jennifer.

Mom was busy straightening up her clothes and getting suitcases out of the way under the cots. "Why are you so interested in the cave?" she asked.

"I dunno."

"Now, Jeff—"

"I *heard* Dad, Mom! I'm not to go in alone."

"And don't go off anywhere else either without telling someone. Sometimes you're too impulsive for your own good."

I flipped over on my stomach, facing the net wall.

"Is something the matter?" Mom asked.

I closed my eyes.

"If you talk about it, maybe you'll find out things aren't as bad as they seem," she said.

Things were bad all right. Either she or Dad or Jen always managed to say something to let me know I had not lived down last year's troubles yet. I probably never would. . . . She and Dad did not trust me because one night last year I had left Jennifer by herself when they were gone for a couple of hours. They had depended on me to stay with her till they returned, but I had sneaked out. I didn't think Jennifer would even know I was gone but when I got back home and saw how frightened she was, it scared me too. Worst of all was the disappointment in Mom and Dad's eyes. The only thing Dad did was to put his arm across my shoulder and say, "I never thought you'd do something like this, Jeff."

I wish he had punished me instead.

Mom's voice broke into my memories. "Jeff, can't you talk—"

"No, I can't because you don't trust me!" I exploded.

Mom was silent a long time. When she spoke her soft voice seemed to blend with the cool breeze.

"The question isn't whether *we* trust you," she said.

"It's whether or not you trust yourself."

"Why didn't you say anything last year when I left Jennifer by herself?"

"Did we have to?"

"I would have known for sure how you felt."

"Didn't you?"

I did. That's what made me feel miserable. Would trusting myself make me feel better? I flopped over and looked at Mom.

She smiled. "You think about what I said."

"OK." I would think about it, but would it change anything? I took the pottery sherd from King Solomon's ancient city out of my pocket. I rubbed it against my cheek and felt its coolness and glazed smoothness. I would lie here the whole afternoon and *think*. How do I learn to trust myself? Anyway, who could sleep from one until four o'clock? That was for infants and tired grown-ups.

When I woke up and realized I had slept through the whole rest period, I was really disgusted. Now it was time for the late afternoon chores and I had not been thinking a bit.

I wished Kerim had been selected for my work team when the group was divided up. But he wasn't. The team I was on washed pottery which was found that day. It had been gathered into buckets according to area and field.

I liked the job of washing pottery best of all. Sometimes it was hard to clean so we used all sizes of brushes—from hand brushes down to tiny toothbrushes to scrub away the dirt. A piece completely crusted over with dirt would often turn out to be beautiful. I played guessing games to figure out what might be under the crust. Running my fingers over the clean sherds, I felt the lines of their design and traced the base rims of bowls and examined lips of vases with my fingers as well as my eyes.

Here in my own hand, I thought, is pottery someone made thousands of years ago. Perhaps it was someone like me or Kerim or Jennifer.

After we had washed the sherds, we laid each one out on the proper pile on straw mats to dry. Each pile came from the same location on the tell.

Jennifer finished her chore of picking up paper and other trash. She and Kerim were watching Mr. McDowell, Mr. Nebergall, and the other archaeologists. When I finished I joined them. Kerim nodded to me but said nothing.

The men were seated around a table "reading" the pottery which was already dry. They dated it—sometimes in a particular century, sometimes even a specific date. I eagerly watched their busy fingers. Mr. Mac especially, since he was the pottery expert, could "read" a whole pile in a few minutes.

The pottery which was not discarded was marked for identification and stored in labeled boxes for further study. From a few pieces a whole bowl or pitcher could be reconstructed in the laboratory in Jerusalem.

Kerim was on one of the teams putting the identifying marks on the sherds with India ink. His numbering was clear and even. I studied his brown hands while his fingers handled the pottery sherds as mine had done earlier to clean them. He glanced at me once.

"The cave," I whispered.

He went back to his work as if I didn't exist.

6

A "Dirt" Archaeologist

STREAKS OF RED AND LAVENDER RADIATED across the Mediterranean Sea. Mom said the sun arranged its spectacular exit—as if it hated to give up its power to the evening coolness. We gazed at the brilliant colors and listened to the evening lecture.

I knew better than to miss the lecture if I wanted a chance to "dig" rather than remain the errand boy. I learned that teams of archaeologists and volunteers like my parents had been working 10 or 12 summers to uncover this layer cake of history.

About halfway through Mr. Nebergall's slide show on the tell's history, I nudged Jennifer. "Hey, this helps me figure out the meaning to some of the stones and holes we saw today."

"Me too—a little," she said.

169

A layer of dung ash, for instance, indicated that fires had once been built on that spot. It was a ground level of some ancient time, and that time could be calculated by the experts. I wondered if the Bedouins at the base of the tell used animal dung for fire as our ancestors did?

Mr. Nebergall's slides included pictures of a burial site containing skeletons, pottery, coins, and jewelry; of walls and gates dating from various times in the city's history; and ancient altars of worship. A row of huge stones might have been altars erected at a gathering of several nomadic tribes. A small stone, probably used as an incense burner, was designed with a crude stick figure that was holding spears or lightning rods over his head.

"This figure may depict the god Baal," Mr. Nebergall explained. "Worship of the god Baal did take place here at various times. You will remember that the Israelites accused King Solomon in his old age of being too tolerant of those who worshiped idols. This stone may have been placed on a Baal altar."

The figure was similar to the ones on my sherd. But several figures—rather than only one—had been carved on my pottery piece, not holding spears but holding hands like paper doll cutouts. I punched Jennifer and whispered, "Are you sure you got this off the discard pile?"

"You can trust me."

Her answer hit a sore spot with me, so I punched her again.

"I'm gonna tell Mom!" she retorted.

"If you do—"

Dad put his hand on my shoulder.

"Dad says get quiet, Jennifer."

"I'm not talking!"

Dad's hand weighed heavier on my shoulder. Mr. Nebergall was still talking about Baal worship. While I listened I also wondered about my sherd. What if it had become a discard by mistake? I couldn't stand to give it up.

By the time the lecture was over, I could have slept on the bare rocks but I wasn't about to let anybody know it. And four o'clock was coming just as early tomorrow morning. I managed to brush my teeth and wash my face and hands at one of the sinks. I hung around listening to people talking for a while, then poked along slowly toward the rows of sleeping tents, glad that ours was nearby. It was getting dark, and the moon was rising. In the distance the lights of Tel Aviv sparkled like the stars overhead.

I could see Kerim walking home to the Bedouin camp. He looked so alone out there by himself. He passed all the black tents huddled close to the earth and entered the gate in the cactus enclosure. Inside where he lived it was dark—like the cave. I hoped he didn't bump noses with a camel. I also hoped his mother was waiting up for him.

171

When I crawled into my cot the dogs from the Bedouin camp were howling. A plane from a nearby air base roared overhead. In the quiet that followed, Dad suggested that we each think about what had impressed us on our first full day in the wilderness of Israel and each select a passage from the Bible to read aloud. I was always impatient at home when we read the Bible at the supper table, but here in the land where the Bible people lived, the writings seemed to come alive.

For my passage I should have selected "Honor thy father and mother" although I would have changed the word "honor" to "obey" because I kept having secret dreams about getting into the cave.

Instead, I read the 23rd Psalm of David because I would like nothing better than lying down beside still waters. Then I turned to my New Testament and read Jesus' words, "I am the bread of life; he who comes to Me shall not hunger, and he who believes in Me shall never thirst."

"I'm sunbaked on this dry land," I said to give my impression of our first day here. "And I'm never again going to take a drink of water for granted."

The next morning Dad suggested that I go to the cave with him after our second breakfast at 8:30. By seven o'clock I decided 8:30 would never arrive. To pass the time I delivered messages back and forth to field supervisors, carried tools, refilled *ibriks*. I even helped clean the latrines; at least *that* daily job was passed around among everyone. Back and forth across the tell I went. Each time I passed over the cave area, I walked along the rim and looked down the hillside at the entrance. I could not get a glimpse of Dad, Kerim, or anyone else.

I walked over and watched Hank break up some rocks with a pick.

"What's on your mind?" he asked.

"There's not going to be an 8: 30 this morning," I replied.

"Maybe so." He pounded on a good-sized rock and split it. The largest piece tumbled over my way.

"Just throw it on the wheelbarrow to go to the dump," he said.

I picked it up. "Hey, look! There are deep grooves on four sides of this rock!"

Hank put his pick down and came over.

I said, "I think we ought to take it to Mr. Mac."

"Go ahead. Probably nothing to it."

I had heard Dad say you don't decide anything is worthless when you're digging, particularly if you aren't the expert. I lugged the huge rock a good city block back to the other end of the tell and deposited it on the "reading" table.

It turned out that the rock was a form for molding tools. Hot metal was poured into the mold,

Mr. Nebergall explained. A handle would be fit into it and held in place by a groove carved in rock. Two molds looked like chisels, another a spearhead.

"Young man, you have sharp eyes," Mr. McDowell said. "We are indebted to you that this did not go on the junk pile."

"Thank you, Sir." I was so excited I could hardly speak.

Mr. Mac pulled on his thick black beard. "I must admit, Jeff, that I had doubts about children as young as you and your sister being here on the dig. But I want you to know that we're glad you came with your parents." He didn't look stern at all now.

"Maybe I can be a 'dirt archaeologist' someday too," I said. I did not add that I hoped it would be soon.

I liked the way Mr. Mac laughed. It was as if we shared something special between us. I gazed long and hard once again at "my" rock and ran off to tell Hank and Mom and Jennifer. I watched where I was going this time and didn't fall sprawling over the wheelbarrows.

7

A Flicker of Light

DON'T FORGET YOUR *IBRIK*!" Dad called. "You'll need it as much in the cave as up here in the sun."

I filled my *ibrik,* spilling some of our precious water in my haste. I ran ahead of Dad and as I started down the hillside, my foot slipped on some pebbles. I slid on my seat all the way to the bottom and came to a stop near the entrance to the cave.

"I didn't break it!" I yelled and held up the *ibrik* for Dad to see.

"Are *you* OK?"

"I think so." But sliding down the stair rail at home was more fun. I rubbed my sore seat.

"I'll lead the way," Dad said, flicking on his big flashlight.

The big mouth of the cave looked like it belonged to an angry giant. I entered the cave more cautiously than I had yesterday. I knew it curved away suddenly into pitch blackness. I shuddered when I lost the sun's direct rays.

"What's the matter, Jeff?" Dad asked. "You haven't been so quiet since we arrived."

"The cave seems to be telling me to shut up."

"We must walk quite a distance before we reach the burial places you saw in the pictures last night. Just because you can't see for miles doesn't mean you need to be jumpy about the underground. I won't run off and leave you," Dad said.

I knew that. After he had told me I couldn't enter alone, he wouldn't leave me for a second, I bet. Not that I wanted him to. I reached out and felt the sandy rock walls and felt a coolness seep into my skin. I could not tell Dad it was Kerim's strange behavior that made the cave seem mysterious. He would probably explain it all away, and I would be left with nothing. Whether the cave held something or nothing mysterious, I wanted to find that out for myself.

We made a turn to the left, and voices echoed through the cave. Sounds of shovels and brushes and scoops rolled out from the distance. Lantern light gleamed. Then we saw Dad's teammates already back at work. First Dad showed me the 15th and 14th century B. C. burial places which had been uncovered earlier in the summer.

"Where are the pottery and jewelry we saw in the pictures?" I asked.

"In Jerusalem. That Egyptian or Phoenician vase and the alabaster pedestal vase were beautiful after they were cleaned up, weren't they?"

Having scrubbed on sherds, I knew the hard work involved in getting to the beauty of those vases. "I just saw them in the picture," I said. "I wish I could have *felt* them."

Dad laughed. "I agree with you!"

He introduced me to Tim and Sally, a couple from a university in Tennessee.

"We've got tons of chunky debris to move out of here," Sally said. "You look like a good strong worker. You're hired!"

I glanced at Dad with hope.

He put his hand on my shoulder. "He's on a tour right now, Sally. Then he'll go back topside. He isn't 18, so you can't hire him unless Mr. Mac approves."

Sally mopped her forehead dramatically. "Even in the wilderness we have to fight the Establishment!"

Everybody laughed, and I asked why they must move so much rubble out. Tons sounded like an awful lot.

Sally grinned and winked at me. "We're going to find water in this here desert, if we have to dig to China."

"But Mr. Mac said there's a good year-round water supply."

Tim said, "What we're actually digging for is

more tombs which we believe are underneath us."

I studied the bones and skulls laid out on the burial mound. One tall figure and one small, perhaps a child, and lots of bones piled up in a corner as if they had been pushed aside to make room for the two stretched out. When I suggested that to Dad, he said I was exactly right.

My eyes were used to the dim light now and I gazed around in every direction from the small chamber that opened up from the passageway we had come through. There were goofer buckets, shovels, scoops and brushes of all sizes, and

screens—the same tools they had on top of the tell. Everything looked quite ordinary. Suddenly my blood felt like carbonated water racing through my veins. Imagine the thought of a 3,500-year-old burial mound being ordinary!

Tim said, "Hello, Kerim. I need you."

I turned. Kerim passed me with a swift glance in my direction.

"Hi!" I said.

"Hello." He wasn't too friendly. Maybe it was because of the language barrier. Maybe.

"Kerim, you look pale. You're not getting

"You look like a good strong worker," said Sally.
"You're hired!"

enough sun," Sally said, as if he could understand her perfectly.

"I am fine, Miss Sally."

"Hey!" I exclaimed. "You *do* know English!"

"Only a little."

"A little, my hind foot! He knows *a lot*," Sally said. "He's just being modest."

"Please, Miss Sally."

"OK, I won't embarrass you, Kerim. But remember that he who runneth down himself will be runneth down by everybody!"

I laughed right out loud.

"I hate to mention it," one of the other workers said, "but we're getting nowhere fast."

"Come on, Jeff, I must get to work. I'll walk you back through the cave," Dad said. "Maybe you can come back another day."

"Right! I'm going to see about hiring you," Sally added.

"If you don't need the flashlight," I said to Dad, "why don't I just walk back by myself? If there was just one way in, then there's just one way out."

"Smart thinking there, Jeff!" That Sally was fun.

Just when I thought I might make Dad forget that I was not to walk in the cave alone, Kerim offered to walk back with me. I wondered why. There must be more to the cave than I had seen.

Kerim walked ahead with the flashlight,

surefooted as one who had walked the path many times. I wanted to ask him why he had stuffed food in his pockets yesterday, but I didn't dare. He was silent and so was I. Here was my chance to talk with him alone and I muffed it. His straight back looked forbidding.

We turned to the right. "Uh, Kerim, uh, did I see all of the cave?"

There was a long silence. Finally he answered, "I do not know what you saw."

I was tired of his little games—pretending he could not understand me yesterday, keeping me out of the cave, being shifty about answering my question.

"For Pete's sake, we walked down this way from the entrance and ended up where you are all working. And all I want to know is if there're any other parts to this cave?"

He shrugged. "Who knows?"

"I bet you do!"

He said nothing.

"The entrance is to the right," he said finally.

I saw only black nothingness ahead and stared into it. He stepped aside and motioned for me to pass.

"You turn right here and you will see light from the day."

I stepped forward where the cave curved to the entrance. Its yawning mouth was bright now instead of dark. For some reason I didn't want to walk toward it and have to admit to myself that the cave was just a plain ordinary cave and that its only mysteries were thousands of years old. So I looked across from where we stood. If we had turned right instead of curving left when we entered the cave, where would it have taken us?

I blinked. Had I imagined a pinpoint of light in that direction? Now there was only midnight blackness. I blinked again and this time there could be no mistake. A tiny flicker of light rose and faded in an instant.

I turned and stared at Kerim but I kept silent. Suddenly I was afraid to say anything.

8

Jeff's Discovery

KERIM WAS SHAKING HIS HEAD. I guessed he meant for me to be quiet. I felt in my pants pocket for my sherd and held it tightly.

I finally found my voice; it had become a whisper. "Are—are you coming outside with me?"

He shook his head again. "You do not need me. I wait here for you to leave. Then I return to work with my team."

His voice sounded pretty normal. Maybe he did not see the flicker of light.

"Go now. We have much work to do."

"Tell my father that I didn't go anywhere by myself," I said. Suddenly I wanted very much to talk with Dad.

"Of course you obey your father. Every boy obeys his father."

That was a help. It sounded as definite as an umpire's decision.

"See you!" I said and ran toward the light.

The sun about struck me down. My *ibrik* of water! I had left it in the cave. I stood in the entrance and wondered what to do. Should I go back to the curve and call Kerim? But whatever caused that flicker of light might hear me. Why not go back? I wouldn't be so far behind Kerim that I could not see by his light. I tiptoed back to the curve and looked down the passageway. I saw nothing. How could Kerim have gone down that long passageway so quickly? No flicker showed up behind me to the right of the entrance. Had I been seeing things? I blinked but saw nothing. I ran back to the sunlight, then pulled off my shirt, wiped my face with it, and tied it around my waist.

When I turned and glanced up the side of the tell, I saw Jennifer sitting on the top waving at me.

"I'm waiting for you," she called.

Nosy. I climbed the hill and lay down on my stomach on top of the tell, covering my face in the crook of my elbow.

"What happened, huh? What'd you do? What'd you see? Come on, Jeff—"

"Will you leave me alone, please?"

"Just for that you don't get any of my water!" She hugged her *ibrik*.

"Don't threaten!" It felt really good to be fuss-

184

ing with Jennifer after my scare in the cave. Safe, that's how it felt.

"Why did you come outside twice?" she asked.

"Quit bugging me."

"Why?"

"So I can think!"

"Wow! Imagine that!"

The rocky ground began to hurt. I sat up and brushed off my chest and stomach. "Jennifer, do you want to go in the cave?"

"We don't have a flashlight. Anyway, I'm scared."

"There's nothing to be scared of, I tell you." I was telling myself too.

"I'm scared of the dark."

"Since when?"

"Since right now!"

Somebody was calling my name. It was Mr. Mac. Jennifer tagged right along with me.

"We need you to fill *ibriks,* Jeff. You can help, Jennifer. And Area Two needs another goofer bucket and hand trowel."

For the rest of the morning I didn't have a minute to myself. When Kerim brought my *ibrik* to me at lunch, he acted as if he didn't even know me.

I tried to put the cave out of my mind. The tiny flicker of light I had seen in the dark just before I came back to the exit kept tempting me. Kerim's definite "Every boy obeys his father" didn't sound

185

so final anymore. It sounded as if you could always know what was right and what was wrong. I didn't believe that. There were many times when I didn't know what was right or wrong, and I tried to convince myself this was one of them. The cave was perfectly safe for human travel; what would be wrong with my turning to the right inside the entrance and following the flicker?

But Dad had said in his most stern voice that I was not to go in alone, so that made it wrong, I guess. If I wanted Mom and Dad to trust me, maybe I should scout around and see if I could find someone else to help me explore. Still, I wanted to find out for myself. The idea of finding someone to go with me put a terrible taste in my mouth, like much too much salt on a boiled egg.

All that day and the next went by while I tried to decide what to do. Now I was hunting for a cave plan and a counter cave plan.

The next morning Mr. McDowell came up to me at the second breakfast. "I've been watching you, Jeff," he said.

My chest got all tight. I had not gone back again to the cave alone, but I wondered if he could read my thoughts.

He pulled on his beard. "You're quite careful when you wash pottery every afternoon; you have a keen, sharp eye. The result of that is this marvelous example of a tool mold. Would you like to try your hand as a 'dirt' archaeologist this morning?"

"Oh, boy! Would I!"

"Come with me."

I followed him to the opposite end of the tell where the wall of one of Solomon's cities had been uncovered. I wanted to run all the way but decided that would not be proper for someone who was just promoted.

"We're trying to get to bedrock down the side of this wall," he said. "Do you know Chris? You'll be working with him and Hank."

Hank. The baggy-eyed one who almost tossed away the tool mold.

Chris told me we were going to use hand trowels now and move slowly. If we were to find anything, we would not want to ruin it with a shovel or pick. I was so excited I did not even mind how long it took us. Every few inches Hank took measurements and Chris wrote them in a book. Volunteers in other squares were finding pitchers and metal blades, but we found nothing important. I would be happy with *anything*.

"You're too impatient," Dad said later in our tent.

I pulled up a second blanket as the cool night breezes moved in from the sea.

"I'll be disappointed if I don't turn up anything," I said drowsily and went to sleep without dreaming about the cave.

The next morning as we dug deeper down the side of the ancient city wall, it got hotter and hotter. The tell's ground level was now over my head.

"We're digging ourselves into an oven," Hank complained.

I kept brushing with a medium-sized brush across the surface of our square area as if I knew my discovery was coming. I uncovered a grayish black layer. I rubbed my hand lightly over the grainy surface. Excitement rippled through me when I recognized what it was.

"Dung ash!" I yelled. "Three thousand years old! Isn't it *beautiful*?"

Everybody around me laughed. I did too. I would be satisfied to find *anything* at all, I had said.

While Chris measured and noted my discovery, I could just see a real live mother like mine or Kerim's, only from a long time ago, who tended this fire for those she loved.

9

Love Energy

THE NEXT DAY WAS FRIDAY. I was looking forward to two things: Dad had said I could go back to the cave that morning—Sally had convinced Mr. McDowell they could use me—and we were leaving that afternoon for a trip, since the weekends were free for travel.

Kerim fell into step beside me on the way to the cave after our peanut butter sandwich breakfast. I wondered why.

Jennifer ran up and grabbed my hand. "I'll miss you, Jeff, but you'll tell me all about it, won't you?"

"Don't get mushy!"

"Quit pulling away. I have something to give you."

I stopped and patiently waited (Dad would have been proud) and said: "What?"

She still held onto my hand. "Do you remember last year when we hiked in the desert mountains in California?"

"So what?"

"You remember how tired we got and you lay down on the desert sand and said you were dying—and how Mom squeezed our hands and said she was passing love energy to us—and how it made us laugh and not feel so tired anymore?"

"Yeah, I remember." I would never forget it.

Jennifer's big brown eyes stared up at me. "I'm just passing you some love energy, Jeff, to get you past the dark down there."

I squeezed her hand in return. "I'll tell you about the cave," I promised.

"Your sister I like," Kerim said as we walked down the hill.

Right now I did too. "Do you have sisters?"

He shook his head. "No, only two brothers. My baby sister died."

"I'm sorry."

"No, it was best. Believe me, it was best."

"Kerim, do you like this work?"

His dark eyes seemed to catch fire. "Oh, yes. I like very much."

When I asked him if he wanted to be an archaeologist someday, he said his father was only a poor Bedouin. "And I have little school. We move by the seasons to the best water supply."

"When will you leave here?"

He shrugged. "My father says perhaps we stay. He finds work in the rich valley. My brothers and I work on the tell in the spring and summer. So if we stay, one day I may go to school. But archaeologist? Oh, I would like. But no—I am afraid it is not for me."

Inside the entrance to the cave I turned to him impulsively and said, "We're going to the Sea of Galilee this weekend. Could you go with us?"

He stood dead still. "Do you mean it?"

"Of course."

"I must ask my father." He smiled for the first time since I had met him. "I think you must also ask your father."

"I will when we catch up with him. Hold that light steady, Kerim. To tell the truth, I'm a little uneasy in here—nothing tough, you know—but I keep seeing things in the blackness. In fact, the other day I thought I saw a light—"

Kerim clapped his hand over my mouth. I lost my balance and fell backward to the ground. Before I could yell at him, he was helping me up.

"You saw nothing!" he whispered fiercely.

Then in a normal voice—a monotone in fact—he said, "Forgive me. I did not mean—"

"That's OK." I brushed my clothes. "It took me by surprise and I lost my balance—that's all."

"What took you by surprise, Jeff?"

Just when I thought I was beginning to know him a little, he came up with a strange remark

191

again. I was churning inside; he had given himself away even if I didn't know why. He knew something about this cave, and I was going to find it out if it took me the whole month.

"Did you answer me, Jeff?"

I was not good at instant answers. Finally I said, "I guess I just got whammied by Jennifer's love energy."

"Yes, I understand."

"I don't!"

"Let us hurry. Miss Sally is waiting for us."

I hoped Dad was also waiting for us.

I felt jittery. Sally's teasing got on my nerves, as Mom says. I finally went over to Kerim and asked, "Why did you act so funny at the entrance?"

"I do not know what you mean."

Didn't he trust me either? Was that why he would not tell me what his strange behavior was all about? If he didn't trust me enough to tell me, I wasn't sure I wanted him to go with us for the weekend.

"You're doing a great shoveling job, Jeff. You're watching carefully and that's important," Sally said. "Say, where did you learn to shovel so well?"

Real funny. I didn't bother to answer. In a few minutes Dad moved over near me.

"It's nice to have you on our team today, Jeff."

Did I look so glum that they had to give me a

buildup? I set aside my shovel and hunted my *ibrik*; I offered it to Dad. While he drank I half-heartedly asked if Kerim could go with us on the weekend. I realized I couldn't back out after mentioning it to him. Next time I wouldn't be so quick to offer.

Dad glanced at Kerim. I could tell he was listening.

"Of course," Dad said. "When can you ask your parents, Kerim?"

"Tonight, Sir, when you are eating."

"Good! We want to leave right after dinner on the bus that's coming out to take some of us to Jerusalem. Tell your father we're going on up to the Sea of Galilee, and we'll take good care of you."

"Oh, thank you. Never in my life have I gone to Galilee."

"Neither have we," Dad said, "so we'll discover it together."

10

The Sign of the Fish

IT WAS NOT JUST BECAUSE OUR TELL was on the edge of the desert. In fact, the rich plain below the tell would not be rich without irrigation. It could not have been because we sometimes ached to shower for hours or splash in puddles. It could not have been these things that made me know the minute I saw the Lake of Galilee why Jesus had spent so much time there.

There was no breeze to wipe away the burning heat from our faces, but the heat did not matter as I gazed at the rich blue water and the Jordanian hills that rose in the distance across the lake. Once the lake had come into view, Jennifer and I had convinced Dad to stop as often as possible. Each time we waded with Kerim on the shore and felt the coolness of all that water on our feet.

It was a long day's journey before we arrived in

Capernaum after spending Friday night in Jerusalem. We had left very early in a rented car—one which Dad had arranged for through a Christian because all Jewish businesses were closed for the Sabbath.

We were there at last, walking along the shore and splashing in the shallow water and exploring the ruins of the ancient Capernaum synagogue a hundred yards away.

"This was Peter and James and John's hometown," Mom said.

It seemed strange to call this place a town when only limestone blocks and a few Corinthian columns of the synagogue remained.

I hated to leave the shore to explore the ruins, but when Dad began to talk about the synagogue remains uncovered only about 65 years ago but dating from about A. D. 200, I got excited.

"See how the blocks of native black basalt contrast sharply with the imported white limestone blocks of the synagogue," Dad pointed out.

"What about these?" I asked.

"That may well be the foundation of the first-century synagogue, the one Jesus would have preached in. You know, He began His ministry here." Dad's excitement rubbed off on me and evidently on Kerim, too.

I had been wondering all day if Kerim, since he was probably a Muslim, had been disgusted with so much talk about Christian and Jewish history.

I hoped not. Maybe I would get a chance this weekend to ask him about his faith. I wanted to know more about Muslims since Jerusalem was their holy city, too.

Now he was asking Dad a question. "Why did Jesus choose Capernaum to begin His work?"

"It may always be a mystery, Kerim," Dad said. "Capernaum was certainly an important city in Jesus' day, and most of His ministry was in the province of Galilee. I would like to know the answer to that question, too. It may lie somewhere in the remains along this shore—those not yet uncovered."

"What do you mean?"

"Just that the ancient city probably covered a mile or more along the lakeshore."

"Why hasn't it all been excavated?"

"Lack of people, money, and time, Jeff. There are centuries of archaeological work ahead."

I liked that idea. His words stirred my mind and I turned to gaze at the harp-shaped lake, called Kinneret from the Hebrew word for harp.

"I found a Star of David!" Jennifer called. It was sculptured in the white limestone.

Kerim was moving his hand over the black basalt of the earliest remains. "It feels different from the limestone," he said.

"Me-ow!"

It was the softest sound, but unmistakable. "I heard a kitten!" I exclaimed.

Nobody believed me.

"Sh!" I moved in what I thought was the direction of the sound, and then I saw a tiny black something running in the opposite direction. I dashed over the ruins and turned a corner in time to see it disappear down a hole in the side of a wall. Calling for help, I started scratching at the hard dry earth.

"That kitten—it has to be a kitten—ran down this hole. I can't see anything. I can't reach my hand any farther than *that*. Oh, for a pick or shovel!"

Dad said the animal—whatever it was—might be half a mile away by now. I said it must be in that hole. I kept digging. Jennifer and Kerim helped—all three of us on our knees scrabbling, with little results. Kerim found a stone with a sharp point to break away the dirt.

"I feel something furry! Maybe I have its tail!"

Kerim's stone made a pinging sound.

"Oh!"

When I saw what Kerim was holding, I jumped up, forgetting that I had *something* by its tail. I yanked out of the hole a screeching black kitten. He hissed and pawed, but when I stuck him in the crook of my arm he quieted down as if he thought he was back inside the hole.

Mom and Dad and Jennifer and Kerim were examining the piece of pottery he had uncovered.

"I saw a fish carved on it!" I said.

Dad held Kerim's outstretched hand which contained the pottery nestled in his palm. Dad couldn't take his eyes off it. Finally he said in a breathless voice, "Let's go wash off the dirt."

The kitten scratched my side, so I rubbed its back to calm it.

On the way to the lake we talked about how the sign of a fish became an identifying mark of a Christian.

"Why?" Jennifer asked.

"Because a lot of Jesus' followers were fishermen, and He asked them to drop their nets and become fishers of men," I said, proudly remembering a Sunday school lesson from last spring.

"Why did they need a sign? Why didn't they just *tell* each other they were Christian?"

"Get this, Jennifer, if you were being persecuted for being a Christian, would you go shouting it around? No! You'd draw a fish on the ground and if the stranger were a Christian, he would draw one back. If he weren't, he wouldn't understand what it meant. Is that clear?"

"But, Jeff, why a fish? Why not a bird?"

"I just told you." Jennifer had a way of asking just enough questions to pull out of me everything I knew about it.

"Maybe I can make it clearer," Dad said. "It was much later after Jesus' death and resurrection that Christians were punished more and more for worshiping Him. They believed He was

"There's a fish on it!"

'Jesus Christ, Son of God, Savior.' And the first letters of each of those words in the Greek language spell *FISH*. So the sign of the fish meant that that person believed Jesus was the Christ, Son of God, Savior."

"Wow, that was like a secret code!"

"They needed one, Jen, for their own safety sometimes."

"I should say so! I wouldn't want to be prosecuted—uh, persecuted—whatever that means!"

We all squatted at the water's edge and watched Kerim dip the pottery sherd into the water. While he scrubbed it with his fingers, Dad told us how some first-century fishermen's huts had been unearthed around the Sea of Galilee, where lamps were found with Christian signs of fish, lambs, or crosses in their designs.

"Those signs are all over our church," Jennifer said. "Now I know why—a little bit."

I held the black furry ball of kitten down for a drink but he drew his head into my cupped hands.

"This sherd may be very significant," Dad said.

Mom laughed shakily. "After this experience, you'll never get the archaeology bug out of your system."

"Never!" Dad said emphatically.

"It *is* a fish!" Kerim said.

Dad took his handkerchief out of his pocket, and Kerim wrapped it around the piece of pottery.

Mom emptied a small purse inside her large purse (her "walking suitcase," Dad called it), and Kerim placed it inside, almost reverently I thought.

"We'll take it to Mac and let him evaluate it," Dad said.

While the kitten snuggled down in the tail of my T-shirt, we sat on the sand and listened to Dad tell about Jesus healing the centurion's servant at Capernaum. A sudden strong wind picked up the water in leaping waves. I remembered the story of how Jesus calmed those waters for frightened fishermen caught in their boat. The breeze was like cold water washing the heat from my face.

The fish on the sherd, Dad's excited voice retelling a familiar story, the wind whipping up the waves—all these made me feel that Jesus must have thought this was the most beautiful lake in the world! I absently drew a fish design in the sand with my toes, remembering our conversation about how the early followers of Jesus had identified themselves to one another with such a sign.

I felt the sudden sensation of someone staring at me and glanced up. Kerim's dark eyes looked straight into mine as he carefully drew the shape of a fish in the sand at his feet.

11

"You Must Trust Me"

THAT MOMENT WAS OURS TO KEEP FOREVER. Neither of us spoke, but we both rose and walked together along the shore. I could not explain my happiness over his being a Christian—it was the *way* he had told me with the sign of the fish, as if we were living back in Jesus' day. There was no need to speak.

I did not know how long we had been walking when Kerim said, "About the cave—you must trust me, Jeff. That is all I can say."

I did not answer immediately.

"I'll trust you, Kerim."

It would have been much easier if he had shared more, but maybe he didn't know how. After all his strange actions and conversations, I was surprised at myself that I could give up all my suspicions just because of two fish scrawled in the sand. Was this how the followers of Jesus had felt long ago? Suddenly I felt very close to them.

We returned to Mom and Dad and Jennifer. Dad put one hand on my shoulder and one on Kerim's.

We drove south along the Sea of Galilee and spent the night at Tiberias, a town right on the shore that was built, Dad said, by Herod Antipas, son of Herod the Great, in the first century A. D. and named in honor of the Roman Emperor Tiberius.

There were hot sulphur springs here, Dad said, in what I called his teacher-happy voice over passing on his knowledge to someone else. He went into detail about the town's history, but I lost him. I was more interested in looking at the buildings and watching the people on the streets. Tiberias was a nice mixture of ancient and modern.

In the cool evening breezes we walked along the seashore; we could not stay away from the water. Sailboats were anchored in the shallows, and lights from the dwellings twinkled like stars.

Stories from the Gospels came alive because we were walking in the land where Jesus and His disciples had walked. Now as we walked along the shore at Tiberias, we recalled stories about Jesus and wondered where they occurred. Once Mom laughed and said: "We sound like we're remembering experiences that happened to us personally."

"That's the way it is with Jewish-Christian tradition," Dad said solemnly. "Their experience long ago 'happens' to us, too, because we're linked to them through faith."

I would have to think about that for a while. I gazed out across the dark water. The Sea of Galilee, or Lake Kinneret, as the Israelis called it. I liked the musical rhythm of the Hebrew word *Kinneret.*

"Kinneret," I said. "The harp lake. I like that, Mom."

"I like Sea of Galilee best," said Jennifer, stroking Something, the name we had given the kitten.

Kerim joined in. "I like them both. The name does not change the lake, does it?"

Kerim was not more than a couple of years older than I, but he seemed so wise. I wished I could be wise. Sometimes one little remark of his would bring out the meaning of whatever we were seeing or talking about.

Dad said we must tear ourselves away from the water and get back to our rooms, for a big day with a long drive was ahead of us the next day. As we walked back to the hotel, I remembered the conversation with Kerim at Capernaum. I hardly knew him and yet I promised I would trust him.

Early the next morning after breakfast, I went

out on the roof of the dwelling we had stayed in during the night. It was fun to look across the lake to the Jordanian hills on the other side, up and down the beautiful lakeshore, and over the whole town of Tiberias. Few people were out on the streets.

I was surprised to see Kerim walking down the street below me which ran in front of the hotel. Where was he going? I started to call to him and wave, but he was almost to the corner. Suddenly a young man—an Arab with a white headdress held in place with a black braid rope—came flying around the corner. He ran smack into Kerim. They each looked as if they were apologizing and going their way; then they stopped and stared.

Kerim tried to run, but the stranger grabbed him by the collar. He talked intensely while he kept his stranglehold on Kerim's collar.

"Hey!" I screeched, then jumped up and down and waved my arms.

Kerim and the stranger jerked around.

"Here I am, Kerim! On the roof!"

Kerim pulled away and ran toward our hotel while the Arab dashed around the corner and disappeared out of sight. I struck out for ground level and met Kerim at the entrance.

"Are you all right?"

Kerim tried to run, but the stranger grabbed him by the collar.

"Come with me!" He wouldn't let me say anything until we were safe in our room.

"Are you all right?" I repeated.

"Yes—yes." He seemed a little angry at my question.

"Well, that man. Who was he?"

"I do not know."

"But he acted like he knew you. And you!" I stared hard at him. "You looked like you recognized him too."

"You must believe me. I do not *know* him!"

"I'll believe you, but it sure is hard. Have you ever seen him?"

Kerim walked over to a small table in the corner and put his hand on Dad's Bible. He then returned and stood directly in front of me. "I asked you yesterday to trust me, Jeff. Will you now make another promise to me?"

"I guess so."

"Please do not mention to anyone what just happened. It is our secret. Will you agree?"

"You must have a reason." Maybe he would tell me.

"Yes, I have a reason. And one more promise?"

His dark eyes were almost slate-colored in the room's dim light. He had really been frightened; he couldn't hide that from me.

I nodded.

"If you ever find somewhere a drawing of a fish—" he paused.

207

I nodded again, my throat suddenly tight.

"You will know by it that danger is near."

"What must I do?"

"You must get help at once, and you must find me."

"Do you mean *you* are in danger?"

"I do not know. I want a signal with you. That's all."

"S-sure, Kerim. But—but if you feel that way, maybe you better not go off by yourself like you did just now."

"I do not intend to."

He sat down on a cot. I sat on another one, feeling sick to my stomach.

We waited for my parents to return from breakfast.

We explored the archaeological excavations out on the mound in Tiberias, believed to be the ruins of the Biblical city of Hammath (which means "hot-spring," for the healing hot sulphur springs, Dad told us). Ruins of a fourth-century A. D. synagogue contained a beautiful mosaic floor. But I was not interested in any of it. I could not get my mind off Kerim and his encounter in the morning with the Arab. I kept trying to figure out for myself who the man might have been. He had looked pretty young. And how did Kerim know anybody in Tiberias?

A fish—"danger is near," Kerim had said. Did

the cave back at our tell have anything to do with this danger?

I shivered when I saw a troop of Israeli youth march in the street. "They're part of a military training program," Mom said.

"They don't look old enough to be soldiers," Jennifer said.

"Their country is in danger. All Israelis are obligated to protect it."

Danger.

"Is that because the Arabs want their land back?"

"Partly, Jennifer. But it's much more complicated than that."

Dad glanced at his watch. "We must leave now if we are to get back to Jerusalem in time to catch our bus to the tell."

I hated to leave the harp-shaped lake, Galilee. But I think Kerim was as relieved as I was that we got away from Tiberias without seeing the Arab again.

12

Distant Gunfire

WHEN WE RETURNED TO THE TELL everything was different. In the first place, we could hear gunfire in the distance. A few volunteers had talked about limited guerrilla fighting by the Arab Palestinians earlier in the summer, but we had seen none of it since we arrived. I had never heard real guns before.

"I'm scared!"

"You're just a baby, Jennifer. Why don't you be strong like the Israeli kids? They didn't get the name *sabra* for nothing." But I was scared too.

"What's that mean?"

"A *sabra* is a cactus, Jen," Mom said quietly. "A kind that is all prickly on the outside, but the fruit inside is very sweet."

Dad added, "*Sabra* also means a hedge of thorns."

"You mean the kids are like a thorn hedge or a cactus? I don't get it!"

"It's a symbolic meaning, sweetheart—that is, they're good defenders, they adapt well to the sunbaked land—"

"I wouldn't like to be called a cactus!" Jennifer said.

"You would if you were sweet inside!"

Mom reproved me with a stiff glance.

"I must go home," Kerim said. He thanked my father and mother for the trip. He shook Jennifer's hand and gripped mine.

"Remember!" he whispered cautiously.

I nodded. My stomach tightened up like a dried apricot. "Are you sure you'll be safe? Don't you want us to walk home with you?"

"No, it is not far. I will go alone."

Jennifer, who had latched onto our kitten all afternoon, held it out gently. "You take Something with you for company and bring him back tomorrow."

He stroked the kitten on the head. "Please keep her with you. I have a brown one at home who sleeps with me every night."

Jennifer smiled. "I'm glad you told me. But if you need Something anytime, you'll ask, won't you?"

"Yes, I'll ask."

"Kerim, it was our pleasure to have you, and I will stand here and watch you walk across the

211

plain," Dad said. "Please tell your father thank you for sharing you with us this weekend."

Kerim's smile spread all over his face. Then he ran down the hillside. It was twilight, and gunfire echoed against the mountains. I stood with Dad until Kerim was safe inside the Bedouin camp.

Most of the tell's volunteers came from the United States with a few from other countries. We all acted jittery. Everyone was talking about the past war, the Palestinian guerrillas, and didn't the guns sound closer now?

The Israelis and Arabs in the group did not pay much attention. They were concerned but they were also used to guerrilla outbreaks, they said; it was a part of living here. No guerrillas had come as far into the interior as the tell (since most of the shelling was on the borders), so everyone could calm down and go about business as usual. It did not pay to go out looking for trouble, Mr. Nebergall said, and particularly where guerrillas were concerned. They could be anywhere—like grasshoppers in the fields. One just learned to live as if his enemy were miles away—or next door.

"I want to know why there's fighting," Jennifer demanded. "Nobody here has enemies; at least, I sure don't."

Mr. McDowell set Jennifer on his knee. "How about a lesson on Israel's history?"

"Okay."

212

I needed it too, but this would be a good time to show my pottery sherd to one of the archaeologists to be sure it was okay for me to keep it. I couldn't bear to think of giving it up, but I didn't want to keep it if it was valuable to the work on the tell. Besides, I wanted to get my mind off guns and guerrillas and anything else that had made the tell so different over the weekend.

I dug the sherd out of my pocket and took it to Mr. Nebergall.

"Son, you look sick."

"Yes, Sir. I mean, my sister found this on the discard pile. She gave it to me our first day here."

"What do you want to know about it?"

"I want to know if it got on the discard pile by mistake."

He took the piece and handled it carefully, lovingly almost. He looked at me as if he were trying to make up his mind about what to say or how to break the news to me.

"Is that all you wanted to know about it?"

"Yes, Sir, it is. I know you could tell me a lot more—probably date it. It's quite old, isn't it?"

He grinned. "A few thousand."

"And you could explain the stick figures—"

"Maybe."

"And you could explain the sun—isn't it a sun glaring down on the figures?"

He turned it this way and that. "Is that what you believe?"

"Yes. And you could tell me about the glaze but—but—"

"But what?" He seemed very patient.

"But I don't really want you to. I want to put my own meaning to it, don't you see? And I want to 'read' it for myself someday. I want to know enough someday to date it myself—and all those other things you do when you read pottery."

"Do you really?"

"Yes, I do." I stood up straight and took a deep breath, surprising myself at all that I was admitting.

"This piece means a great deal to you."

"Yes."

He motioned me to a table where we washed pottery late every afternoon. I sat on a bench beside him.

"I want to show you something." His long fingers rubbed the sherd. He showed me its curve and traced the lip of the piece and then the opposite edge where a rim or base was located on one corner. He showed me how, with some indication of the base and the lip, I could follow out the curve's measurement and reconstruct a bowl the exact size of the original.

"You must come to the laboratory if you are in Jerusalem next weekend," he said. "You will be able to see some of our workers actually reconstructing pots or bowls or vases from such a beginning as this piece."

214

"Could we visit?"

"Of course."

"Then this must be a valuable piece."

"Yes," he admitted. "It is most valuable to you. I can see into your future, I think, and I believe you are going to reconstruct that bowl—and perhaps not too long from now. How old are you, Jeff?"

"I'm 12, going on 13." I added, "going on 13," like my mother does when she wakes me at 4:05 and says it's "going on 5:00."

Mr. Nebergall placed the sherd gently into my palm. He said, "Jewish boys have a religious ceremony, a bar mitzvah, when they're 13 to celebrate their coming to manhood."

"At 13 years old?"

He nodded, still holding my hand with the sherd in it.

"Bar mitzvahs are beautiful. So is this sherd. And it is yours because it was given to you and because you accepted it. You're discovering many things on the tell, Jeff, and I'm confident that one day you'll be able to 'read' this gift for yourself."

"Oh, thank you, Sir." Words seemed so inadequate. I figured, though, that Mr. Nebergall knew exactly how I felt.

When I passed them, Mr. Mac was still trying to explain to Jennifer why fighting erupted regularly in Israel. For a few minutes I had forgotten all about it. But now I heard some distant firing.

I went off to the showers and then got ready for bed. I wanted time to think about my sherd and my dreams I had shared with Mr. Nebergall, and to think about Kerim and all that had happened during the weekend.

But mostly I wanted the comfort of my own sleeping bag to blot out the flares against the dark skies and the gunfire in the distance.

13

Kerim's Sherd

I WOKE UP WITH AN UNEASY FEELING the next morning before the alarm jangled. Mom and Dad were already stirring around, but I snuggled back under the covers to listen for sounds of shelling. Guerrilla raids were sporadic, Dad had said last night, and probably would be over almost as quickly as they had come.

I didn't hear anyone talk about last night's gunfire at breakfast, but there was none of the laughing and joking that usually went on in the dining shed. The silence was difficult to live with, too, I discovered.

After we finished eating, Dad motioned for all of us and Kerim to stay with him. He wanted us in on the conversation with Mr. McDowell, the pottery expert, about the sherd with the fish sign which Kerim had found at Capernaum.

When he heard that we had been to Capernaum on the weekend, Mr. Mac pounded us kids with questions. Did we see all the rich sculptures in the ruins—palm trees, clusters of grapes, and the seven-branched candelabrum? We nodded and added the Star of David to his list.

Dad said, "I think they went over those synagogue ruins with a fine-tooth comb. Kerim uncovered this when they dug a hole to rescue a kitten."

Mr. Mac held the piece as carefully as Mr. Nebergall had held mine last night.

"Beautiful! Beautiful!" He asked us to tell him exactly how we found it. He then got a small box and laid the piece inside.

"What are you doing with it?" Jennifer demanded.

"We'll label this box so that the sherd is identified as thoroughly as possible. Then it'll go to the laboratory in Jerusalem."

"But it belongs to Kerim!"

"Now what would we archaeologists do, Jennifer, if everyone who happened on a find such as this kept it to himself? We wouldn't discover nearly as much about our heritage, would we?"

"I guess not."

"Do you think it's first century?" I asked.

"No. I would say early third century. Pottery with many Christian motifs—such as the fish, lamb, cross—has been found in Galilee."

"Then you don't really need this sherd." Jennifer still sounded worried.

"That all depends. Usually loose pieces found on top of the ground aren't important because they aren't related to any particular earth stratum. That makes accurate dating more difficult."

"But we—I mean Kerim—didn't find this on top of the ground."

Mr. Mac nodded. "That's the reason it's going to the lab."

"What if you decide to discard it?" I asked.

"I doubt that will happen. But we'll put Kerim's name on it, and if it isn't kept we'll return it to him."

Jennifer went over and stood beside Kerim. "That's better," she said. "I hope the sherd isn't important."

"It already is important to me," said Kerim softly.

Mr. McDowell summoned the team photographer to take pictures of the sherd Kerim had found and the one Jennifer had given to me from the discard pile. I was pleased that they were taking pictures of them together and asked the photographer to give us copies of the photos. Kerim's sherd then went back into the box, properly labeled, and mine back into my pocket.

We grabbed our *ibriks* when Dad said it was time to get to work. I was glad Jennifer was going

219

into the cave with Dad and me since Mom could not look after her down in her trench.

It was going to be another hot day—bright and beautiful with a blue sky above, streaked only with jet streams. As we headed down the hill to the cave entrance, I gazed off toward the Mediterranean Sea. Tel Aviv, 15 miles away on the coast, was in clear view. The radio, Dad said, had reported this morning some guerrilla activity near Tel Aviv. I decided that 15 miles away was too close.

It was obvious why our tell had been such an important location for a city. An enemy would have a hard time approaching it because the view was unlimited from the tell in three directions. To the west lay the plains and Tel Aviv on the coast. North one could follow the Mediterranean coastline all the way to the hills of Judah, and to the south as far as Ashkelon. The mountains were right upon us to the east. Two major roads crossed on the plains between us and the sea, and since the ancient border of Egypt was not far away to the south, the roads carried trade and armies within a few miles.

I could stare over the plain and almost see the armies of the pharaohs and of Saul and Solomon and David pass by.

When we arrived at the section of the cave being excavated, Sally and Tim and others were hard at work. I worked near Dad and asked him to tell Jennifer and Kerim and me more about the city's history. I had forgotten some of it from the evening lectures, and I especially needed it to take my mind off the tension around us. Dad retraced how the city had been conquered by the Egyptians off and on between 2,000 and 1,200 B.C., that it was a Philistine city for several hundred years, that King David had engaged its Canaanite peoples in battle many times, but it became a part of Israel when the pharaoh of Egypt gave it to King Solomon, when his daughter became Solomon's wife.

"It was a strong city for hundreds and hundreds of years—an excellent location with fertile valleys and a year-round water supply. What more could it need?" Dad asked.

A shade tree, I thought.

Dad continued, "And it didn't die out permanently until the first century A.D."

"Then people were living here when Jesus lived?"

"Yes, but we have no record that Jesus ever passed this way during His ministry."

"This place has been dead 1900 years!"

"Until our archaeology teams came 12 or more years ago," Dad added. "Now it's very much alive—at least every spring and summer."

I shuddered to think this city and plain were the locations of so much warfare in ancient times.

I asked Dad anxiously, "Does history often repeat its bad mistakes?"

Dad went on filling his goofer bucket with debris. "I'm afraid so, Son. I'm afraid so."

14

Danger

At LUNCH MOM BROUGHT ME a large round stone. "For your slingshot, Jeff."

She wasn't joking, I found out, when Mr. Mac explained that it was used in ancient times as a slingstone. My fingers could barely reach around it.

I dropped it into Jennifer's hand, and it caught her off balance.

"Is that ever heavy! Wow!" She returned it to me.

Mr. Mac said, "We've found enough of these around the old fortress wall to fill several buckets, so you may keep this one."

"Let's see you carry *that* in your pocket!"

"Worry about your own pockets, Jen!" I said and then could have bitten my tongue for sounding off over nothing.

"I'll hunt up Kerim. You're nicer to me when he's around."

"I'll help," I said to make up with her. "I haven't seen him since we left the cave." I checked out the sinks and up and down the tables. Surely he would be here in a minute. I was certain he had left the cave with the rest of us—well, almost certain. I was worried for a reason. Coming out of the cave just now, I had seen that pinpoint of light again to the right of the entrance. I tried to tell myself that it was a wisp of light from Dad's flashlight playing against the blackness, but I knew it was not.

Somehow I made it through lunch, although Kerim never showed up. This wasn't like him. He always ate lunch and usually hid food in his shirt and ran off afterward. Once he had headed toward the cave with the food, but I never said anything about it. Where was he now? Was he all right? Nobody else but me seemed concerned about him.

"Where's Kerim?" Jennifer asked after our meal.

"I don't know, nosy. Maybe he went home." Couldn't she see I was already worried sick about him?

"I don't like you, Jeff, when you call me nosy."

"I don't like you either when you ask stupid questions."

"So what's stupid about it?"

"I don't know."

224

*Coming out of the cave, I saw
a pinpoint of light.*

"Well, if you don't know—"

"Will you please stop?" I yelled.

I looked up to see Mom staring at us.

"Jeff, come with me to our tent. Jennifer, go take your shower."

I was in for it now. I scuffed at the rocks along the path. If I hadn't gotten into trouble with Mom, I could go look for Kerim. I knew I could not take the four-hour afternoon rest without knowing he was all right.

Inside the tent I had my mind so much on Kerim I didn't pay attention to Mom's verbal spanking until she said, "I know something is bothering you, Jeff. Every time you get up-tight about one thing or another, you start treating Jennifer like the dirt under your feet."

I opened my mouth to protest, but she continued: "It may be too much to ask a 12-year-old to grow up, Jeff. But at some time you'll have to learn how to settle the thing that is *really* bothering you without taking it out on Jennifer." She turned and headed for the showers.

I sat on my cot, feeling miserable. All right, I thought, I'll settle what's really bothering me! But right then my worry was Kerim, so I decided I would have to postpone my misery until I had found him. I looked out to be sure Jennifer and Dad were not coming down the path; then I grabbed a towel so they would think I was on my way to the showers if I ran into them. I rolled

Dad's flashlight and the slingstone Mom had given me into the towel and dashed out of the tent.

"Watch it, kid!" Hank exclaimed as I rounded the corner.

"I will! I will!" He'd better not delay me.

At the showers I turned and headed out the gate to the fields, praying that no one would see me and call me back. This was the first time I had struck out alone. I wouldn't really go into the cave by myself, I kept thinking over and over. The important thing was to get there. I looked out toward the Bedouin camp but Kerim was nowhere in sight.

Running down the hillside, I slipped and fell, but I finally reached the cave. I peered into its big black mouth and saw nothing.

I could hear Dad's firm voice, as strong as if he were saying it right in my ear: "Do not go into the cave alone." Kerim could be home resting or tending the animals. Or he might be somewhere on the tell by now. I was stupid. What was I doing here anyway? Turning my back on the cave and gazing out on the plain, I shifted the flashlight and slingstone in the towel to my left hand, then reached down and picked up a rock to throw.

I stared. Drawn on the rocky soil beside the entrance to the cave was the distinct outline of a fish. Danger! I wanted to run for my life, but my feet were glued to the ground. My head pounded.

227

Kerim had said danger is near if you ever see the sign of a fish. I stared at it . . . The head of the fish was facing the cave. Did that mean anything?

The sun beat down on me, hotter than ever before. I wiped the sweat gushing down my face and neck with an end of the towel, then I unwrapped the flashlight.

"O God," I prayed, "I don't want to disobey Dad. I want him and Mom to believe in me and trust me, but if I do the wrong thing, Mom and Dad—" I shut my eyes against what they would think. "But Kerim needs me. I know he does. I made him a promise about the fish, and now I don't know what to do. Do You know what to do, God?"

I hoped God could understand prayers that didn't make much sense.

Flashing through my memory came Kerim's words: If I saw the sign of the fish, I must get help and *then* find him. I glanced up toward the deep blue sky and hoped that was my answer.

I blinked. At the top of the tell, with her chin propped on her knees, sat Jennifer staring down at me.

15

Inside the Cave

I DROPPED MY BELONGINGS on top of the fish design and dashed up the hillside.

"Am I glad to see you! Now, Jen, listen
carefully—"

"Jeff, you're white like my Easter bunny.
You're going to have a sunstroke."

"No, Jen, just listen."

I dug my pottery sherd out of my pocket and
laid it in her palm. "Jen, I'm giving this back to
you so you'll know it is important for you to do
exactly what I say."

"OK, Jeff." Her big brown eyes widened in
fright. She must have felt how scared I was.

My words couldn't tumble out fast enough. "I
am going into the cave—no, no, don't say anything. I think Kerim is in some kind of danger.
I'm going in alone because if I wait for someone to

come it may be too late. But you're to run and tell Dad I've gone inside and that he is to get help and come down fast. Tell him to be careful—and tell him, Jen, he's to turn to the *right* inside the cave, not left. Have you got that?"

She nodded, one big tear rolling down her cheek. I rubbed it away with my thumb.

"Hurry now, we have to think about Kerim."

She pressed the sherd back into my hand. "You keep it for love energy, Jeff. I'll do everything you said."

She raced toward the other side of the tell. I moved cautiously back down the hill, mopping my face on my shirt. The slingstone was still wrapped in the towel. I checked the flashlight to be sure it was working, then I moved inside the cave. When its cool shade struck me I shivered.

I kept the flashlight off and moved snail-like. Where the cave curved to the left toward our diggings, I turned to the right and gazed into midnight blackness as if my eyes had been punched out. I waited and listened, afraid to turn on my light. At first all I could hear was my heart thudding against my ribs. Then a scurrying sound— like field mice on the run—came through the dark. I had to get my mind off my own danger—if there were any—and think only about Kerim.

Finally, with the light turned toward the ground, I moved the switch—my thumb stiff against it. I forced my arm up slowly so that the light split the darkness straight ahead. A plain cave wall ten feet ahead stared back at me. I crept down the passageway. Where the cave curved to the left, I drew a fish on the wall with my sherd to give me direction for going back. Then I inched along the passage.

The passage was endless. Finally a stone wall stopped me. I raised the light and discovered that the wall was cut away about three feet from the ceiling and exposed another passage at the higher level. I climbed the rock wall, clinging to the jutting stones and using them for steps, then I drew another fish on the ceiling and crawled on my hands and knees down the narrow upper passage.

Several new smells hit me—not the moldy odor of the passage—but the smell of sheep, of gunpowder, of smoke . . . I wanted to turn back but instead I shut off the light and shuffled ahead, my fingers sliding along the floor to guide me. By now I had hitched the slingstone inside the back of my pants, lost the towel from around my neck, and clamped my teeth around the handle of the flashlight. The ragged edges of the sherd cut into my hand. I must remember the way I had come. I drew another fish on the floor although I could not see it. A pale light seeped through the passage ahead. The smell of smoke was stronger.

Suddenly I came out into a large cave chamber and stood up. Stones encircled a small fire. Pottery jugs stood nearby. The only light was from the fire, flickering against the walls.

My gaze shifted cautiously around the room.

"Kerim!" I said. All caution left me. I dashed across to the opposite side beyond the fire where he lay in a heap. He did not move.

"Kerim! Kerim!" I put my head on his chest to listen for his heartbeat. I was sure he was dead.

I froze when he whispered: "My arms are tied behind me. Keep your head on my chest."

I stayed there motionless. He whispered again, "I was knocked unconscious. *He* thinks I still am."

Who? I wondered. I had seen no one else, but I was afraid to ask. I moved to pick Kerim up when a voice echoed through the chamber. I whirled around although I could not understand the foreign words.

Facing me was a young man—not much older than Kerim—with a rifle in his hand. A Palestinian guerrilla!

"I have to get my friend out! Don't you understand that? I must get him out!" I shouted, moving back toward Kerim.

The stranger snarled, and motioned with his gun for me to stay where I was. How could I call his bluff?

I gestured wildly. "My friend is dying! I must get him out!"

An evil grin crossed his dark face. I lunged for the fire to beat it out with a stone. Perhaps Kerim and I could get away in the darkness. The guerrilla aimed his rifle at my chest, then suddenly swung the butt at my head. I lurched backward just in time to miss the blow. Snarling again, he motioned me away from the fire with the butt of the rifle. I crawled back to Kerim and laid my head on his chest, feeling his pulse at his wrist.

"We'll find a way," I whispered. "Help is coming."

"Be careful!"

Another snarl. I had to move away from Kerim; the guerrilla was telling me with a motion of the rifle. I did. Shaking my head to clear it, I realized he wasn't going to fire that gun! Of course not. He was afraid that it would be heard outside the cave. If I could stamp the fire out he would have no light. I wanted to lunge for it again, but the sick grin on his face stopped me. I had read that guerrillas did not put a high price on their own lives. This one might be willing to risk shooting the gun if I pressed him—a shot for each of us.

"Sometimes you're too impulsive for your own good," Mom had told me once.

I sat and waited.

Finally I could not stand the silence, the eerie flickers on the walls, the gun pointed at my forehead. Dad must be coming with help; could he hear me if I shouted?

I began to talk loudly—gibberish, anything that came into my mind—as I kept my gaze fastened on the gunman. Kerim did not move.

"I hear a noise!" I yelled. "It's mice! It's rats! No, it's little black kittens!" I yelled till I was exhausted.

The guerrilla knew. He *had* to know that way back in this dark room no one could hear me if I shouted till doomsday. When I turned my head from side to side, the rifle moved back and forth with my movements. His hateful grin told me he was enjoying my torture.

I cautiously moved my hands behind me to reach the slingstone lodged under my belt. Clamping my fingers around the stone, I pointed toward the entrance with my free hand and screamed, "Watch out! Watch out! He has a gun!"

The guerrilla jerked and opened fire on the entrance. I flashed my light into his eyes to blind him and heaved the slingstone at his head.

He fell.

I dashed to Kerim.

"Knife in my pocket—" he gasped. "Cut the ropes!"

I reached for the knife. A loud splintering sound above us shattered the silence. We crouched together looking upward. Light streamed in from an opening in the roof of the cave chamber.

"Jeff! Kerim! Jeff!" Jennifer's shout was the sweetest sound I had ever heard.

16

Linked by the Fish

I DON'T KNOW WHY YOU FAINTED after you were safe," Jennifer said, sitting on the edge of my cot in the nurse's tent.

"I was scared, Jen."

"And you wouldn't be hurt at all if you hadn't held that piece of pottery so tight."

I looked at my bandaged hand. "I needed lots of your love energy," I said. I figured as long as my sister was sentimental, I could be too. "Is Kerim okay?"

"He's right over there."

I was so relieved I could have cried at the sight of Kerim across the tent on another cot. He looked just as happy as I felt but he didn't say anything. I knew he wasn't going to say any sticky words about my coming in the cave to find him. He knew they would just make me feel funny.

"Boy, I'm glad to see you," I said.

"I knew you would come, Jeff, when you missed me at lunch."

He *knew* I would come.

Mom and Dad were standing in the doorway. They didn't say anything, but I didn't feel any shame about going into the cave alone. It seemed right. For once I trusted my own decision. I hoped they would understand but if they didn't, I knew it was exactly as Mom had said the night I left Jennifer alone last year. They might be disappointed in me for what I had done, but they still loved me. I didn't know it then, but I certainly did now.

They came inside and sat on stools beside me.

"I had to go in the cave alone, Dad, but not before I sent for you."

"And you were right," Dad said. "As soon as Jennifer told me you had gone in, I knew you had decided it was the thing you had to do."

He *knew*. He had trusted me.

"A tough decision for a 12-year-old," Dad added.

"Jennifer made it easier by following me to the cave. If she hadn't, I would have had to go up on the tell for help." I hesitated before I added, "It was because of the fish that I hunted for Kerim."

Dad looked completely surprised. "What's this fish business?"

"Do you remember what you said at Capernaum about us being linked to Jesus and other people of long ago by faith?"

He nodded.

"Well, Kerim and I were linked by the sign of a fish."

"I'm just thankful you and Kerim are safe now," Mom said.

"It could have been different," added Kerim from his cot.

Dad's voice was low. "Yes. Sometimes we don't know if a decision is good or bad when we must make it. We just have to trust, don't we, Jeff?"

They understood. I looked from Dad to Mom. "Thanks," I mumbled, my throat suddenly scratchy.

"All the shouting you did, Jeff, pinpointed where you were," Mom explained. "We could hear you above ground, and Mr. Mac knew exactly how to get there from above to save time."

"From above?"

"Through a tunnel dug years ago by archaeologists. We passed through a stone shaft that led into a cistern—"

"Which had an opening to that cave room," Jennifer interrupted.

"I am glad Mr. Mac knew about that entrance," added Kerim. So was I. It was a simple one compared to the long torturous route along the passages we had come through.

Now that I knew how my parents felt about

237

what I had done, I was eager to know what had happened after I passed out.

"I didn't kill the guerrilla, did I?"

"No."

I shuddered at the memory of his evil face but was glad that I didn't kill him. He had been tied up with Kerim's ropes, Mom said, and was now in the custody of the military. Soldiers were already spread out in the mountains around the tell, hunting the rest of the band.

"But we aren't in danger now or they would evacuate the tell," she reassured us.

"What were the guerrillas doing here?"

"Hiding out—no one would suspect them of being on a tell where there were so many people. At night they moved out undetected to raid the countryside. They just happened to find a perfect hideout in an unexcavated section of the cave."

"How did you get into this, Kerim?" I was as full of questions as Jennifer.

He said, "One day I followed the pinpoint of light I saw at that end of the cave."

"That's what I saw! What was it?"

Mr. Mac entered the tent in time to answer. "This cave system is intricate and interlaced with cisterns and tunnels built to bring in water underground from a source outside the city walls. It is impossible to know where that tiny spot of light came from in all that labyrinth."

He sounded like a teacher. I grinned at Dad.

"I wish I had not seen that light!" Kerim said. It led him accidentally onto the guerrilla band. They then blackmailed him into bringing them food and keeping their hideout a secret.

"If I had not," Kerim added and his eyes filled with new fear, "they showed me the grenades they would use. They would blow up the tell, they said, and my people's tent homes, even if they killed themselves when they did it."

"Kerim—"

"I was afraid, Jeff, that they could hear everything I said even when they were far away. That is why I did not speak with you freely about the cave."

"All those strange conversations!"

"I could not let you talk about the cave. They might overhear and think that I gave them away."

"Who was the man in Tiberias?"

"One of this band. Two of them had gone there to connect up with another band. When he accidentally bumped into me, he was suspicious about why I was there. He threatened me. And then you saw him—and he saw you—and I was frightened for everyone here."

I was thoroughly confused. "But—but I don't understand how you got yourself tied up down in the cave."

Kerim was suddenly tongue-tied. Finally he said, "I love my land. I love my people."

"I still don't understand."

He was groping for words. "I—I stayed behind today at lunch. I went to the hideout to tell them that I will not bring them food again. That they must leave. That I cannot help men who kill the people of my land—"

"But you are an Arab too!" I said.

"Not a guerrilla! I made my decision," he said firmly. "My life I can lose—that is nothing. But I do not live another day in fear and shame that I am slave to evil men who kill my people."

No wonder he seldom smiled.

I said, "There's the sign of a fish along those cave walls for direction. They'll be there forever."

"I love my land," Kerim said again, his eyes lighting up with excitement. "The Jews love my land. Christians and Muslims love my land. It must be the best place on earth."

I smelled the dust on this desert tell and said, "It must be."

Kerim raised himself up from his cot. "But I will not kill. I wish my whole land were like the people who work together right here."

Jennifer and I exchanged glances. We had once said the same thing.

"To think that the guerrillas making raids at Tel Aviv yesterday were living right under us," Mom said.

I shuddered.

"They could have turned us into goofers!" Jennifer grinned at me and slung her *ibrik* up for a drink.

They held us in the nurse's tent overnight for observation although Kerim and I were aching to go home. His mother and father came in the evening when his father returned from work in the valley. I could not understand what they said but I did not need to.

Mom never left the side of my cot. Sometimes as I dozed off to sleep I could feel her rubbing my back as she did when I was little and couldn't go to sleep. Sometimes she rubbed Kerim's back too.

The next day we stayed so busy I hardly saw Jennifer. Soldiers were in and out of the unexcavated tunnels, clearing out ammunition left by the guerrillas, asking Kerim and me and Mr. Mac and others a million questions. I did not know much to report, but I learned a lot by listening to everyone else.

It was late afternoon when I hunted out Jennifer.

"Let's go sit on the other side of the tell," I said.

We didn't say anything all the way over. We sat on the edge, threw pebbles down the slope, and gazed out across the plains.

I wanted to talk to her but couldn't find a way to say what I felt, so I took the pottery sherd she had given me out of my pocket and drew a fish on the ground beside us.

"What's that for?"

"Oh, I like to think Jesus once walked here just like King Solomon and David did hundreds of years before Him."

Jennifer took the pottery sherd and studied the stick figures. Mr. Nebergall had said that some-day I would be able to "read that gift for myself." In a sense I figured I already could because of the giver.

"I sure am glad nosy old Jennifer followed me to the cave yesterday," I said.

"Huh! I knew you weren't supposed to be out there during rest time."

"I can depend on you to tag along after me."

She looked hurt.

"It's a compliment," I said quickly. "I needed you and you were there."

"Oh!" She brightened and handed my sherd back to me.

I had not said what I wanted to very well, but we gazed out from our tell. Suddenly we didn't need to talk. The view over the Mediterranean Sea was magnificent with its fiery red sunset.

The artillery-shell gong sounded for the evening lecture. Kerim lifted the shovel to bong it again.

I turned and challenged Jennifer.

"Race you across the tell!" I said.

242

ACKNOWLEDGMENTS

I am deeply indebted to my husband, Geoffrey L. Story, Jr., Chairman of the Department of Religion, Illinois Wesleyan University, whose experience in Israel made this book possible. The location for this story is Tel Gezer where he participated in an archaeological excavation. The historical background, geographical location, and archaeological findings included in this story are true to the Tel Gezer site, although fictional descriptions of the Tell itself do occur.

My thanks are due Madeleine L'Engle and Penny Anderson for their helpful criticism and suggestions for revision.

River of Fire

BETTIE WILSON STORY

1
YELLOW FEVER

MALINDA SHARP SAT ON THE EDGE of the cane chair. Hearing the mournful call of a hoot owl at the edge of the clearing, she dropped her head in weariness. Her fingers absently traced squares on the quilt that covered her mother as she watched her familiar face on the pillow. Seven days of fever had drained the rich color from mother's skin and turned it yellow. Her large, generous mouth and firm chin were lifeless.

Please, God, mama must live! Malinda prayed. *I need her. Papa needs her.* It was a litany Malinda repeated over and over.

Mary Sharp slowly opened her eyes and turned her head to look at her twelve-year-old daughter.

"How do you feel?" Malinda placed a hand on her mother's hot, dry forehead.

Mary closed her eyes briefly. "I'm fine," she whispered.

"You told papa that just before he left to repair the traps. Are you sure?"

"Yes. I want to talk, Malindy."

"Save your strength, mama. It'll keep till you're stronger."

"I'm afraid it won't get said. You're growing so, child—you're almost grown. And you haven't had a speck of schooling."

"You and papa—"

"We taught you to read, but there's much more to learn. We can't teach it all." Her breath came in short gasps.

"Please, mama, rest—"

Her mother's eyes held hers. "They have schools down in Mobile, Malindy. I've been plannin' for you to go live with your Aunt Eliza for a while—"

"I don't want to leave you and papa!"

"Promise to remember my wishes, child."

Malinda gripped her hand. "Yes, mama." She would say anything to save her mother's strength, but she would never leave them. Never!

Numb with fear, Malinda pushed back her mother's brown hair, which sparkled with gold and amber. Her mother smiled at her touch.

"Now that you have promised, please read to me. I want . . . to hear the Twenty-third Psalm."

Malinda knew it by heart, but she picked up the worn Bible from the lamp table beside the bed and turned to the psalm, forcing herself to hold the book steady.

"The Lord is my shepherd; I shall not want."

The lamplight cast eerie shadows on the cabin wall and filled Malinda with a lonely dread.

"Yea, though I walk through the valley of the shadow of death, I shall fear no evil—"

"He knew, Malindy," her mother interrupted.

"Who knew, mama?"

"The psalmist. Some folks think we find God in all the beautiful, lovely things of life. But the wilderness, Lindy—that's where we find God."

"But, mama—"

"Read, honey."

"For thou art with me. . . ."

Malinda wanted to cry out in desperation.

When she finished the psalm, her mother was in a calm sleep. Malinda picked up one of

249

the ocean stones from the lamp table and studied its designs of grey, wine, and crystal, rubbing her palm over its sea smoothness. She had treasured the stones after finding them that day on the North Carolina coast—the day Aunt Eliza had set sail for the far-off port of Mobile.

Two years later papa had moved his family overland from North Carolina to a place near the Tombigbee River. Mobile was only a few days' journey down the river, but it might as well be on the other side of the world. In five years of living in the west Alabama wilderness, they had not been able to visit Aunt Eliza.

Malinda set the ocean stone aside and laid her fingertips on her mother's cheeks. They were hot and flushed. Her fever was rising again.

There was no tea to give her; they had used it all up as the days of mama's sickness wore on. Water would never do. Mama had always said it was fatal if you had the fever, and her mother before her.

Her heart pounding, Malinda grabbed the warm herb broth she had made. "Please, mama, try to drink this," she cried.

The broth would not go down.

"Swallow, mama!"

She did not.

Malinda set the broth back on the stove, then dipped up a pan of cool spring water to bathe her mother's face and arms.

Papa! Papa! She wanted to shout and have him appear instantly in the doorway. But only the July flies filled the night with their sound.

Soon mama was delirious. She thrashed wildly about, then changed to fevered listlessness and drifted into unconsciousness.

A voice inside Malinda said, *Find papa,* but she wasn't sure that was the wisest advice. She had never gone into the forest alone at night—a rule papa demanded she obey without question. But tonight was different. It would take both of them to pull mama through this new crisis. The inside voice might be right; she needed to find him.

After bathing her mother once more with cool spring water, Malinda placed another damp cloth on her forehead. Then she closed the cabin door softly and dashed up the creek. When she did not find her father at the first trap, she followed the creek a while before deciding to strike off through the woods in search of a short cut. The image of the flushed face on the pillow drove her on to find a familiar trail.

But she did not. The forest was a strange world of its own in the dark. Soon she was entangled in dense undergrowth; twisting and turning she made her way beyond briars and swamp dogwood. Vines climbing among the smaller trees made a canopy that hid the moon. Once she thought she heard the *ha ha* sound of a Choctaw Indian's call for caution.

She pushed ahead, totally confused. In her struggle she forgot the things papa had taught her in case she lost direction. She could hardly see at all.

Then the smell of woodsmoke drew her forward, her nose searching out its location. She stared beyond the trees as she walked, and soon saw a dim fire sputtering through the branches. Was that papa? She began to run, then tripped over a log and fell head first into a clearing. The fire on the other side of the clearing was tended by several men who were shouting obscenities.

"That runawayer won't run no more!"

A colored man dangled by a rope over the fire.

Malinda curled up in revulsion and squeezed her eyes shut.

A scream split the air. It crossed the clearing in a second, bumping the tree trunks around Malinda and striking the high branches. No other sound existed, she thought. No wind, no songbirds, not even a lone coyote.

The familiar fragrance of pine smoke

She stared beyond the trees where a man dangled from a rope.

turned to stench. It filled Malinda's nostrils. Gasping for breath, she opened her eyes. The slave's feet and hair had been set on fire, enveloping him in flames.

The men laughed and cursed. "No sir! He ain't runnin' no more! I coulda took it from just him! But the fool tried to start a risin' of the field hands!"

Malinda retched.

She crawled to her feet in a daze and began to run. One of the lynchers crashed through the underbrush, clamped his arms around her, and slapped a hand over her mouth.

"You git outta here! You didn't see nothin'!"

Malinda struggled, kicking at him.

He loosened his grip. "Well, if it ain't Jeremiah Sharp's gal! What you doin' so far from home? You tell your pa we caught our nigger! You tell him, you hear?"

When she finally found her father, Malinda was sobbing, but she could not tell him what she had seen.

He held her close for a brief moment. "For sure, Malindy, you're brave—and foolish, too—to come alone. These old woods scare grown men."

If only she could feel comfort from his hug.

"There's wild animals, maybe unfriendly Creek Indians around."

Malinda wiped her eyes with a balled-up fist. "It's mama—run, papa, run!"

As they rushed home, he tried to reassure her. "It touches me deep, Malindy, that you braved the night. Don't cry now. We'll reach mama in time."

She doubled over, vomiting again. "I hate the woods! I hate them!"

When they reached home, mama's fever had risen still higher. Her skin was dry like an August creek bed, and she lay listless as death.

Papa knelt by her side, bathed her face and arms and body in cool water, and whispered his love. Malinda stood by handing him cloths, helplessly gripped in loneliness. She tormented herself with the thought that mama's worsened condition was her fault for losing her way in the forest.

She could not take her eyes away from mother's face. Papa suddenly let the cloth drop. His hunched shoulders sagged; his head dropped to his chest in despair. *Mama won't pull through,* she thought.

She reached for the Bible on the bedside table. Without opening it she whispered, "The Lord is mama's shepherd. She shall fear no evil. Is that a promise, papa?"

"Yes, honey. It's a promise."

The next day her father dug a grave by the cabin while Malinda carved on a simple wooden marker:

MARY SHARP
1804-1836

2

NO TURNING BACK

MALINDA GRIPPED THE HANDRAIL on the deck of the *Alabama Queen* as she watched slaves—no, papa called them roustabouts— load on wood for the furnace. Other slaves stacked bales of cotton that reached as high as the upper deck on each side of the steamboat. Clerks were checking goods and passengers on and off.

Most of the travelers watched the commotion on this October evening from the upper decks. But not Malinda. She wanted to be in the middle of all the excitement. It kept her from remembering that she and her father had only a few remaining minutes together.

She walked along the narrow path between the rail and the stacked cotton bales back to the huge paddle wheel. Roustabouts, dripping with sweat, stoked the furnace. Flames were visible through the doors, and the boat shuddered as if impatient to be on the move again.

But where was papa? He should be done talking to the captain by now. She ran back up the boiler deck, wistfully looking at the passengers standing above her and wishing the trip held the same gaiety for her.

The boat was huge—two-and a-half decks and a pilot house. Above it a smokestack rose on each side of the boat whistle, which had already given off a shrill blast.

She did not see papa. Instead she caught the eye of a young colored girl who was staring at her.

Malinda had never seen so many Negroes. Their nearest neighbor ten miles up the creek owned a slave, and Malinda had seen him once. She had gone with her parents sometimes to see Running Bull, their Choctaw Indian friend, and seen a few Negroes living among the Choctaws. Papa said they were runaways. The only others were several miles down the Tombigbee River on a plantation. But Malinda had never been there.

The girl still stared at Malinda. Why had

she let papa out of her sight, and why was he talking so long with the captain? As if she read her thoughts, the black girl nodded toward the main deck. Malinda looked up and saw papa coming down the steps.

She ran to him. "Papa! Where were you?"

"Just checking out your cabin room once again, honey. Are you all right?"

"Papa, I'm so afraid!"

"All aboard!"

The steamboat blew another splitting whistle in the evening air. It muffled the wild laughter in the gambling room and quieted the roustabouts on the deck.

"Come, walk with me to the gangplank," Jeremiah said. "Why are you afraid, Malindy?"

How could she explain that the boat would lose all its excitement when he left, leaving only her memories of her mother's death and the runaway slave?

"There's nothin' to be afraid of, Malindy. The captain's a good man. He's been on the river a long time and knows it well. He's promised to deliver you safe and sound to Eliza at the Mobile dock."

All the same, Malinda's throat ached. She changed the subject. "Is Aunt Eliza like mama?" she mumbled.

His arm tightened around her. "There's nobody like your mama, Malindy."

"Then I reckon I better go with you."

Jeremiah put his big, strong hands on her shoulders. The shock of black hair falling over his forehead did not hide the ache in his eyes.

"Malindy, gal, we've been over this again and again. Your mama wanted you to get some schoolin'." His gaze roamed her face as if to etch it in his memory. "I promised her years ago that we wouldn't let the move west keep you from gettin' it. Neither one of us forgot; we just couldn't let you go."

"You can teach me better than anybody."

"You're almost grown up, child, but you need a mama for a while yet. Anyway, this wilderness is too hard a life. I'll go on farther west, find a place, and clear some land. I'll come for you when the time is right."

"But, papa, I can help you clear the land."

"Malindy, we both made a promise to your mama."

Her misery pushed her on to say, "Then you come with me." But she knew he could never be happy in Mobile. All those townspeople would crowd him too close. He was a trapper and farmer, always pushing farther west when too many settlers moved in. Tomorrow he would begin his trek west with the few cattle and hogs left after paying for her passage.

He was right. They had been over and over the decision in the three months since mama had died. There was no turning back now.

"Papa—"

"Did you bring any of your stones from the ocean?" he interrupted.

"Yes." She had placed most of them at the foot of mama's grave.

"It pleases me you brought them."

Malinda tried hard to smile. "And you're takin' your fiddle along. You promised."

"Malindy—"

"I can see you goin' through the woods hollerin' and singin' and playin' your fiddle to drown out the blue jays."

"My fiddle is for happier days."

"Running Bull would like it."

His hand clenched around her hair. "Nobody can outholler a Choctaw Indian."

She looked up at his rich brown eyes, his high cheekbones, and his firm mouth, once so accustomed to smiling. "You sure did outstubborn Running Bull, or he would have never been your friend."

Papa's eyes crinkled in remembered pleasure. "That old mule! I'll never forget him stoppin' us on the Georgia trail. He got us safely across Creek Indian country, too."

"He wouldn't have, though, if you hadn't outbluffed him."

"How was I to know it was a game? That's one time, Malindy, your pa did the right thing without knowin' it. Did you know old Chief Pushmataha once took a lighted torch in his hand and invited a white man to join him on a keg of dynamite?"

Malinda smiled. It was her father's favorite story.

"What bluffers those Choctaws are! And now Running Bull is out west somewhere in another forest."

"If you holler and fiddle loud enough, maybe you'll find him again."

"Is that what you want?"

Malinda nodded. "You won't have mama and me travelin' with you this time." She could hardly bear to say it. "But if he hears you comin', he might even find you."

Jeremiah held her face and kissed her forehead and then each cheek. "I'll try, Malindy gal, I'll try."

"You can do it, papa."

"All aboard!"

"She's amoving," someone shouted behind them.

"The plank ain't up!"

Papa hugged her roughly. The boards beneath them shuddered.

"You're going to make it. You're going to come through on the other side," he whispered in her ear. "You're all I have, Malindy, and oh, how I'll miss you!"

He ran down to the landing just before the gangplank was raised.

"Stoke her up, boys! Stoke her up!" someone encouraged the firemen at the furnace. The paddle wheels began to turn, and the boat moved slowly into the current.

Malinda gripped the rail with both hands until they ached. She could see papa on shore in the twilight, his hands deep in his pockets. He was still standing on the landing when the steamboat passed around the bend.

Malinda gazed at the now blurry tree-lined shore and tried to remember everything her father had said . . . "You're going to make it." If only she could believe that, too. Once she was at Aunt Eliza's perhaps she would not have to go into the hated woods again. She clung to the thought; it eased the pain of leaving papa.

She had not always been afraid—only since that frightening night alone in the forest, the night mama died. In the three months since, she had not stayed by herself in the cabin or walked alone in the woods.

"What's got into you, Malindy?" papa would ask. "I've taught you all I know about these woods, and you can't get lost in the daytime. You know everything I've learned from the settlers and from the Choctaws. So how come the devil rides you every time you step foot out there?"

Finally one night she broke down and told him what had turned the woods into her enemy.

"God have mercy on their souls," papa had whispered. "Why didn't you tell me about the runawayer before now?"

"I couldn't."

"You rest on me and try to forget."

But she could not. And soon he began making plans for her to go to Aunt Eliza's.

It was a sleepless night. The bed was so tiny that Malinda dared not turn over for fear of falling out. Whenever the fiddlers struck up a familiar tune in the main cabin on the other side of her door, it recalled painful memories of the times her parents had danced to the same music.

The songs and shouts and boisterous laughter and sometimes the crying of a young child on the deck below also reached her. This night was nothing like ones at home where in the stillness she often heard a hoot owl or coyote or a lone wolf cry.

To escape the sound—and the memories—Malinda slipped out the other door, bringing her directly onto the upper deck to watch the passengers below. Flaring torches on rods extended out over the water. Papa had said that sometimes they were used to guide the pilot through a black night.

Restless, she returned to her cramped sleeping quarters.

She picked up an ivory-handled hair brush, the only possession of her mother's she had brought. Slowly she brushed, her head tilted sideways—the way she and her mother let their amber-brown hair fall to their waist. She had mama's hazel eyes, too, and a spattering of tiny freckles across her cheekbones. Papa had said she was going to be as pretty as mama. She hoped so.

Then she thought of her father. Tomorrow he must face the wilderness alone.

3

A NIGHTMARE
OF FLAMES

BY THE SECOND NIGHT on the *Alabama Queen,* fatigue and grief had overwhelmed Malinda. She fell across the tiny bed without bothering to undress. She even felt feverish.

That did not surprise her. It must be one of her "upsetting fevers" as mama called them. They would come unexpectedly—such as the time Aunt Eliza left on the ship and when she and her parents uprooted their home in North Carolina and headed west. Or whenever father was away for several days to sell animals or pelts or to buy supplies.

The fever could vanish just as quickly. If she

266

gave in now to her drowsiness, perhaps tomorrow it would be gone, and several more hours of this lonely trip would have passed.

Malinda awoke choking and coughing. Smoke was suffocating her like the times she tended fires and a wind change engulfed her in heavy smoke. Frantically she snatched open the door to the deck and gasped for breath.

An explosion rocked the *Alabama Queen,* sending the rear section up in flames. The fire spread quickly to the bales of cotton stacked seven or eight tiers high. Passengers spilled out onto the decks, screaming and cursing. They jostled Malinda as they ran past.

The tortured face of the runaway slave stared out at her from the flames. His image seemed as real as the frantic passengers on the boat.

The entire steamboat would soon be in flames. She did not board this vessel to be burned alive like that runawayer. She scrambled wildly over the rail of the upper deck to the top tier of a bale of cotton, which was just beginning to topple.

She jumped.

She did not think once that the river was wider and deeper than the creek behind the

log cabin at home, that her skirt and petticoats would tug like undertow, or that she
might be hit by burning cotton bales toppling
over the sides.

She thought only of escape.

Water closed in around her. She dragged
one arm over her head, pulled the other down,
then drifted with the current in quick exhaustion. The water in her ears muffled the cries of
others and the crackling fire. She was enveloped in another world that tugged at her.

But she would not let herself drown, either.
Her legs kicked in slow motion. Slowly her
chin rose above water, and she inched toward
the distant shore.

An overwhelming splash deluged her, but
she thrashed to the surface again. Heat
burned her face. Flaming cotton bales hissed
as they hit the water not three feet away.

She was dragged under by the current.
Don't fight it! Set the rhythm! Did her brain
still function or had someone shouted? But
those were her father's words.

Malinda Sharp! Malinda–she stretched her
limbs as she sounded each syllable. *Sharp*–she
kicked her legs together, pulled with her
arms. If she could remember her name, maybe
its rhythm would be her salvation. *Malinda*–
she stretched. *Sharp*–she kicked. *Malinda . . .
Sharp!*

Her hands finally struck roots. She pulled herself up but fell exhausted half in the marsh, half in the river's edge. Water gurgled in the grass under her ear.

Shrieks slashed the darkness, and Malinda tugged at her water-soaked dress and struggled to her feet. She bogged her way through the swamp grass to the cypress tree. Then she zigzagged deeper into the woods, fleeing from what seemed to be the runaway's image rising in the flames of the steamboat. Slowly her wet skirts twined around her legs, and she fell.

Were those footsteps crashing through the forest after her? The woods were haunted with her nightmares of the past; she staggered to her feet and spurted ahead. She must find a planter's house in the bottoms. Vines whipped at her like a cat-o'-nine-tails, and she fought them off as she stumbled on.

Looking back she saw nothing but darkness and fog slithering in among the tree trunks. Muscadine vines plaited the giant foliage overhead together, sealing in the oppressive October heat. Malinda slipped on brown pine needles and wrenched sideways to catch her balance. Frogs croaked somewhere in the bogs, and a distant wolf howled in the darkness.

She turned all the way around and sobbed in terror. The river had vanished! The fog and the black night yielded nothing. No cultivated fields. No trails in the undergrowth. No cabins. Nothing.

Panting, she wiped her face with her wet skirt in an attempt to gain control of herself. Where was she? And where was the *Alabama Queen?* The dark woods were worse than the flaming ship. She ran to escape them. She tripped over vines and fell again.

Why not give up? She felt her eyelids close, locking out the night's horror.

When she awakened, she would be back home. Mama would be churning and papa trapping or fishing at a creek in the backwoods. When he came in, mama would feed them all to bursting. Then papa would make the fiddle croon a tender love song while mama sat at his feet. Later he would swing into foot-tapping music that would send Malinda reeling round the room. And then strike the minor tone of a ballad or a slave melody—a tune that pushed out at the darkness beyond the firelight in their cabin.

The scene changed abruptly. In her dream Malinda was pounding on the door, imploring someone to open it so she could join the song and the firelight. Mother was inside to teach her the steps, and father's gay tunes would turn their cheeks rosy . . . if she could only reach them. But they did not hear. She con-

270

tinued to pound on the door as fingers of the night reached out to grab her.

Her cry as she beat on the locked door of her dream awoke her. Scrambling to her feet she tore through the brush to escape her nightmare. Although her arms were stretched out ahead, they did not protect her. When her head crashed against a low oak limb, she folded to the ground as if into her mother's soft feather cushion.

While she slipped in and out of consciousness, she thought she heard cowbells across the meadows back home, then the soft music of lullabies, until daylight and night were the same in their passing.

PEBBLE TEA

SOMETHING INSIDE MALINDA stirred. Her eyelids fluttered. Her fingers moved, and her nose twitched. She smelled woodsmoke, and rolling over, she stared at the small fire in the center of a ring swept clean of leaves and scrubs.

Beyond the flames a face stared back at her. It was a black face, and she knew this was no dream.

"Are you a ghost?" she demanded, struggling to rise. Her weak arms and legs did not respond.

The face did not answer.

"I got to know! Are you a ghost?"

"I ain't no hant! But if you wants to get out of here alive, you better not yell again!"

"How come?"

"You find out soon enough."

"I want to know now!"

"Wait till your feeblements be gone. We is safe here."

That was strange. What was this Negro doing with her? Why didn't he take her to the big house to be cared for? She wanted out of these woods.

Malinda forced herself to stare across the fire. The face did not look black now but burnt rich brown, like the crusted sugar in the bottom of mother's cane syrup jug. The lips were still, expressionless, but the eyes commanded her attention. They were large and round as walnuts, midnight black, and they glanced at her briefly, then flicked away.

He stood. A homespun shirt and pants covered the strong body that was not much taller than she. Her heart thumped wildly as she tried again to sit up.

"I be back." He turned away from the fire and walked deeper into the woods.

Malinda could not look through the trees. The Negro might not be a ghost, but the woods were still haunted, of that she was sure. She struggled to sit up, her gaze darting around the campfire where a rack made of reeds held dried apples. Nuts and acorns filled two large gourds. Another gourd had been carved flat like a frypan, and smaller cupped dippers were near by.

Suddenly dizzy, she lay back on the bed of moss under her. How long had she been here? These supplies had not been gathered in a day. And where had the young man gone? Had he abandoned her with only a few nuts and apples? If only he would come back.

Before long he did.

"Drink this," he said.

Should she or was this some poison? But the apples and nuts, the moss bed and the fire—surely they were evidence that he had cared for her. She leaned on her elbow and took the gourd he held out. It felt cool in her hands. Inside it were water and several stones.

She glanced up at the large walnut eyes.

They avoided hers. "Pebble tea for your fever. I think it be the yellow fever!"

Oh, mama, no, no, no! She swallowed the cool liquid and stared at the smooth stones in the bottom of the cup.

The dark hands took the gourd, and once more the stranger slipped away into the forest. Malinda felt in the pocket of her dress, but her ocean stone was missing. She hid her face in her arms.

When the stranger returned, he placed the dipper of water on the fire and resumed his position across the flames.

Malinda could not stand the quietness. "What's your name?"

The face looked uncertain. His eyes darted to and fro like a hummingbird and soon focused on the dark green leaves of a jasmine vine. "Jasmine. . . . My name be Jasmine."

"A girl! Are you a girl?"

A corner of the stranger's mouth twitched. "I be a woman!"

"Oh, I'm so glad! My name's Malinda Sharp."

"I knows."

The pebbles in the gourd clattered as the water began to boil.

"How did you know my name?"

"You say it for days—Malindy . . . Sharp . . . Malindy Sharp—like you gonna forget it if you quits."

"*Days?*"

"It been ten days. You last out the fever ten days, so you gonna live."

Malinda shook with chills and sank back on the moss, too weak to do anything else. Tears stung her eyelids.

It was morning when Malinda awakened

again. The black girl was cooking over the fire. Jasmine, she said her name was, but Malinda knew better. She glanced over at the jasmine vine, remembering the sweet scent of its white flowers in spring. From the olive family, mama had once explained when she placed a bouquet in the center of the supper table.

"Jasmine?"

"Is you awake already?"

"I didn't hit my head here, did I?"

" 'Course not. Nobody hits their heads in a good hidin' place like this."

"I don't understand."

"This be a good place. Deep enough in the woods and close to a spring."

"Why didn't you take me to the big house?"

The long slender hands stirring the mush were still.

"What big house?" she finally asked.

"Don't you live around here?"

"I lives right here in this spot!"

"How long?"

Jasmine pointed to a pine. The bark had been cut away in ten short lines.

"Ten days?"

Jasmine nodded.

"But you said I had the fever ten days."

"That be how long I lives here. After we eats this mush, I'm gonna add a line for today."

"Where do you live, Jasmine?"

"Here!"

"Then where did you live?"

"My mercy me! I thought I couldn't wait till you gets over that fever. But there was blessings. I sure don't like questions."

Malinda lay back, her head swirling. What secret did Jasmine know about fevers? They had tried every potion for her mother but water—that was fatal everytime. Malinda sucked in her breath, and the other girl turned at the sound.

"Was . . . was that water you gave me?"

"No! It be pebble tea, boiled and boiled. It save you from the fever."

"Is the tea different from water?"

"Ain't you never seen tea?"

Tea. The kind that arrived on the steamboat too late for mama.

"Of course, but this pebble tea didn't change color."

"Just you never mind that. When you gets fourteen years on you like me, then you knows tea can be a heap of colors."

Jasmine was not going to answer a direct question no matter how she worded it. "Thank you for making me well," Malinda whispered.

"Oh, hush! It was the pebble tea." Jasmine handed her another gourd full, cooled at the spring. Malinda slipped her fingers into the water, removed one of the pebbles, and enclosed it in her hand, remembering her father. This one would have to take the place of her ocean pebbles.

"Are you sure I had the yellow fever?"

"Huh! That ain't all you got. Talk about hants—you got them in your head. Such goin's on I ain't never fell across before."

Remembering mama's delirious thrashings, Malinda drank the whole gourd full without removing it from her lips.

Jasmine bent over the fire. The meal was ready: bread cooked with acorn flour, catfish, and fresh apples. Malinda was ravenous, but Jasmine gave her only small portions. She pushed Malinda's questions aside while they ate.

Afterwards Jasmine folded her hands, one on top of the other in her lap, and focused her big round eyes on Malinda. "In two days you be stronger. Then we go downriver by night."

Downriver. Mobile, where father was sending her to live with Aunt Eliza, was somewhere downriver. Two words suddenly struck like cockleburs in her mind: *by night. Travel by night.* Only a fool—or somebody pretty desperate—would travel through this wilderness by night. Her eyes wandered slowly from Jasmine's leather moccasins, up her baggy pants and man's homespun shirt to the bridge of her nose and the bonnet of black curls.

Malinda was not fooled. Jasmine's words confirmed her suspicions. She was a runaway slave! She must be a runaway!

Malinda jumped up. Suddenly dizzy, she steadied herself.

"I'm goin' *up* river to my papa, and you ain't gonna stop me! He sent me away, but I'm going back! You can't keep me here!"

Jasmine did not move. "G'bye," she said.

Malinda stumbled through the carpet of fall leaves and needles, setting the jays to chattering in the trees. She gritted her teeth in misery when she was forced to stop and lean against an oak to rest. Where was the river, and which direction was north? Why couldn't she think clearly? She plunged ahead, her breath coming in rough gasps.

The trees began to turn flips in the sky like buzzards circling over a carcass. She clung to a limb.

"We wait three days instead of two." Behind her, Jasmine's voice was firm. "You can't get nowhere without me, so don't try no more."

The forest closed in on Malinda as her fingers slipped from the limb. Jasmine took her arms and sat her down against the live oak.

"I loses ten good days to save you," she said. "Now you got to stay with me."

"No! Leave me alone! You're a runawayer!

They'll cut your tongue out! They'll burn you to death—"

"Last time he just beat me with a cat-o'-nine-tails."

"They'll set a torch to you! Me, too! They'll kill me for helping you!"

"He won't catch us, I tells you! Where be your papa and mama?"

Malinda turned her head away. Her ear pressed against the washboard bark of the oak until it ached.

"My mama's dead," she finally whispered. "The yellow fever. You should have let me die, too."

5

JASMINE THE RUNAWAYER

FOR THE NEXT THREE DAYS Malinda wished she could think Jasmine without adding runawayer, as if Runawayer were her last name. What was she going to do? "You got to stay with me," Jasmine had said. And Malinda wanted to. She could no more go through the forest alone than she could fly like that hawk overhead. But once they got to the river, that was something else. She wasn't going to be caught with a runaway.

Jasmine had found a good hiding place. Nobody could find them in this undergrowth. Since they had been here more than ten days without being found, they must be the only ones for miles around.

Jasmine never stopped for a minute to rest. She would climb a tall pine to gather muscadines from the vines entwining its branches. She brought in apples she had picked somewhere and stored them in a sack that looked like one of Malinda's petticoats and boiled pebble tea until Malinda figured she was fated to drown in it.

"You make me tired just watching you," Malinda said once.

"Huh! It be the fever make you tired."

"Maybe so."

"Is you strong enough to pick berries?"

"I reckon so." It would make time pass faster.

"Come on, then."

Not far from the campfire, Jasmine showed her the berry bushes. She gathered walnuts, too, to add to their horde.

Malinda would search for berries and nuts when Jasmine was nearby. But when alone, she stayed at the campfire, hating herself for being afraid. Sometimes Jasmine would go off for hours at a time—simply disappear—while Malinda clung to her moss bed and listened to every sound in the forest. Long before the other girl's return, Malinda began to watch for her through the dark woods. Jasmine always reappeared, shining with sweat and drooping with tiredness—but still watchful.

Feeling stronger, Malinda stayed up a little longer each day. Whenever she trembled with weakness, she slipped back onto her soft moss bed. Then she would lie on her back and watch squirrels chasing and leaping at one another from limb to limb high overhead. Her mind sometimes absorbed itself with Jasmine, the Runawayer, and her heart thumped hard at the thought of leaving their safe hideout.

Thinking of Jasmine reminded her of a time before mama had taken sick when night riders had broken into their clearing chasing another runaway slave. Mother had lit a lamp, sat on Malinda's bed, and held her tightly as the lamplight spilled feebly out the open door to where father stood on the front step.

"You can't go roaring through my sheds and smokehouse," Jeremiah Sharp had said in a friendly enough voice. "But I reckon my wife and girl are the only humans I've seen today."

"We didn't say no human—just a stinkin', runnin' nigger. We gonna take a look-see anyways."

Jeremiah drew himself tall like the straight pine across the way. "You might better trust my word. It's been good for thirty-five years, and I reckon it's good now. You just step your horses right off my place and be on your way."

The men threatened and grumbled. Then a muffled voice conceded, "Awww, Sharp's okay. Leave him be."

"We need help. Git your horse, Sharp, and come with us."

"Not this time," answered Jeremiah. He had stood on the step for an hour after the riders had left.

Now Malinda gazed at their campfire. She must get away from this Jasmine as soon as she could after they reached the river. Never mind that Jasmine had cared for her and had risked getting the fever herself. Malinda had seen what happened to runaways.

When Jasmine returned, Malinda was adding the berries and nuts she had gathered to the ones already stored in the gourds.

Jasmine stirred the fire to cook the fish she had brought, and Malinda tried to grind acorns between two rocks for flour. It would bring the strength back, Jasmine had said, but it only showed Malinda how weak she was.

Jasmine viewed Malinda as she worked. "You is better. Tonight we be leavin'."

Malinda nodded. "I'm ready to get to the 'Bigbee."

"How come?" Jasmine asked suspiciously.

"Maybe we'll find somebody—"

"No! You ain't gonna turn me in!"

"But I am gettin' help."

Jasmine's chin set in a firm line. "Help?" she said scornfully. "Me and you's all the help we needs."

"That's not what my mama and papa taught me."

"If you gonna talk about help every minute, I thinks maybe I shoulda left you with the fever. Here, eat this!"

They ate the fish, a few berries, and apples in heavy silence. Afterward, Jasmine began tying vines to a stout pole she had brought to the campfire that morning. Malinda helped her tie the other ends to the filled gourds. When the moon rose, Jasmine put one end of the pole on Malinda's shoulder and the other on hers, part of their supply of gourds and the petticoat filled with apples hanging between them.

"We carry more this way," Jasmine said, "and we's goin' slow." She set a labored pace through the trees, stopping often to rest but saying nothing. Finally reaching her destination, she untied the gourds from the pole and placed the supplies carefully under a log.

RIVER OF FIRE

Malinda slumped to the ground. So what if the river were near? She was too exhausted to care.

They made three trips to the log that night—slowly, painstakingly, halting, stopping. By the last trip Jasmine was carrying most of the weight. When they returned to their smoldering fire, Malinda sank on her moss bed and slept all the next day until dark.

That evening the moist air was cool and misty, clinging to their skin as if to stifle movement. Now their fire was covered with leaves and straw as if it had never existed.

They made their way one last time to the Tombigbee River. Malinda did not once look back.

ON THE TOMBIGBEE

WHEN THEY REACHED THE LOG that covered their food supply, Jasmine whispered, "Help me turn this here log over."

Carefully they tugged and pushed until it rolled over.

"A dugout canoe!" Malinda gasped. "Like a Choctaw's!"

"It sure be a canoe all right!"

"Did you do this?"

"I sure didn't! I found it."

"Then somebody lives around here!"

"No, they don't. There was a hundred years of cobwebs coverin' this boat."

"Choctaw Indians aren't here, or they would have found us long ago."

"How do you know about Injuns?" Jasmine threw a string of gourds into the canoe, and then turned to Malinda, "Is you gonna help me load?"

"I'm gonna help."

They began packing their goods inside the canoe, being careful to balance the load.

"I learned some Indian ways from papa," Malinda explained. "Choctaws and Creeks burn out logs like this for canoes "

Jasmine shrugged.

"Were you working on the canoe when you left me for hours?"

"Yep. I cleaned it up. And it don't leak neither. I reckon it will get us downriver."

Malinda stood up straight to stretch. Reaching out for a cypress trunk nearby, she ran her hands around it in both directions. A thick layer of moss grew on one side but not on the other.

That's north, she thought, holding her hand flat on the moss. If you ever get lost, remember how the Indians tell direction, her father had told her: by a moss that grows on the north side of trees. Excitement rippled through her. Now she felt less helpless.

Placing two long poles—each with a sharp pointed end—into the canoe last, they tugged

288

it into the marsh. When the water was deep enough, Jasmine held it while Malinda climbed inside. Then Jasmine followed.

"Don't tip it!"

"I ain't!"

"This thing's goin' to dump us in the water!" Malinda cried.

"Shhhhhh!"

They pushed the canoe clumsily with the rough poles, moving it through the high marsh grasses. Soon they edged into the Tombigbee River. The current carried them along as they fearfully stabbed the river bottom with their poles. When Malinda grew tired, she laid her pole inside the wobbly canoe and took the white pebble out of her shirt pocket. Rubbing its smooth roundness with her shaking fingers, she tied it inside a knot in the tail of her shirt in case the canoe tipped.

In a sweet gum tree behind them, a screech owl screamed.

"Screech owl say somebody gonna die." Jasmine moaned but did not break the rhythm of the pole.

Malinda tried to reassure herself. "I don't care what the screech owl says. We won't die."

The owl called again and again, and Jasmine's low moan continued until the canoe had moved well downstream.

Suddenly Malinda saw Jasmine's back

stiffen as she strained ahead to listen, the pole idle by her side.

"Steamboat be coming!"

No lights appeared through the thin mist.

"I never thought we'd find anybody on the river at night."

"You think a boat stop just 'cause it night?"

"No." The *Alabama Queen* hadn't stopped.

"Well, then."

Malinda wanted to reach out and wipe at the fog that surrounded them. "I can't see it."

"It be there!" Jasmine moved her pole, directing them nearer the tree-lined shore. They nudged the canoe under low-hanging limbs where gray, crinkly Spanish moss cascaded down among the branches to hide them from the river. The sawing of insects and the gentle lap of the water against the canoe were the only sounds at first. Finally Malinda, too, could hear the steamboat making its way upriver.

Upriver. Toward home.

Malinda counted the days since she had seen her father: two on the *Alabama Queen,* three since her ten days of fever—fifteen in all. It must be the middle of October.

"Papa's gone now," she said quietly. "He's been headed west for fourteen days."

"Then why you make like you want to go home? What be at home?"

Malinda could not answer. All she knew was that she was sick for home—the way it used to be.

The steamboat was parallel to them now, but its lights did not pick them out behind the mossy leaf curtain. The paddle wheel slapped the water, and its wake rocked the canoe. The smokestacks belched black smoke into the fog. Malinda watched it out of sight. Even if she were traveling north on that boat, she would never reach home. She had no home now. Mother was dead, and with father deeper into the wilderness, he might as well be dead.

Jasmine was looking at her. "Has you got good memories?" she suddenly asked.

"Yes." She wouldn't think about the bad ones.

"You is rich then."

Jasmine's face was a blur. Malinda brushed at her eyes.

They took their poles in hand, pushed out from their covering, and headed downstream. Later other man-made sounds rose from the shore. A bell rang and a horn blew somewhere over the bluff.

"It be a hour to dawn." Jasmine was suddenly tense. "This drift's too slow."

"What's the matter?" Malinda clutched the sides of the rocking canoe.

"That was a overseer's horn calling the field

hands for the day's work."

"A farm can't be anywhere in these dark woods."

"Huh! He ain't a-blowing to the chickadees!"

"You said we'd hide before daylight."

"Not here! I ain't stopping ten miles to a big house." Jasmine took up the pole again, pushing hard against the bottom. The pull of the current twisted one end of the canoe.

"Watch it, Jasmine! Be content with the drift."

Jasmine hunched over. "Come on, river. Move faster!"

Daylight slipped under the mist and lifted it from their shoulders. Still Jasmine made no move to bank and hide.

"We must stop!" Malinda couldn't keep her voice steady. She wanted help from somebody, but what would she do if they ran into someone in broad daylight?

"No! We ain't gonna stop yet!"

Stubborn runawayer.

Malinda's arms sagged with fatigue. The forest looked dark and ominous. Was someone in those woods watching them now that day was dawning? A crow cawed. Malinda wanted to fold up like a croaker sack and disappear in the bottom of the boat.

Slowly they rounded a bend in the river as

pink streaks shredded the horizon as far as they could see.

"Ye ding-busted, dag-blamed females! Git outta my trot lines!"

They were caught! Malinda jerked around. Her eyes swept the river bank. There he was. Hunkered over the edge, he clung to a taut line, his face blown into a rage. A low moan escaped Jasmine's lips.

7

A FEMALE
AND HER WENCH

MALINDA STARED AT the stranger. His eyes
were sunken pools in a sharp, lean face. A
homespun coat and slouch hat hung on him
like on a nail behind a door. Jerking a line
caught on the end of their canoe, he waved his
other fist at them.

"Did ye hear me? You is playing with my
trotlines! Now git! I'm gonna slap ye right up
into them woods. And don't poke my traps
with them poles!"

Jasmine, hanging her head, did not move.
Malinda leaned over to free the line. The
canoe wobbled.

"You is playing with my trotlines! Now git."

"I been outsmarted by Injuns, and I done had my goods burnt up on a steamboat. But I'll be danged if I'm gonna lose my lines to a female and her wench!"

Malinda flinched. Jasmine looked indifferent.

"Git! Git! My family's got to eat. I got nine chillun to hold in the hollow of my hand—"

Malinda jerked the line free. Under the water she saw box traps built like log cabins and a live trap in the shallows, all similar to papa's. A huge catfish, spreading its bubbles over the surface, was moving away from the live trap.

Maybe she had better capture it for the nine children. Remembering how papa had taught her, she turned her pole upside down and quick as lightning speared the fish with the sharp end.

"For your trap. It's a nice one!"

"Well, I'll be a hornswoggled goose!" The man tipped his hat to the girls. "I'm mighty obliged to you."

He pulled up the trap. Malinda stretched the pole out as far as she could reach. He added the muddy-colored catfish, half the length of his leg, to the trap.

"Do you live here? Do you have a boat? We need help—"

Jasmine grunted and pushed them away

from the shallow water near the shore.

"What you say?" the man called.

Jasmine lifted her head. "She say, 'Good luck to you!'"

Malinda looked back at the stranger. He was scratching his beard. Why had she said anything? He didn't look like the kind that could help, anyway.

After they had drifted in silence for several tense minutes, Malinda whispered, "We have to stop somewhere, Jasmine. I could have eaten that catfish raw."

"We get away from him. We crosses to the other side." Jasmine set her pole in motion.

It was useless to argue with her.

The canoe moved into deeper water and floated downriver. When Malinda let her pole straight down and it could no longer touch bottom, her stomach clutched in a knot. The opposite shore seemed miles away.

Finally Jasmine exploded. "I got somethin' to say to you! You was gonna turn me over to him. I could tell by the way you was actin'! You was gonna say, 'Here be a runawayer. Let's go get the reward.'"

Malinda bristled.

"Why didn't you, huh? Why didn't you holler for help to drag me in?"

"Get one thing straight. I'll never turn you in to anybody."

"If you goes for help, that be the same as turnin' me in. You was gonna do it the first chance you got. Why didn't you force the canoe to shore?"

Malinda could have kept Jasmine from pushing them away from the trapper, but it would have been a struggle. "I don't know, Jasmine. I guess I felt beholden."

"Beholden!" Jasmine snorted. "Ain't nobody gonna feel beholden to me."

"But you said I had to stay with you because you saved me—"

"So I say it once. That don't mean I got to say it now. You ain't gonna be beholden."

"Why?"

"Because you sit there all beholden like till you burn your insides out, and in the end you call the dogs on me anyhow."

Malinda jabbed her pole into the current.

"You gonna double-cross me, do it right now! Just get!"

"You chose a fine place for your sermon," Malinda retorted. "Right here in the middle of the river."

Jasmine wiped her face with her shirttail and lapsed into silence.

Her back to Jasmine, Malinda thought about her dark face, the long lashes that framed her large walnut-shaped eyes, the stubborn thrust of her chin. "I do thank you for takin' care of me all those days."

"It ain't no thanks if you gonna get help."

"But didn't that old man think just what you thought he would? The reason you saved me was so I could pretend to be your mistis. Don't deny it! And that's just what he thought, too. So will everybody else."

"Huh! You don't know nothin'! If that old goat wasn't all tied up in his trot lines, he be lookin' at us real hard. And he see all right that I be a runawayer. He got eyes like fire."

Malinda didn't want to say that Jasmine had acted like a runawayer, too. She kept silent.

Finally they reached midstream two miles below the trot lines. The day's sun was bright in its newness, and they were alone. Or were they? Surely a thousand eyes must be watching them from the woods.

The onrush of the water twisted the canoe into a spin.

"Watch it!"

"Oh, lawsy mercy!"

"Don't fight it!"

The canoe turned two complete circles. Then the current headed them toward the opposite bank.

Jasmine's knuckles were shiny from her iron grip on the pole. "And God say, let the dry land appear," she intoned like a preacher.

"Amen!" Malinda swallowed the knot in her throat.

They were too busy keeping the canoe upright in the swifter current to speak. A mile of shore had slipped by when they nosed the canoe into a bayou where water invaded the low land far up among the cypress trees. They maneuvered between the trunks until a slow slope framed the water's edge. Surveying the land far ahead, they saw tall sweet gums and pines among an undergrowth of swamp dogwood and red maple. Squirrels barked as they leaped like a whirlwind through the branches, and overhead in a cypress, a possum stared at them with beady eyes. A fox yelped in the distance.

When they had pulled the canoe completely out of the water, taken out all the supplies and turned the boat over on top of their rations, Malinda shook her finger at the snout-nosed possum.

"That's to keep you out of our apples!"

"You go hunt for fish since you is so hungry," Jasmine said, picking up a large gourd. "I's goin' over the hill."

"Be watchful!"

Malinda followed the riverbank with her pole until she found a shallow pool where bushes hung over the water. Soon she returned to the canoe with a large trout she had speared, but Jasmine was nowhere in sight.

How were they going to start a fire? She had never questioned how Jasmine had started the fire that had burned all those days and nights. It just was. She gathered brush and dry maple leaves and pine needles to pass the time until Jasmine returned. Ravenous, she ate an apple and snubbed her nose at the possum who was now hanging by his tail. Finally she heard the cracking of footsteps as Jasmine approached with fresh clear water.

"I come across a spring!"

"I found a trout, but I didn't find a fire." Malinda drank from the gourd.

Jasmine pulled out a small leather pouch that was tied to the inside of her pants, untied the string, and displayed a piece of flint, her knife, and a notched stick.

"I come prepared this time." She made a notch on the stick with her knife and put them back in the pouch. They cleared a place for the brush and leaves Malinda had gathered, then struck the flint between two rocks endlessly until its sparks finally lit the pine needles Malinda held.

When the fire caught up, Malinda asked, "How many times before this did you run away?"

Jasmine handed her the knife to clean the trout, then got out the gourd frypan and an apple. She ate the apple down to the core and added it, sizzling, to the flames before answering, "Once."

"How far are you from home?"

"I ain't got no home."

Neither did Malinda. She shrugged sadly. "From your master then."

Jasmine did not answer.

Malinda put the fish in the pan and placed it over the flames. "I need to know. Would they be huntin' you here? Would anybody around have descriptions of you?"

"How come you wants to know?"

"I'm wondering if night riders are out for you." She shivered at the thought.

Jasmine traced the outline of a fish in the cleared space by the fire. "I's pretty far from my big house, and I got my own plan."

"You'll still need some help."

"Huh! Help, help, help! That be the only word you knows. Last time I got helped right back to my massa, and I don't need that kind no more."

They ate the fish, another apple, and some berries.

Jasmine tossed her head. "Did you ever have a wench?"

"No!"

"Next time we runs into somebody, you better act more like a mistis."

"Who says I'm stayin' with you?"

Jasmine's black round eyes looked twice as large across the fire. "I ain't nobody's slave—if I don't get caught. Even if I has to play like you is, I ain't nobody's!"

"I ain't gonna get caught with a runawayer, either. Can't you get it through your head that they'd kill us—"

"You talks so biggety! You don't know nothin'. You ain't never felt a cat-o'-nine-tails on your back. You ain't never seen a lynching."

"I don't want to hear—"

"Keep your voice down! So you don't want to hear. You don't want nothin', does you, but your ma and pa. Well, you better figure out I's all you got right now."

Malinda tightened her fist around the pebble knotted in her shirttail until her fingers ached.

"While I'm with you, we ain't runnin' across anybody," she said. "I'll see to that."

"Who say? We has already done it once."

"We'll have to be more careful."

"But if you plays mistis properlike, who gonna know I's a runawayer?"

After a long silence Malinda said, "You'd have to teach me how to act."

"Oh, lawsy mercy! I's beginnin' to wish I had saved somebody else."

"Did you have any choice?"

"Does I have to tell everything?"

Malinda felt the tension between them drain away.

Much later Jasmine said, "I remembers how turnip greens smells cooked outdoors in a big black washpot. I sho could stand some."

"And corn bread crumbled up in the potlicker," Malinda added, savoring the tasty liquid left in the pot after the greens were cooked.

"And buttermilk!"

Malinda lay down near the warm coals. "We're homesick."

Jasmine hooted. "Tell that to the possum!"

8

STORM CLOUDS

THE CLAMOR THAT JANGLED Malinda awake set her heart pounding like an ax hitting a tree. She controlled her first impulse to spring up and turned her head unobtrusively. Jasmine was awake, too. No one stood within her range of vision, so Malinda raised her head slowly. A wiry, dirty gray-haired possum was clattering their gourds as a dozen squirrels flitted around the canoe.

She jumped up. "Go find your own nuts!"

The squirrels scattered like chickens. The possum jumped to the nearest tree and swung by his ratlike tail from the highest limb.

"Just waiting for us to turn our backs," Malinda sputtered.

A scratch sounded from inside the canoe. She raised one end, and a red squirrel with a nut in his mouth darted out. She dropped the canoe and hunted until she found the place where the squirrel had weaseled through. Jasmine clogged the opening with the frypan.

Malinda returned to the fire, which was only a bed of coals now. "Last night plain tuckered me," she said as she lay back down.

"I got a pain from restin'. I's gonna look around."

"Oh?" Malinda hesitated, then added softly, "If you happen to meet anybody, please don't act like a runawayer. Hold your head up and look them right in the eye. If you have to give your name, say it's Jasmine even if it really isn't."

Jasmine stood as if her feet had taken root. "Now you done gone to preachin'."

"You don't want to give yourself away, do you?"

Jasmine only grunted and turned toward the slope.

It was almost dusk when Jasmine woke Malinda, her hands loaded with ripe persimmons.

"C'mon," she said. "Help me."

They hid the persimmons under the canoe. Then Jasmine led the way over the slope and turned south. Crickets and red-winged blackbirds sang, and in the crevice between the hills, daisies and goldenrod bloomed. When they reached the spring, Jasmine and Malinda drank from their cupped hands and washed their faces.

"I feel as dirty as when the sweet-potato hill caved in on me," said Malinda.

"Don't your pa know how to store taters right for the winter?"

"Sure. But once when I was little, I thought if I kept diggin' in the side of the hill, I might reach the other side of the world. It didn't work."

Jasmine chuckled. "A tater hill is a tater hill. It sho ain't the doorway to the other side of creation."

Malinda nodded.

Lying flat, her dripping face hanging over the spring, Jasmine looked at her. "My name be *Jasmine!*"

Malinda raised her head, her own face dripping wet, and stared at Jasmine a moment. She didn't know what to say. They wiped their faces on the tails of their homespun shirts.

"The persimmon tree is yonder." Jasmine pointed to a tree fifty feet away.

RIVER OF FIRE

Malinda stripped off one of her two remaining petticoats and tied a knot in one end so they could fill it with persimmons. Later when the fruit had been placed safely under the canoe, they made another trip to the spring to fill three gourds with water.

That night they cooked up a mush with persimmon pulp. It was not tasty like corn bread and pot liquor, but it filled their stomachs. Afterwards when they put out the fire with dirt and scattered leaves over the clearing, Jasmine said, "I didn't run across nobody today, 'cept a turkey buzzard in the sky. He not flap his wings while I's looking at him, so my wish gonna come true."

They turned the canoe over and reloaded it. As they pushed off between the cypress trees in the water, Malinda wondered what Jasmine had wished for.

The moon looked like a large orange ball suspended in the sky while the twinkling stars and the fireflies in the woods seemed to be kin. Wind sent crinkled leaves scuttling across the surface of the water. Buoyed by a night's experience, Malinda and Jasmine moved with the current as if on a charted course. They took cover under branches twice when other boats passed and relaxed enough to eat fruit and nuts occasionally.

Once Malinda ventured enough confidence to ask Jasmine if she had heard anything about a steamboat explosion before she had found her in the woods.

"I reckon so. I seen it."

"You did?"

"I sho did! All that noise and fire and yellin'. I knowed the world be coming to a end, and I runned lickety-split."

"Do you know if most everybody got free?"

"Not me. I's too far back in the woods, and I's not stayin' around to see. Anyways, the night be too dark." Jasmine gave her a hard look. "Has you got friends on that boat?"

"Not really. When the boat exploded, I was too scared to think. But now I keep worryin' about the others."

Jasmine brought her pole down strong in the river. "I reckon you just gonna have to leave them up to the Lord. Ain't that what they's having to do with you?"

"I reckon so. Jasmine, how long had you been runnin' when you saw the steamboat?"

"A few days."

"Where did you come from?"

"I ain't sayin'."

"Do you even know?"

" 'Course I does. I knows a heap."

"Then tell me."

The silence grew large between them. Malinda tried another subject.

"Since you must be a long ways from home, we can get help—"

"No we ain't!"

"Maybe nobody knows about you down here."

"Maybe, you say. But we got to be for sure."

"We can't stay in this canoe forever."

"I got a plan, and we's all the help we needs."

Malinda knew better. She hadn't lived for five years in this wild country for nothing.

They banked before daybreak.

The sky clouded over in the early afternoon. Darkness seeped through the milk glass cloudiness long before it was due, forcing the girls to huddle nearer the fire.

"I wish there was a way to warm both sides at once. My backside's cold."

"Mine, too. . . . Jasmine, we been together a whole lot of days, and I don't know nothin' about you."

"Sho you does. I be a good nurse for you, and not a bad cook, either."

"I mean *before*. You wasn't born by our first camp fire."

Jasmine set her jaw in a firm line. "I be

310

more interested in how we gonna survive on this river."

"Me, too. And I know we won't make it by ourselves—"

"Now wait a minute!"

"But I think I have a right to know something about the slave girl who saved my life."

"I ain't a slave no more! And I got a right to tell you nothin' if I don't want to."

She surely had Jasmine's back up now. She ran her fingers through her long matted hair and wished for her mother's brush. Tying her hair in a knot to keep it out of her face, she stared at Jasmine across the flames.

"We might as well be travelin', Jasmine. I'll put out the fire."

Jasmine turned away. "I's gonna warm my backside first."

They traveled several hours that third night before they heard a roll of thunder and saw a crash of lightning streak through the gloom. The wind rose, and the rumble of thunder rebounded in the wilderness. Rain fell in torrents. Firebolts lighted up chalk cliffs far ahead in the river's bend.

Suddenly the dark water turned into a monster, swirling and rising to batter everything in its path. Malinda's hands clamped like steel on the pole, trying to control the canoe.

Jasmine moaned.

Malinda yelled, "Watch it!"

The canoe twisted and pitched.

"Hold on!"

The boat capsized.

Malinda fought the frenzied, churning water to reach the surface.

"Grab the boat!" she shouted. Lightning picked out the canoe humping a wave. She struggled to reach it, then looked around wildly for Jasmine.

"Help! Help me!" The cry came from behind her. Jasmine was thrashing the water, then she disappeared under a wave. Malinda struggled against the current to reach her, straining to find her again. Jasmine's head bobbed up suddenly, her arm smacking Malinda on the shoulder.

"Help—I can't swim—"

Thunder clapped. Jasmine grabbed her around the neck, choking her. Malinda forced herself to go down deep underwater until Jasmine let go and began thrashing again. Then she surfaced, gasping and spitting. She came up behind Jasmine, slung an arm across her chest, and headed for shore.

"Relax! Don't fight!" Malinda managed to gasp. Her legs tired under the weight as she pulled at the water with her free arm. Her head went under, and she sputtered for breath. One more stroke . . . one more . . . and another . . .

When an oak limb scratched her face, she dropped her legs but could not touch bottom. Waves beat against the bank with a force that sent them reeling in retreat, and the lashing crosscurrent threw Malinda off balance. She flung out her free arm and hit the bank. Lightning laced the sky so that she could see a sheer cliff through the trees and bushes above them.

Jasmine lay limp on her overburdened arm. Malinda reached for a limb. It broke off in her hand. She fought the slashing waves, flung out her arm for another support.

"Jasmine . . . help! Take hold!"

Jasmine stirred and stretched out, clenching the oak that grew out from the cliff parallel to the raging river. Malinda pushed with her foot against the bank to boost herself over the trunk. She hung limp. How good to feel the wet ridged bark scratching her.

"Is the land flooded?" asked Jasmine.

"No. It's overhead—a hundred feet it looks like."

"We ain't gonna make it."

Malinda pulled herself up and searched for a place to climb. Her foot secure on a root, she reached for a limb above her and called for Jasmine to follow. The river hit the banks from below, and the rain slid down from above as Malinda dug into the sticky clay to find roots to grip. When she moved a foot upward, Jasmine's hands clutched the support for her own. They stopped on another strong tree trunk growing out from the bank and rested.

Able to see only when lightning slashed the storm, they groped their way upward—slipping and sliding, clawing and digging.

"Watch that bush!" Malinda shouted against the thunderclap. "It gave a little with me."

Her warning was too late. The bush pulled loose from the wet soil, and Jasmine plunged downward.

"Catch a tree! Catch a tree!" Malinda clutched her own support in terror.

The tall pines moaned in the wind. The thunder rolled. The river roared. And Jasmine crashed down the cliff, wailing.

One sound ended. Jasmine's cry.

9

CONQUERING THE TOMBIGBEE

"I'M COMIN', JASMINE! Hold on!" Malinda screamed into the void. She hunted for another place to put her foot. She turned her head sideways, straining to hear, as she inched downwards.

"Jasmine—"

"Malindy—" The sound was so weak that she did not trust her ears. "Malindy—"

Then the unsteady voice sounded once more. "Go—on to the top. I'll make it."

Relief flooded her. She wouldn't climb on. She'd wait for Jasmine.

Jasmine did not call again. Malinda dug

315

both feet into the clay above the root support and shouted encouragement when she could hear nothing beneath her but the roar of the river.

Finally Jasmine drew near. Malinda still could not see her, but she felt her presence, heard her every move. So she searched for another root and planted her feet there instead. Then she leaned over and grasped Jasmine's hand, placing it on the root she had just abandoned.

"Pull up—there. Now there's another one a little higher."

Jasmine eased flat against the cliff and rested. "I caught on to the oak."

"The one just above the river?"

"Uh-huh."

Malinda shuddered, and when Jasmine did not stir for some time, she said, "You lead now. I'll stay below."

Jasmine moved, reached upward to a scrub, dragged her feet higher, and dug in where a tree root corded the bank. Malinda followed.

By the time they reached the top, the rain felt matted to their eyelids. Clay and soggy leaves plastered their bodies. They crawled on their knees to the base of the nearest pine, collapsing onto the solid earth and retching for breath.

"Scree—screech owl—were right," Jasmine

gasped after a long time. "Death's a-comin'."

Malinda heaved, feeling blended into the soil and soppy pine needles. Her body shuddered with each gasp. She could not think beyond that moment.

"Death's twistin' my—breath out and—"

"Save your strength!" Malinda warned.

Lightning crackled and thunder rolled.

"Malindy! My plan done gone. I was goin' to Mobile—to stowaway on a boat."

Malinda pushed her straggling hair back from her face. Where could Jasmine go, and what would happen to her? Surely it must be hard to slip unseen onto a boat.

Jasmine lay still as death. In panic Malinda leaned over and pressed her ear against her back and was finally rewarded by hearing her breathe.

"Jasmine, we—are you hurt?"

"Scratches."

"Where do you hurt?"

"Just scratches."

Thank God she was alive. Malinda rested her head on her arms, her body oblivious to the rain pelting it.

"My rib bones aches. I thinks they's fr-freezin'."

Malinda lay an arm across Jasmine to warm her cold rain-soaked body. "You're getting your breath back."

She raised her head as lightning lit the sky. Then she stared and squinted her eyes, rubbing them with a fist in disbelief. She shook Jasmine's arm. "I saw a cabin—ahead of us."

Jasmine looked up.

"Straight ahead!" Malinda peered into the darkness until a lightning streak appeared again.

"There be more than one," Jasmine said. "I see lots."

"I can't. Come on, lightnin'."

"Let there be lights in the firmyment!" Jasmine intoned, but the flashes came less often.

"Come on! We're gettin' out of the rain."

"No! I ain't goin' to no cabins."

Malinda sneezed. "There's no light in any of the buildings. We got to see if they're deserted."

Jasmine struggled to her feet. "Oh, lawsy mercy, I don't like this." She followed well behind Malinda. "If anybody be there, I's runnin'!"

The first structure they came to was a windowless double cabin with a breezeway porch between. Malinda eased up the steps onto the breezeway, then to a door that hung crazily on its hinges.

She peered inside the cabin. A crude wood bed frame draped in cobwebs was all she could see. She motioned to Jasmine to come inside.

Malinda worked with the door until she got it latched upright while Jasmine stumbled around the room. Aided only by occasional lightning through the cracks between the logs, she found three dusty quilts heaped in a corner.

"Let's stay here, Jasmine. This settlement must be abandoned—there's no lamplight or woodsmoke. I feel no life; at least nobody is in this cabin."

"We need to shake the earth out of these." Jasmine held up the quilts.

Malinda unlatched the door, and they took the quilts to the porch and shook them until their arms ached. Jasmine winced. "My side don't feel too good," she said.

They choked on the dust. The wind and rain blew through the passageway making them lose balance and setting their teeth to chattering. Malinda sneezed and coughed again.

Jasmine stopped short, suddenly alert and tense. "Did you hear a groan?"

"It's just the wind in the trees. C'mon!"

"Mebbe. Mebbe so."

Once inside Malinda again latched the door. They rung out their clothes and hung them over the bed frame to dry. Malinda unknotted the white pebble from her shirt. Holding it in her hand, she curled up in a quilt to sleep.

Favoring her left side, Jasmine clawed at a cobweb, the lightning through the cracks highlighting her body. Then she rolled up in another quilt beside Malinda on the floor.

The storm raged overhead, but Malinda began to feel warm inside the blanket. With a roof over them and the coziness of four walls, she began to doze.

"Where was you headed?" came the muffled question from deep in Jasmine's quilt.

Malinda hesitated. Should she tell her? "I was goin' to Mobile, too."

Nothing moved inside the other bundle, but now that she was awake again, Malinda wanted to talk. She remembered the warm times at home after the lamplight had been turned out when papa and mama would share their dreams and stories of their slow trek from North Carolina to the lush lands of the West, a land flowing with milk and honey they had been told. Nobody had mentioned the yellow fever, Malinda thought bitterly, just milk and honey.

"What are you goin' to do now, Jasmine?"

There was no answer, but she spoke up again, ignoring Jasmine's silence. "What, Jasmine?"

Still no answer. She would change the subject.

"Now I know how mama and papa felt when

they had beat the forest back one more acre for planting. We conquered the Tombigbee tonight!" She felt a weary pride.

"Huh!" Jasmine suddenly grunted. "It took all our food, and tomorrow we got to build a raft."

Malinda sat straight up. "No we don't! I'm not gonna get on that river with you again. Why didn't you tell me you couldn't swim?"

Again Jasmine ignored her question. "G'night, Malindy."

If Malinda wasn't going on the Tombigbee again and was scared of the forest, what was she going to do? She couldn't stay here. She closed her eyes and held tightly to her pebble. She would face that question tomorrow.

HANTS!

WHEN MALINDA AWAKENED several hours later, Jasmine was sitting against the door.

"You tryin' to hold it up?" Malinda asked lazily. She bundled up tighter in her blanket.

"There be hants in this here cabin!" Jasmine's round black eyes were larger than usual. "They been groanin' and moanin', and they not like us. So we's gettin' out of here!"

"I don't believe in hants. Besides, we can't leave. It's still rainin'."

Jasmine's eyes rolled. "That don't make no difference to hants."

"It does to me. I'm sleeping another twenty

322

hours." Malinda moved around in her blanket, settled finally into a comfortable position, and closed her eyes. But not before she heard it—a groan as clear as if it had come from the corner of their room.

The skin on her scalp crawled. "Jasmine—" She sat up, clutching her quilt under her chin.

"Huh! Didn't I tells you?"

"I ain't afraid of hants. I don't believe in them." Her voice quavered. Her throat was dry.

"You sho don't sound like it." Jasmine pushed her back harder against the door.

Malinda flung off the quilt and grabbed her clothes, shivering as she pulled the clammy underpants and petticoat over her skinny body. She pitched Jasmine's baggy trousers to her.

"Come on out of that blanket."

The groan again.

"I'm movin' out!" Malinda jerked on the long homespun shirt Jasmine had put on her during her fever days and slipped the white good-luck stone into her shirt pocket.

"Not without me you ain't!" Jasmine jumped up and was in her clothes by the time Malinda unlatched the door and opened it a few inches. She saw nothing on the breezeway, so she eased through the opening with Jasmine right behind.

The moan sounded again, louder than ever. "Oh, lawsy mercy!"

"Somebody's in that room." Malinda pointed to the other side of the breezeway. "Don't you think we ought to find out what's in there?"

Jasmine turned her head sideways, listening. When they heard the moan again, Jasmine said, "Is we or is we ain't a scaredy-cat?"

"We is."

Malinda stepped aside. Jasmine stuck her thumb in a knothole and pushed with the palm of her hand against the door. It moved with excruciating slowness. Malinda could hardly bear the odor seeping from the room. Jasmine held her nose with her free hand and pushed her head in cautiously, then jerked back frantically trying to get her thumb out of the knothole.

"Injun! There be a Injun in there!"

"What kind?"

"I say what kind! A Injun!"

"Let me see."

Jasmine extracted her thumb from the knothole. Malinda held her nose to block out the stench and cautiously looked inside. Heaped in a corner, as if waiting to die, was a body dressed in a printed calico shirt, buckskin leggings with beaded ornaments, and a white turban on his head.

"It's a wounded Choctaw instead of a hant," she whispered. She pushed open the door and eased over to the Indian who seemed to be unconscious. But when she put her hand on his forehead, his eyes slowly opened. His lips formed the word, *"water."* Malinda smiled, trying to reassure him, although she wanted to retch from the smell.

"Well—" his lips barely whispered. She checked beneath his shirt and found blood-soaked rags covering his chest from just below his left collarbone to underneath his arm. She closed his shirt.

"We'll find water for you."

The eyes opened again.

"We'll be back."

The eyes closed, then opened. Was he signaling that he understood? She rejoined Jasmine. "Leave the door open to let in more fresh air."

"Where you goin'?"

"He says there's a well, so I'll have to find it. You look for something to carry water in—and dry wood for a fire. I got to find some herbs—"

"Whoa! How we knows every cabin ain't plumb full of Injuns? We's leaving and ain't coming back."

"But he's wounded and I promised. A Choctaw hates a white who lies."

"I ain't no white. And he can hate me all he

wants to. I don't trust him."

"You don't trust anybody, do you?"

"I don't have cause to trust nobody," Jasmine answered. "I's goin' and I ain't comin' back."

"Don't you trust me?"

"When all you does is talk about gettin' help and ask me more questions than tadpoles in a creek? You got to take me as me without no more questions before I trusts you."

Malinda's chin set in a firm line. "Well, I promised the Choctaw and I'm stayin'." She marched down the steps and headed north toward the well, forcing herself not to glance back at Jasmine. She would have to gamble that Jasmine would not leave without her. But she looked warily at the other buildings she passed. Grasses and weeds grew high in the pathway and around the cabin doors. There was no sign of life anywhere.

Finally she found a well located in what seemed to be the center of the abandoned settlement. A chain hung down in the well from the center pulley. She leaned over, trying to look into it, but not trusting the planks to support her. She pulled the chain up until she saw with relief that a bucket was attached to the end. She lowered it until it smacked the water below, then raised the full bucket and set it on the ground while she headed for the

"It's a wounded Choctaw instead of a hant."

woods behind the well to look for herbs.

But she stopped before she reached them. She could not go on into the forest alone. There was a chance she could find herbs for medicine in the weeds between the trees and the settlement. When she was almost ready to give up, she discovered two peach trees behind a cabin. She gathered as many leaves as she could carry in the tail of her shirt and returned to the well for the bucket of water.

It was not there. She rubbed her eyes and walked all around the well, stared at both ends of the chain that dangled from the pulley, walked around in the opposite direction, and leaned over as far as she dared to peer into its dark depths again.

Then she turned down the path toward their cabin with a sinking feeling, looking back at the well every few steps but not daring to face the question of who had taken the bucket and, more importantly, where that person might be. Were eyes staring at her through the chinks in the cabins? She shivered and hunched her shoulders. With Jasmine she had never felt so afraid.

She smelled woodsmoke! It was filtering up from the direction of their cabin. Holding fast to her shirttail full of leaves, she sprinted down the path, bounded up the cabin steps, and then stopped. Jasmine must not see how elated she was that the black girl had stayed, at least not now. Malinda walked nonchalantly across the porch and into the room where they had slept.

Jasmine was adding more wood to the fire and did not glance at Malinda. "Huh! Chickens that fly the coop always cacklin' that they be comin' back—they sho do. I bet you wouldn't a-come back if you hadn't smelled the smoke."

Malinda grinned to herself. "Is that why you built the fire?"

"That ain't for you to know."

"Look, I found peach leaves. How's our Indian?"

"He ain't my Injun!" Jasmine nodded to a cup and two crockery bowls by the fireplace. "I found them and dry wood in one of them cabins. Don't say I didn't give him some water."

"Thanks. I'm glad it was you that got the bucket at the well."

Jasmine's hand lay still on the cup for a long moment before she handed it to Malinda. "Well, don't just sit there! Get this to him."

"Okay."

Jasmine added, "I come across a crow's nest in the tip-top of a pine out yonder. So I climb up."

"Whatever for?"

"Eggs. I's looking for crow's eggs."

329

"Crow's eggs in *October?*"

"Well, I didn't find none, but then I remembers about birch bark, so I cuts some of that and is gonna boil it into a thick soup."

"Why didn't you catch the crow instead?" Malinda was enjoying the talk. It felt good after the scare she'd just had.

"Always wantin' something you ain't got. Now get! But first—" Jasmine turned suddenly solemn. "How does you know he be a Choctaw?"

"His turban for one thing and his long hair."

"You sure?"

Malinda held the cup steady. "I'm sure." She headed once again for the room across the porch.

11

NISH'KINHALUPA

By putting her arm under the Choctaw's head and holding the cup to his lips, Malinda finally got him to swallow a little water. His eyelids blinked.

"I found water, and we're making a peach leaf poultice," she said.

He swallowed again, and she set the cup down, opened his shirt, and removed the rags to get a closer look at the wound. Gangrene—that putrid odor was gangrene. She had seen enough animals with gangrene to know the poultice was too late to help him.

His eyes were staring at her, and she pretended to be busy with the wound to avoid them. He murmured slowly in his own language, his lips barely moving, but then whispered, "Too late. You come too late." He didn't sound sad.

She shook her head and said the only Choctaw words she could remember from the few papa had taught her. "Hello. I am your friend."

The man trembled and poured out a stream of low guttural Choctaw phrases. She strained to hear; he seemed to be asking her a question. She shook her head again and told him she could not understand as she gave him another sip of water. His eyes closed and again he whispered, "Too late."

Malinda jumped in surprise when she heard Jasmine behind her. She was holding out a couple of hot wet rags, torn from one of the blankets.

"Thanks, let's try—"

"*You* can try.".

Malinda turned back to the man. His glance had shifted to Jasmine.

"If you help it will be easier to clean the wound," Malinda said, but she wondered why she was undertaking the hopeless task.

Jasmine did not move. "You sure you ain't a Injun?" she asked suspiciously.

"I'm sure."

"I ain't never seen a white who could talk Injun talk."

"I have. Papa taught me just a little—"

"If your papa Injun, then you be Injun."

"Papa had friends among the Choctaws, especially Running Bull."

"How come you know Injun talk and don't know nothin' about being a mistis?"

Malinda set the cup down deliberately, aware of the man's eyes on first her and then Jasmine. "Will you please understand that my papa was a herdsman?" she asked irritably. "He lived by raisin' cattle, growin' food for us, and huntin' in the forest where a few Choctaws still live. They were his friends."

"Huh!"

Malinda's lips drew together in a tight line. "I don't know anything about bein' a mistress because we didn't have slaves, and I don't know anything about runaways either."

"You sho don't!" Jasmine snorted.

"Are you goin' to help me or not?"

Jasmine wiped her damp hands on her trousers. "I reckon so—this once."

They set to work to clean the wound, the Indian not wincing a single time but his eyes never leaving their faces.

Jasmine broke the silence. "He voodooin' us."

Malinda felt his weak pulse.

"I wish we had all them apples and berries and persimmons and the canoe we lost in the river," Jasmine whispered as if uncomfortable with the silence.

"Where's the birch bark?"

"They's boilin'. How long we got to stay here?"

"I figure this is a good rest place from last night's fight with the 'Bigbee."

"Two words you always spitting out—*rest* and *help*. I's gettin' tired to the bone of hearin' them."

Malinda grinned, her impatience gone. "*Rest* your tiredness then."

"Oh, lawsy mercy!" Jasmine stood up. "I gonna feed him and see if I can break his voodoo spell."

"Those leaves ought to soak for hours but bring them in anyway. We can't wait that long."

When Jasmine left, the man moved his hand along his right side, muttering incoherently with his gaze still tense on Malinda. Painstakingly he grasped something and moved so that she could see it. She drew back from the hatchet in his hand.

"You . . . take. You need," he managed to whisper.

She cautiously reached out and took the hatchet from his grasp, laying it on the floor behind her. "Thanks . . . thank you." After losing everything in the canoe, an Indian hatchet was welcome.

He had spoken in English again, and she wondered how much he could understand. She asked gently, "Where are we?" His eyes closed for the first time since she had begun working on his wound. She tried again, "Do you know this place?"

Mockingbirds sang in the pines.

"Ho-hobuckintoopa."

She did not know the name. "I do not understand." She waited to see if he would speak again.

"Saint Stephens."

The first capital of the state? She remembered papa saying once that it was fast becoming a ghost town, just as the circuit-riding preacher Lorenzo Dow had predicted. She had pictured Saint Stephens as being larger than this.

"Are you sure?"

"Saint Stephens," he repeated. "I . . . die . . . in Hobuckintoopa."

Malinda felt his pulse again, put the cup to his lips, and waited impatiently for Jasmine.

By the time Jasmine returned, the man was beginning to feel feverish. "These hot leaves ain't gonna do no good," she said matter-of-factly. "I's got thick soup now."

"I think his fever's risin'."

"You give him this soup so's I can hunt pebbles for tea." Jasmine looked relieved to have another excuse for leaving.

"Here." Malinda took her white stone out of her shirt pocket and gave it to Jasmine.

"One ain't enough. I hunts for more." Jasmine slipped the stone into her own pocket and patted it. "I not lose it," she said as she left.

Jasmine had been scavenging again, for cattail roots seasoned the warm soup that had been thickened with the inside layer of birch bark. Malinda fed him sip by sip. Her own stomach lurched; she could not remember when she had last eaten. Yet the stench of the wound took her appetite away.

"You look better," she observed as he finished the soup. "What's your name?"

"Nish'kinhalupa, the one with the Eagle Eye."

"Why did you give me the hatchet?"

The staring eyes focused on her. "You need it. You will go on long journey—perhaps."

"Why do you say perhaps?"

"Nish'kinhalupa sees two ways stretching out arms to you. One trail from Hobuckintoopa follows the river to the big waters. One trail follows the sun to a plantation."

"How far is the plantation?"

"Two, perhaps three hours."

"The big waters—is that toward Mobile?"

Eagle Eye nodded, struggling to raise himself.

"You must rest. The talk is taking away your breath."

"No, I die here. The ashes of my people are here." He raised himself until he was supporting his weight on his elbow. Malinda understood how he had acquired the name Eagle Eye; she squirmed under his gaze.

"You won't need hatchet if you go west to the plantation. My people go west. Now we are broken."

She moved the hatchet from behind her to his side. Looking into his eyes, she wished she had paid more attention to the stories papa had told her about the Choctaws and Creeks who lived in Alabama. Saint Stephens had been a large trading center long before the white man moved into the wilderness. Indian trails from every direction crossed there. She also knew that most of the tribes had been moving west for several years. Her parents were guarded in what they said in front of her about the removal of Indians from their lands. But papa's face always looked bitter and grim after a visit with his friend Running Bull.

"Some of your people live a-half day's travel from my papa's cabin," she said.

"I come back to get all my people." Nish'kinhalupa lay back exhausted, beads of sweat standing out on his forehead.

"How were you wounded?"

He ignored the question.

"Six winters I am away from this land of my people." His hand clasped tightly around the hatchet. "I hear their voices. I see their tears."

Malinda wiped his face with one of the clean wet rags, then added more hot leaves to his wound.

"The plantation. Is it just two hours from here?"

His eyes seemed to stare right through her. "You take the trail west. Do you go without the slave?"

She had no answer.

"You go west, and perhaps you, too, see tears."

She nodded, goose bumps popping out on her arms when he turned the hatchet in his hand and laid it on the floor pointing south. "You know Choctaw trail signs?"

"My papa taught me."

His words tumbled out as if he expected each one to be his last. There was a good trail to Mobile, he said, but if she knew the signs she could take a short cut and pick it up farther south, thus saving a day's travel. Follow the river one day, cross a swamp, and pick up the signs southwest at the Choctaw cabin, one hour's travel past the swamp. Exhausted he fell back.

"Take gift," he added.

Malinda wiped his face again. Did she dare give him sips of water instead of pebble tea now that his fever had risen? And where was Jasmine?

The eagle eyes rolled back; his eyelids closed. "Go now," he whispered.

WHICH WAY?

MALINDA SAT IN FRONT of the fire in the cabin where she and Jasmine had slept the night before, shivering as she fingered the hatchet and waited for Jasmine to return with pebbles for tea. She turned it so that the head faced away from the river—west, toward the plantation Eagle Eye had mentioned. She wanted to strike out in that direction. Turning it clockwise, she changed the hatchet head to point south—toward the wooded trails, the swamp, the days of travel with a runawayer to Mobile.

Why should she go on downriver when help

lay two hours away? She could tell Jasmine the trail Eagle Eye had described, and even give her the hatchet so she could go on alone. Eagle Eye had said Malinda would not need it if she traveled to the big house. What else had he said?

"You go west, and perhaps you, too, see tears."

What if she did? She had seen plenty in her lifetime. She was sick of her constant fear, of cringing in the woods whenever she was alone. Besides, she was weak from hunger, and food and shelter lay only a short distance away.

Eagle Eye had never pointed the hatchet west, only south. Malinda picked it up and deliberately set it down pointing west. Then she tasted the thick soup Jasmine had left warming in a tin cup on the coals, relaxing now that she had made her decision. She handled the hot cup with the tail of her shirt and sipped the soup slowly. Holding it in her mouth until it penetrated every spot and her teeth ached from its heat, she savored each drop until it cooled. Only then did she swallow it, concentrating on the soup and avoiding a glance at the hatchet.

"What about the Injun?"

Malinda jerked guiltily, hugging the warm tin cup with her palms.

Jasmine stepped closer to the fire. "I can't find white pebbles for tea."

"We don't need them now."

"What does you mean?"

"He told us to go."

"Is we just gonna leave him to die?"

Malinda sipped slowly from the cup. "That's the way he wants it."

Jasmine slipped by Malinda and crossed the porch. She tried to peek through the knothole before she opened the door, moving cautiously toward the Indian's outstretched body.

"Malindy!"

Malinda set the cup down and joined her.

"He dead, ain't he?"

Malinda placed her hand on his forehead, his fever replaced by an icy clamminess. "He's dead."

"Now what we gonna do? With just that hatchet, we be diggin' a grave till old Joshua make the sun stand still."

"We'll leave him here."

"Right here on the cold floor? You's tetched in the head."

"That's the way he wanted it."

"How you know?"

"I just know."

"Huh!" Jasmine turned on her heels and left. In a minute she returned with one of the blankets and carefully placed it over Eagle

Eye. "You and that Injun sho don't know much about dying."

"Somebody'll come along one day and burn this place down. Then his ashes will join those of his people. It's what he wants, I tell you."

"It still ain't human. Now let's git! I ain't mouthin' off no more in this room." Jasmine bolted out the door.

Malinda looked at Eagle Eye's calm features, then stepped outside. Sticking her thumb in the knothole, she closed the door carefully. She glanced at the hatchet in the other room and on beyond it to the bed where the dress her mama had stitched by hand hung.

"Jasmine, if you knew a plantation were close by, would you go there for help?" Her voice shook as she struggled to keep calm.

Jasmine looked at her with suspicion. "Me go to a big house? How come you ask?"

"I just wondered."

"You know I ain't joinin' Daniel in the lions' den. I ain't goin' to no big house neither."

But if she went ahead and found out they were friendly, she could return with help, Malinda convinced herself. She could pose as Jasmine's mistress, and no one would be suspicious. If the folks at the big house weren't kind, she and Jasmine could follow Eagle Eye's trail. It sounded sensible, but Jasmine would never agree to it. For once she must follow her own feelings.

"I'm going to draw some water," she said quickly and walked into the room for the bucket.

"I ain't stayin' here with no dead Injun."

"Go on ahead then. I'll catch up. Eagle Eye told me how to save a day's travel." Malinda shifted the bucket to her left hand. She did not look at Jasmine as she continued.

"Listen carefully now. You need to know the directions, too. We follow the river one day to a swamp, then one hour past the swamp we'll find an Indian cabin and signs to the Mobile trail. Why don't you check along the river for a trail?"

"Why you talkin' lickety-split? Don't you remembers? The river is the trail."

"It may be too thick with underbrush."

"I give a look-see. Don't get plumb lost on the way to the well."

Once outside Malinda jumped the last three steps to the ground, splattering water and mud from a puddle over her one remaining petticoat. She would not look back as she hurried down the path between the deserted cabins. Did Jasmine suspect? "Don't get plumb lost!" she had said, and she shouldn't expect Malinda to get lost going to the well.

Malinda drew the water slowly so the bucket would not hit the sides. She was shaking as if with cold.

"Quit the quaverment," she said as she set the bucket on a plank shelf at the top. The circuit-riding preacher used to say water was the staff of life. Or was it bread?

She was not really leaving Jasmine, she reassured herself, just going to get help.

She turned and, without glancing to either side, crossed the road, skirted between two cabins, and set her direction straight into the woods. It was the first time she had been in the forest alone since the night mama had died. No, it was the second; the first time came after her escape from the *Alabama Queen*. She must not panic as she had then.

She walked under the dark pines and oaks, her heart pounding like a war drum. Little of the day's gray cloudiness seeped through the heavy foliage, but she must have several hours of daylight before it got dark. She must! Her hands, clammy with sweat, clenched into fists.

The storm had fizzled out like a slow fire, but the wind was rising again. She stopped dead still and hid behind an oak as a creak, like a sagging door, sent chills through her. Then she tried to isolate the sound. Finally she gazed upward where the trunks of two dead giant oaks rubbed together, creaking eerily when they crisscrossed in the wind.

She pressed her forehead against the washboard ridges of the oak in relief. She had come perhaps a hundred feet. Could she survive two hours more in the woods just to reach the plantation? Still, fields cleared for planting might not be far away. A dense forest did not last forever; one could stumble into a clearing without even seeing it—she had that night last summer.

She shuddered, then stepped out from the oak. For the first time, she noticed streaked scratches on the oak's surface, as if it had been clawed by a wildcat. She moved on, stumbling over a log as she searched for a clearing ahead. She would *not* jump like a jack rabbit at every sound.

Her fear tasted like bitterweed. It followed her every footstep until she could stand it no longer. She turned and fled back the way she had come.

Tears blurred her vision. The forest seemed denser. She was defeated. She would never reach the plantation and never learn to control her fear either, for she was running back to Saint Stephens and Jasmine. Storm-drenched leaves and mud weighed down her feet.

The gray cloudiness seeped in among the trees ahead. Still she ran as if she were being chased until she was out of the woods and near the row of huts by the well. There she stopped long enough to snatch the bucket and fling out the water; then she dashed wild-eyed down the road to the last cabin.

The girl on the breezeway shouted, "What got into you?"

Malinda took the steps two at a time in a dash for the fireplace, where she grabbed Eagle Eye's hatchet. Sobbing, shaking, and sweating, she raked pieces of burning logs and coals from the fire into the bucket.

"What you doin'?" Jasmine kicked a log that had rolled out on the floor back into the fire, watching her with alarm.

Malinda could not bring herself to burn down this cabin, not with Eagle Eye's body in the other side. But her only hope was to whip up a fire large enough to draw the plantation folks here to their rescue. She could not travel another step through this wild country.

"What you doin'?" Jasmine demanded.

In a frenzy Malinda headed for the door with the coals. "If you have to know, I'm goin' to another cabin—" Her voice was shrill.

Jasmine latched onto her shirttail. "How come?" She, too, was near panic.

"I have reasons!" Malinda twisted away.

"You gonna burn it?" Jasmine's voice rose to a wail.

When Malinda didn't answer, Jasmine snatched at the bucket.

"You ain't gonna burn it! I not let you!"

Malinda tried to run, sobbing. But Jasmine jerked her arm. A smoldering wood knot flipped out of the bucket onto a quilt; then the quilt puffed into flames.

They stomped it, but the fire quickly spread to another quilt lying in a heap on the floor. In panic Malinda dropped the bucket, spilling red coals out in the room. She grabbed up the hatchet and her dress hanging over the bedstead as smoke filled the room.

"You crazy!" Jasmine yelled.

"I didn't mean to—"

Suddenly the whole room seemed to burst into flames. They dashed out to the rain-soaked ground.

"The devil got you! That fire bring out the whole countryside."

"Yes yes yes! We'll get help now. It's our only chance!" she shrieked.

"It ain't mine! I's runnin' before the whole woods crawls with slavers."

Malinda clutched the hatchet. "I'm stayin' here till help comes."

"You ain't closin' me in no trap with your help." Jasmine's eyes were wild. "I's leavin' for good, you hanted witch!"

Tears spilled out over Malinda's cheeks.

Jasmine was fleeing through the pines.

"Don't leave, Jasmine," Malinda sobbed hardly above a whisper. "I didn't mean to do it."

THE VIGIL

MALINDA WATCHED JASMINE disappear out of sight, heading south toward the river edge. I didn't leave Jasmine. She left me, Malinda thought, sucking in deep gulps of air between her sobs but feeling no relief. She only felt abandoned. The white stone she instinctively reached for was gone. She had given it to Jasmine for Eagle Eye's pebble tea. She had nothing left to cling to.

She circled the cabin endlessly. There was something beautiful, yet sad, in knowing that Eagle Eye's ashes would mingle among the cabin's remains and eventually return to the

350

earth that had belonged to his people. Setting the cabin on fire had been an accident—would Jasmine ever believe that?—but it had seemed right for Eagle Eye. He had wanted to die in this place; otherwise, he would have gone somewhere for help rather than burrowing himself up in the corner of a cabin. Her sobbing ceased, and a calmness and peace surrounded her. This fire was so different from the violence she had associated with fires.

Although she was exhausted, she kept a vigil in all directions, anticipating someone—anyone—to be summoned by the fire. When that someone came, she would sleep in a warm room for days, eat until she ached, and be given safe travel to Mobile. She could turn her back on the wilderness forever.

At the thought of eating, the ache in her stomach returned. Somewhere nearby she had seen some checkerberries, so she headed toward the well. She moved along the edge of the pines to look for them as she had when hunting herbs for Eagle Eye. When she found them, she ate like a wild pig stripping the berries, then hoarded the rest in the dress she still carried. She gathered the bright leaves to nibble on later.

Jasmine was probably hungry, too. She might be running so hard she wouldn't find anything to eat, or she might cross trails with someone attracted by the cabin fire. Suddenly the checkerberries tasted like potash. How could she eat when she would never know what happened to Jasmine?

She stuffed a handful of berries back in her dress. The burning logs sizzled and hissed as the last of the flaming cabin sank to the ground. The milky sky darkened; soon night would settle in.

Night. A creeping fear shivered along her spine. What if no one came?

She had not considered that possibility. Stay here alone? She gazed in the direction of the river, which she could not see below the bluff. Would any river travelers pass by and find her? Surely they could see the fire.

The cry of a hawk filled her with dread.

Timbers fell and resettled as they burned, while Malinda stared shivering into the fire. The same helpless loneliness that she had felt as she watched father kneel beside mother's bed last summer washed over her.

Malinda buried her face in her hands. She sobbed for all her named and unnamed terrors, for mama and all the losses she had known, for the long months of separation from papa that now stretched out into eternity, and for Jasmine.

She blinked at the embers shimmering before her eyes.

The hatchet felt heavy in her hand. Eagle Eye had been right all along. The only trail she could rightfully follow and still live with herself was through the hated woodlands straight south—with Jasmine.

There seemed to be enough woods to test her a hundred times over. Papa had said she could not run from the wilderness and survive, and mama had said it was in the wilderness that one found God. All she could say right now was that she and Jasmine needed each other.

She shivered, chills like a creepy crawling vine moving through her again. The hissing flames seemed to be the only noise in all the woods. The birds had stopped singing; no winds rustled through the trees; no squirrels skittered from limb to limb.

She juggled the hatchet in her hand. "Thank you, Eagle Eye, for the hatchet," she said aloud to the flames. "And g'bye—as Jasmine would say."

The fire no longer evoked images of a runaway's torture and that was a good omen as she moved away from the heat.

The forest seemed as deserted as ever. She darted through the pines toward the river. It was not a question of could she find Jasmine. She must find her.

The pines grew right up to the riverbank. She glanced quickly over the bluff and wondered how she and Jasmine had ever climbed to the level ground in that vicious storm.

She kept her gaze out toward the river as she ran on the soggy pine needles, trying not to think about the woods around her. The bluff continued as far downriver as she could see, past the white cliffs she and Jasmine had viewed from the canoe.

The bend in the river seemed endless. Pains pinging her ribs slowed her pace, but soon she was streaking through the trees again, realizing that the twilight was disappearing. She found no trace of Jasmine. She wanted to call her name into the darkness, but she did not dare.

She tangled in cobwebs and stumbled on roots. A hoot owl called from the dark recesses of the forest beside her. A fox yelped. Tonight there would be no moonlight. How long before total darkness? Malinda moved blindly ahead, her chest aching, her throat closing tight.

Suddenly she heard a bell ringing. People were shouting. Lights were visible far below on the river. A large boat was pulling away from shore. Ahead a moving line of slaves carried supplies away from the river as their masters waved and shouted back to the boat. How long had they been hauling supplies, and where were they going? Had they stumbled on to Jasmine? *Oh, God, where is Jasmine? If you have anything to do about it, God, don't let her get caught!*

Malinda ducked behind a tree. As she slid down to the ground near a bush, she toppled over a body hunched up in a knot.

14

TOGETHER AGAIN

MALINDA HUGGED the soft brown body. "It's me—Malindy," she whispered in her ear. "Don't be afraid."

Jasmine pulled away. "I ain't scared!" she whispered in contempt. "There they is, the help you always cryin' for. Now git!"

"Hush! You want them to hear us?"

Jasmine fell silent. Malinda waited. Several minutes later she whispered, "Maybe they've gone. I'll take a look."

"Hush! I hears voices."

They strained to hear.

". . . girl lost. What'd cap'n say the name was?"

"Sharp, was it? Yeah, Sharp. Only passenger unaccounted for, eh? Probably drowned."

"Cap'n's passing the word along up and down the river. As a favor to her old man, he says."

The voices dwindled away into the forest.

Malinda's blood pounded. "Did you hear that?" she whispered.

"Sho I did. What you gonna do?"

"We're gettin' out of here lickety-split. They know I was travelin' alone on that boat."

Their glances met and held.

Jasmine finally said, "I wonders if they knows it all down the river."

"There goes our help, Jasmine. We don't have any hope for it now."

"But, Malindy, all you got to do is follow them voices. Tell them who you are, and they get you on a boat right down the 'Bigbee to Mobile."

It sounded tempting.

"And what would happen to you?"

Jasmine hung her head. "I made out all them days before I find you. I reckon I can get to where I be goin' without you."

Malinda had never heard such loneliness in Jasmine's voice. "I reckon I better stay with you. Now, come on! Follow me."

Jasmine stopped her. "You ain't acting like

357

no hanted witch now, Malindy."

"No, I'm just myself."

"You sho you ain't doing this just 'cause you feels beholden?"

"How could I feel beholden? You'd have been drowned long ago if I hadn't pulled you outta the river. I figure we're even."

Jasmine grinned. "I remembers. Okay, then I follows you."

Malinda raised slowly so she could see over the bush, hidden by the darkness that had enveloped everyone. She remembered the Choctaw movements papa had once taught her—the games she had played with him, disappearing instantly and turning up minutes later somewhere else without his detecting her.

She inched along on all fours for several feet and then stood straight as an arrow behind a pine, waiting several seconds before looking out around the trunk. She motioned for Jasmine to follow, then stooped and crawled off to the left and flattened herself beside a log. If he were watching her now, Running Bull would have roared his approval.

Jasmine joined her, copying her same movements. "I can't stay here," Malinda whispered. "Let's stoop low, keep our direction by the river, and go as far as we can."

"What if they's dogs around?"

"Did you hear any before I found you?"

"Nope."

"Let's go then." Malinda moved out from the log. They ran stooped over until their backs and legs ached, then flattened themselves on the ground and rested. They heard only the quietness of the forest.

Sometime later they straightened up behind a live oak tree, its huge craggy limbs covering them like an umbrella. "Let's sleep here," Malinda said on impulse. "We can travel faster at dawn."

"We ain't too far from back there."

"Don't you think we're safe for now?"

"I reckon."

"Let's fox any snoopin' dogs." Malinda led the way far down the trail and then doubled back to the giant live oak.

"Don't touch the tree trunk, and our scent will end way down there on the trail."

She swung up on a low broad limb with Jasmine following her. They walked the limb and climbed to another higher one and yet another until they each found huge comfortable forks to support them for the night's rest.

Malinda passed the berries to Jasmine. "For you."

Jasmine ate in silence; Malinda liked the sound.

Finally Jasmine said, "G'night, Malindy."

It sounded as if she was glad they were back together. Malinda smiled up at the black sky.

"G'night, Jasmine."

Malinda was awakened by Jasmine pulling at the tail of her slip. "I's got a feeling dawn's a-comin'."

Malinda yawned. "We hardly got a mite of sleep."

"We better eat these berries so's you can put this dress on."

"First meal we've had together since before the river storm," Malinda said sleepily. "The Lord's been good to us."

"Uh-huh." Jasmine paused, then added in a tense voice, "I asks you, does you reckon the Lord intended for some peoples to be slaves and other peoples free?"

"I reckon not, Jasmine. Why?"

"Well, the preacher what comes to my massa's, he always tellin' us the Good Book say God made us slaves, and we gotta stay slaves. We preordered, or something like that."

Malinda held her breath. Jasmine was telling her something about her past life.

"If it be so, then we's goin' against the Good Book's preachments."

"My papa read us from the Bible every night," said Malinda. "But he never read anything like that. Maybe your preacher—"

"He ain't *my* preacher!"

"Mine neither. I can't believe God preordered mama to die from the yellow fever, so I reckon I can't believe he preordered you to be a slave either."

"You better hush that kind of talk."

"You started it."

"Good! Then I's stoppin' it."

Malinda stretched stiffly, slipped off the shirt she had worn over her slip, and pulled her dress over her head. It hung looser than when she had last worn it. Now it was all grubby and berry-stained. She touched the folds of the skirt and the lace on the bodice, remembering how pleased she had been when mama first tried it on her. She tied the shirt around her waist.

Jasmine was digging into her pants pocket. "Here. I reckon you wants this back." She dropped a white stone into Malinda's hand. "I's sorry not to find pebbles for tea for that Injun. Reckon it coulda done him good?"

Tears blurred Malinda's eyes. "No, Jasmine."

"But I not look too hard for them pebbles."

"That's not the reason he died."

Jasmine was gazing at the smooth white stone. "I hope not," she said. "I sho hope not."

Malinda tied the stone up in a shirt sleeve

that dangled from her waist. Reluctantly she said, "Dawn will catch us soon. Let's go."

As they descended along the oak limbs, they heard a bell far in the distance.

"Time to get to the fields," she whispered. "Let's run fit to kill."

They traveled quickly to put as much distance as possible between them and the boat dock they had passed the night before. Intent on their watchfulness, they seldom talked. Malinda's guilt over leaving Jasmine yesterday was replaced by a relief that she could not explain or understand.

The day turned into thick, muggy heat, an aftermath of the storm. By late morning the moisture in the air felt like a physical force the girls must penetrate.

"It isn't natural," Malinda said, wiping her face with the shirt tied around her waist.

"That sun be pullin' up the storm and flingin' it at us all over again."

The bluff wasn't so high now, and before them it sloped easily to the river. They raced ahead, left their clothes on an overhanging bush, and slid silently into the cool water.

"Just don't whoopity 'round!" Jasmine said, ducking under the water.

By midafternoon the heat was oppressive;

no breeze gave relief. Just when Malinda
thought she could not walk another step, she
saw the swamp Eagle Eye had mentioned,
swimming before her vision like a mirage.
The river ahead curved like a snake.

"We can cross the swamp like Eagle Eye
said and cut off several big bends in the river,"
she said.

"We goes straight across like the crow
flies—if the canebrake ain't too thick."

"Let's try," Malinda said. If she was going to
conquer the forest, she might as well keep at it
until she dropped.

The canebrake, a swampy land covered
with bamboolike cane, was thick enough to
give them firm footing as they started across.
But Malinda did not like the boggy unknown
under her feet.

"Are you afraid we'll see water moccasins?"

"I just see cane grass below and that devil
sun above," said Jasmine.

By the time they reached midway, Malinda
decided it would have been faster to follow the
riverbank. She had never known such stifling
heat even in midsummer. Suddenly a droning
noise pricked their ears, and a cloud passed
under the sun. They stared in horror as the
cloud moved swiftly across the swamp.

"Skeeters! Skeeters!" Malinda sobbed. "Run
for your life!"

SKEETERS

BY THE TIME they reached the riverbank on the other side—fighting and scratching and flailing at the mosquitoes through the tough canebrake, vaguely aware of the danger of broken cane stobs that could go right through a foot—the cloud of mosquitoes had devoured them. The whine pierced their brains as if they could never rid themselves of it. The mosquitoes' lifeblood was theirs—coming off on their hands as they wiped at their arms and beat the air in front of their faces. They scrambled up the sloping bank into the forest, and the swarming insects veered off out over the river.

Then by instinct Malinda and Jasmine turned back to the river and fell into the water, dunking their heads and swishing their hair about to get the mosquitoes out and wiping away the blood and insects from their bodies. Out on the bank they whimpered like pups and packed mud on their skin to take away the sting. They helped each other wring out their wet clothes and sobbed in their weakness.

"Under your eyes," Malinda gasped and patted mud high on Jasmine's cheeks.

Jasmine picked at mosquitoes still lodged in Malinda's drenched hair. Their eyes met.

Exhaustion squeezed Malinda's chest; her legs trembled. She shivered in her wet clothes but was devoid of feeling—suspended and numb. When was it ever going to end? The fear that had stalked them—the pain and agony and guilt in all their running? Her gaze clung to Jasmine's for support.

A wave of depression enveloped Malinda. She looked down at the mud in her hand.

"Jasmine! Your foot's bleedin'."

Jasmine had long since lost her moccasins. Malinda dropped to the red clay ground.

"Skeeters didn't do that." She turned Jasmine's foot and found the gaping wound on the underside.

Jasmine's eyes widened. "Cane stob, I reckon. But it not be hurtin' bad till now."

Malinda tore out the back of the shirt Jasmine had given her and cleaned and wrapped Jasmine's foot. She must not think about the torn wound or what lay ahead, or she would give in to nausea.

"I still hear the skeeters in my head," she whispered as saliva ran fast in her mouth.

Suddenly Jasmine whimpered, and Malinda glanced behind her. The cloud of mosquitoes had turned on the river and was heading back in their direction. She grabbed Jasmine's hand and Eagle Eye's hatchet, and they scrambled—haltingly this time—back up the slope and into the woods.

She felt beyond nausea and tears now— beyond despondency and fear. She knew only that she must not stop, that she must place one foot in front of the other, that she must hold on to Jasmine. When Jasmine faltered, Malinda held her arm so that Jasmine could hobble on one foot, then supported her as she hopped. Later, looking behind to be sure the mosquitoes were not on their trail, they stopped and rested—too weak to say anything. The only thought that held Malinda together was the hut: Eagle Eye had said a Choctaw hut lay an hour beyond the swamp. Never mind that the swamp now seemed six hours behind them. The hut must be there, and it must still be unoccupied.

Finally Jasmine rose, and they continued, the heat oppressive under the foliage but still hardly penetrating their consciences. The hut drew them on. It seemed their only hope on a trail that held out no hope, no assurance at all.

When they finally reached the hut, they could do no more than stoop and enter the low doorway as if it were as familiar to them as home. They fell exhausted across beds covered with cane shucks and slept in a stupor.

When she awoke, Malinda's gaze canvased their refuge, seeking out the light through the doorway and the holes at the top of each gable. As her eyes adjusted to the darkness, she discovered Jasmine across from her on another cane bed.

"Jasmine!" she whispered urgently, alarmed that she was outsleeping her for the first time. There was no answer.

The cane shucks rattled as Malinda dragged herself up and placed her feet on the dirt floor three feet below the bed. She swallowed, her throat feeling tight and raw. By the time she reached Jasmine, she was exhausted, but she placed her hand on Jasmine's forehead. It was hot and dry. She pulled her gaze away from the serene face; she must find water—and a poultice for her foot—and food. But first of all she needed containers, and the strength to carry them.

She found utensils in a corner of the hut: a pottery bowl and a pot, a gourd dipper, a wooden spoon, which looked recently used. Neither were the ashes in the round circle of stones old. Was it Eagle Eye or someone else who had built the last fire?

She must keep moving for Jasmine's sake. Jasmine had saved her life once. It seemed so long ago. . . . Now Jasmine needed medicine and food, and she must not fail her again. She stooped as she moved through the low doorway to the bright sunlight, she herself feeling alternately flushed and chilled.

It took three torturous trips to bring the clear spring water, the apples, checkerberries, ground ivy, and cattails to the Choctaw hut. While Jasmine still slept, she finished gathering dry limbs and leaves for a fire. Suddenly dizzy, she leaned against the mud wall, too weak to make another move.

The fire, Malindy. You must start the fire, she was telling her dulled senses as she shuffled over to Jasmine and retrieved the flint from the pouch tied at her waist. It seemed to take forever to get any sparks.

Put the water on, Malinda implored herself grimly. She bruised the ground ivy leaves as the water boiled in the pot, and soon she had a poultice for Jasmine's wound. In another container she made tea with the checkerberry leaves.

Jasmine moaned and awoke as Malinda was wrapping her foot with the hot poultice. Neither spoke until Malinda was finished.

"Now some tea," she said gently, bringing the dipper to her.

"Pebble tea?"

Malinda could not lie. "No. But mama used this kind for aches and pains."

Jasmine turned away.

"Please, Jasmine. You need it for strength." She supported her, raising her enough so that she could sip from the dipper. Malinda's arm trembled with her weight.

Jasmine's eyes above the dipper studied her carefully, and when she lay back down, she said, "You is sick, too."

"It's the skeeters," Malinda said.

"Is we safe here?"

"Eagle Eye thought we'd be."

Jasmine's eyes closed. Before Malinda had finished an apple, Jasmine was asleep again. Malinda ate another apple and some berries and drank some tea. She woke Jasmine and held the dipper for her once more.

"Thanks," Jasmine mumbled.

As she crawled wearily back on her cane

bed, Malinda was silently joyous. Her sick fear of the woods, worse than the sickness, had clawed and beat at her outside the hut. But she had thought of Jasmine's face on the cane shucks, pretended Jasmine was walking beside her, and talked aloud to her for courage. Best of all Malinda had forced out the strength to move, to hunt, to carry, to nurse; and if she must, she could do it again tomorrow.

TICKLING TROUT

THE NEXT TIME Malinda awoke it was dark, and Jasmine was boiling cattails over the fire.

"What you doin' up?"

"Don't you talk biggity to me just 'cause I had the feeblements." Jasmine stirred the cattails and then hobbled over to her with the gourd dipper. "Drink!" she commanded.

The gourd rattled suspiciously. "Where'd you find the white pebbles? I couldn't."

"When you really needs pebble tea, you finds the pebbles."

Jasmine put the dipper to Malinda's lips. Beads of perspiration clung to Jasmine's forehead, and her hands shook.

"It's your turn. Drink it all," Malinda likewise commanded.

Jasmine hesitated only an instant before she raised the dipper to her own lips. Returning to the fire, she sat cross-legged and slumped for some time before checking the cattails for tenderness and removing them from the fire.

Malinda joined her, also sitting cross-legged. "You need to lie down and stay off that foot."

Jasmine ignored her, lifting cattails out of the boiling water with two sticks stripped of bark, which they used for stirring. When the cattails had cooled in the bowl, she popped one in her mouth and handed one to Malinda.

"Sho would taste good in chicken stew," she said.

"I could fix a trap like papa's for a rabbit or squirrel."

"No, you is too poorly."

Malinda stuck her chin out defiantly. "I am not!"

"Don't blaze up like a kindling fire," Jasmine admonished. "We not need meat bad enough to tucker you plumb flat." She shook with chills although she tried to control them.

"I'll lie down again if you will," Malinda said, trying to crack Jasmine's stubbornness.

"You's the one that needs it."

They finished off the rest of the cattails, reveling in them despite the flat flavor. Then they ate fruit and drank tea from the dipper.

"If you not rest unless I does, I reckon I will," Jasmine finally admitted and hopped to her cot.

Malinda smiled wearily to herself and fell asleep as soon as she lay down, her hunger halfway satisfied for the first time in days.

The next day a coolness tinged the air, sweet relief from the storm's oppressive heat. Each girl had risen in the night to tend the fire and give the other sips of pebble tea. Malinda put another hot poultice on Jasmine's wound. Now that it was daylight, she was determined to make a trap and snare meat for a special feast.

She had not been wielding the hatchet long, however, when she was forced to abandon the project, tears of frustration and fatigue blinding her as she checked to see if Jasmine still slept. The least she could do was catch a fish. She could imagine Jasmine's joy in waking to the smell of smoking cat or trout; it might make her forget chicken stew.

As she considered how she would make the catch on her way to the river, Malinda's memory flashed back to a time when papa had first taken her to the creek.

"You master this old Indian skill, and you'll be the best fisherman around before you're knee-high to a grasshopper." Papa's face had crinkled in pleasure.

"As good as you, papa?"

"Heap better than me," he had said. "But you got to be still like a sleeping alligator for this one."

He had taken her to two logs that extended out over the creek—"I placed them here just to try this trick." When they were stretched out flat on them, papa had said, "Now dangle your hand down beside the log, and when a trout comes along, tickle his belly. He'll lie so still you can grab him right out of the water."

Malinda had laughed. "How will we get the trout to come by?"

"We wait. Most of fishin' is waitin'."

They had lain on the logs two hours, past mama's dinner bell. When she had finally found them, she laughed, too, and tumbled papa right off the log into the water. Before their water fight was over—in which they both were soundly dunked—Malinda had decided they had scared the trout off anyway; so she had joined in the frolic.

Stretched now on a pine freshly fallen into the Tombigbee River, Malinda smiled to herself. Papa's patience had finally won out. Later, when he brought in trout he had tickled into submission, mama had admitted he was not just joshing her with a tall tale. But she had always teased him about it.

Now Malinda dozed in the sunshine, and when a turtle nibbled her fingers, she caught it and walked as fast as she could back to the Choctaw hut. Turtle soup would be the first, and only, course for their feast.

"I thinks I has you figured out. You could have left me for good back yonder, but you didn't," Jasmine said later as they drank the soup. "So I reckon you ain't leavin' me no more."

It was not a question, but Malinda nodded anyway.

"But you ain't stickin' to me just for *me*," Jasmine added firmly. "You got another reason."

The soup suddenly tasted like mud.

"And you want me around to pretend to be your mistress if we're caught," retorted Malinda.

"So we's two of a kind? Huh!" Jasmine's voice regained some of its old fire. "With them boatmen's tootin' your name up and down the Tombigbee, you ain't nothin' but a millstone around my neck."

"Are you sure?"

"I reckon." Jasmine's fevered face faltered.

"Well, just as long as you just 'reckon' and aren't dead sure, I guess we'll get to Mobile together."

"You *guess?*"

"I know."

Jasmine carefully examined her as if desperate to read her mind.

"Does you think your papa is turned around from the West and huntin' you?"

"I don't know. I can't get my hopes up, so I won't let myself think about what those men said. But I've been thinkin' about my mama and papa. Do you want to hear how to be the best fisherman around?"

Jasmine only grunted, but Malinda told her everything she had been remembering all morning about tickling trout.

Jasmine's laugh began deep in her throat, musical and rich like honey in a honeycomb. "I's glad that turtle come along."

"You just wait. I'll get you a trout yet."

"Ramble on, child. Ramble on."

17

SOME ANSWERS

THE NEXT DAY both girls felt stronger, although each had pushed beyond their limits to nurse the other. Their fevers were waning, and they ate better. Thanks to the hot poultices and Malinda's care, Jasmine's wound was beginning to heal, but she could not yet put her weight on the foot. They were still weak enough, however, that neither girl had suggested that they leave the security of the hut for the southern trail.

They kept a fire going night and day for warmth and to keep animals away. The bowl and pot were turned upside down over nuts,

377

fruit, and berries when they slept. The squirrels, coons, and possums were evidently satisfied harvesting from the same trees and bushes for they seldom bothered them. Occasionally they heard a fox yelp or a cat scream in the distance, but the ancient hut with its mud walls covered outside with cypress bark protected them.

One day Malinda lay again on a pine, which had fallen out over the river. She was determined to catch a trout by tickling its belly. She dangled her hand into the shallow water and rested. Ever since the mosquito attack, every bit of energy used meant twice as much rest was needed.

Waiting for a fish would give her time to figure out how she was going to ask Jasmine some questions.

She lay there, half sleeping in the morning sun as minnows nibbled at her fingers. She almost missed seeing the first trout, and the involuntary jerk that brought her mind back into focus scared it away. The next time, she vowed, she would be more alert.

Malinda concentrated on the murky water below her, straining her senses as she kept awake by going over again the little she knew about Jasmine.

She was determined to catch a trout by tickling its belly.

Then the ripples in the water below her increased. Slowly, gracefully the large light-streaked body moved toward her.

She held her hand and body still. Even her breath came infrequently and only in a steady rhythm. Now she could see the tail and belly close by her hand. Carefully she stroked the soft under portion with one finger. The trout lay still, suspended in the water and time.

Quickly Malinda turned her hand over and grabbed the trout, locking him in from above with her other hand.

The trout thrashed up and down, but Malinda held on, raising it out of the water and carrying it quickly back to the cabin.

She greeted Jasmine, who was by now awake, not with an abrupt I-told-you-so but with the joy of someone who has a treasure to share, one that would ease the vague ache of hunger that still permeated each day.

Once the trout was cleaned and cooking on a rack over the fire, Malinda began changing the bandage on Jasmine's foot with a clean piece of shirt.

Finally she asked, "Jasmine, where are your mama and papa?" Her heart pounded for fear she would not answer.

Jasmine stopped cracking the nuts they had found yesterday under the walnut tree behind the hut. "Your face be still swoll up with them skeeter bites. You looks like a squirrel with two handfuls of nuts in her jaws.... I ain't got no ma and pa."

Malinda bent lower over her task. "Are they dead?"

Jasmine resumed her nut cracking. "You done gone to meddlin'."

"I told you about my folks."

"You sho did! You was so feverish back in them woods you not know who you was talkin' to."

"I also told you about them when I wasn't feverish."

"Will you finish wrapping that foot so's I can move this rack off the fire properlike?"

"No!" She could be as stubborn as Jasmine.

"That trout you tickled to death gonna burn to bits.... No they ain't dead, I reckon."

Malinda waited.

"My massa sold them away when I was a young'un, no more than two."

"Why?"

"Oh, lawsy mercy, I hates meddlers." Jasmine rolled her black eyes toward the mud roof.

"Are you huntin' your mama and papa?" Malinda persisted.

"Huh! It be easier to find a pinch of salt in a flour barrel than find them."

Malinda had finished with the bandage, but

381

she still held Jasmine's foot.

"Well, don't look so sickly," Jasmine snapped. "And so I has no remembers, good or bad, of my folks. Ever since I was knee-high to a gnat, I been sewin' on lace and ruffles for my mistis and her gals. And so now maybe I got a man, and this fish am burnin'." She pulled her foot away, turned and poked at the fish smoking over the hot coals.

Jasmine had shared more than Malinda had dared hope for. Her mind was reeling with the information. Was Jasmine married, and where was her man? And what was she doing on the run like a wild rabbit?

Feeling that she would burst out with dozens of meddling questions that might keep Jasmine from sharing again, Malinda picked up a pottery bowl and disappeared out the door.

"I'm going to the apple tree," she said.

Malinda awoke long before Jasmine the next morning, with a prickly wariness like a cat's fur rubbed the wrong way. For the first time, she did not feel safe in the hut. Had the skeeter fever and the Choctaw shelter taken away her watchfulness? Or was it because she had discovered well-trodden trails, crisscrossing in all directions, not a mile away?

She had ventured farther away than usual yesterday, looking for the Choctaw trail signs and testing herself against the strange, hovering forest. Alone and out of sight of the hut, she pushed herself beyond her dread until she happened upon the well-used trails too near their hut for comfort. The discovery sent her scurrying back to Jasmine. Now she fussed inwardly everytime she rustled the cane shucks beneath her. They scratched at the silence.

She bolted out of bed. There was no silence now. The birds had seen to that.

"Jasmine! Wake up! Somebody's comin'."

Jasmine did not move, but she was breathing heavier. "Don't hear nothin' but jays squallin'."

"That's what I mean. They're warnin' us."

"Since when the jays start talkin' to you?"

"Never mind. I just *know*. C'mon, we can't stay here." She kicked dirt over the hot coals before they stooped cautiously through the low entrance, looking first in all directions.

"Listen!"

"Somebody's south of us—away from the river."

"Maybe it be a bobcat?"

"Papa said you can trust a jay, and they're sayin' it's a human comin'."

She headed up the river, back in the direction they had come a few days before, with Jasmine hobbling along close behind. The sound of pounding hooves sent them scurrying behind a clump of holly bushes. When voices sounded in the distance, Jasmine whispered, "We got to figure how to get out of this here pickle."

Ah! Jasmine had said "we."

"We can sit still as a Choctaw for hours if we have to." Malinda tried to sound reassuring.

Suddenly a call broke into their whispering.

"Howdee! Howdy there!" The horses were trotting closer again. The voices were clearer.

"Let's poke around a mite. 'Twasn't no hant built that fire."

"You fan out that away, Jess. I'll go up river. If all's clear, we'll just help ourselves to some vittles."

"Oh, lawsy mercy!" Jasmine made no sound, but Malinda read her silent lips. They crouched lower to the ground, the squirrels barking in the treetops adding their warnings to those of the jays. Then a horse sounded nearby. It snorted as it passed them, moving on north.

"Anybody could hear that racket," Malinda whispered later as she wiped clammy hands on her sleeves. "He's headin' away from the river now. Maybe he won't come back this way."

Again they heard voices.

"Howdee! Anybody home?"

The girls shuddered. Malinda resisted the urge to run farther upriver.

"They's back at the hut."

Malinda nodded and slumped. "Now we wait."

It seemed hours but must not have been much more than one when the riders returned to their horses and took off west from the river. The girls raised only high enough to gaze through the holly leaves.

"Now we go."

"Not yet. They might be tryin' to flush us out by pretending to leave."

The squirrels quieted, the jays disappeared, and the girls relaxed. Malinda pulled off a dozen holly berries and stared at them as she rolled them in her hand.

"Jasmine, how old are you?"

"I told you long time ago. I's fourteen."

"I forgot. I'm twelve."

"Maybe so."

"I was born in 1824."

"Mistis say my ma and pa was sold in 1824."

Perhaps she would answer another question. "Are you married?"

The silence made Malinda shiver.

"I got a man."

"But—"

"Well, I jump over the broom with a man, but my massa took him away."

"You what?"

"Let's go back to the hut now."

"No, we have to wait longer." Malinda gazed at Jasmine's brooding face. "Jasmine—"

"It say in the Good Book that the Lord don't like pushers."

"You sure don't like them." Malinda vowed once more not to question her again, knowing full well she would the next chance she got. She turned away and threw the berries one by one toward a hollow log several feet away.

Suddenly Jasmine chuckled. "Look at you! Face swoll up like a chipmunk, hair tangled like a thicket, shirt half tore up for my bandage. And that dress now—you's just about fit for a boggle-eyed coyote!"

Malinda ran her fingers through her hair. "You could stand a little fixin' up yourself."

"You got a nice laugh, Malindy. I ain't heard it in a long time."

"So what are you butterin' me up for?"

"It ain't no butter; it's the truth. But I got another truth—we better not stay in that hut too long. We was just plain lucky this time."

18

BACK ON THE TRAIL

AN HOUR LATER, carrying the pottery bowl, pot and dipper, and all the foodstuffs they could handle, Malinda and Jasmine left the Choctaw hut, following close to the river.

If only we weren't so weak yet, Malinda thought. *If only Jasmine's foot were completely healed.* They moved slower than before, but Jasmine did not complain as she hobbled along. In the lead Malinda stopped often for them to rest.

"If the moon shine tonight, let's keep goin'," Jasmine said the next time they stopped, crouching under a tree.

"What does your foot say about it?"

"It say, lead me to Mobile." Jasmine chased an ant with a twig. "You want to hear about my man, Malindy?"

She would hear anything freely offered. "If you want to tell me," she answered.

"I reckon I's huntin' him, and I gonna find him, too."

"I hope so."

"I made myself a promise, Malindy. I's dead sure I gonna find him, then him and me's gonna be married properlike."

"You aren't married?"

Jasmine's eyes flashed like lightning. "Sho we's married, but we just jump over the broom. That ain't like massa done for all the others."

"The others had the preacher?"

"Sho they did. Whenever the preacher ridin' by, massa snatch him by the coattails and drag him in. And he do up the whole thing with the Good Book, nice and solemnlike—pretty, too—and then everybody have eatin' and dancin'." Jasmine stood up. "I's rested now. Let's git."

They walked side by side.

"Oh, massa give us partying all right. He laugh his fool head off and say we can jump the broom. Jeb say in my ear after we done it that when preacher come, we get him to do it up

388

proper. Then we dance and sing and eat most all the night."

Jasmine stopped suddenly and scowled. "I hears a boat."

"I hear a bell ringin', but it's far away." Malinda's gaze scanned the river. "I see a big steamboat. It's on the other side."

"Ain't it fine that river be so wide?"

"I didn't think so when we were crossing it in the canoe. But yes, it's fine."

"Malindy, a whole big bunch belonging to massa jump over the broom," Jasmine said as if their conversation had not been interrupted. "But later the preacher always take care of them."

"Maybe your master was going to do that for you and Jeb, too."

"Huh! You's just fooled! When all the party be over, Jeb just disappear."

Malinda stared at Jasmine.

"Come on! Don't stumble on the root, or I has to carry *you*," Jasmine warned; then she continued, "He just disappear like a hant."

They sat on a log to rest and watched the steamboat, Jasmine talking so low and fast that Malinda leaned nearer to hear. "Massa lock him up and trade him off like a hoss—"

"Why, Jasmine, why?"

Jasmine hung her head. "Massa say I too pretty for my Jeb."

"Do you know where he is?"

"Sho I knows. After he be sold he runned away, and he get word to me that he go north."

"Where?"

"Well, I can get there by boat. I runned, too, after that, but I be scared of my shadow—"

Malinda could understand that. "And you tried to get help and got sent back home—"

"Uh-huh."

That night they built a fire back in a bayou and rested till dawn, Malinda dressing Jasmine's foot and feeding the fire, their only protection from the cold. At best it kept them only half warm.

Malinda could not sleep. She suspected that Jasmine did not know for sure where Jeb was. She was probably running away from her master as much as she was hunting Jeb and freedom.

"Jasmine, you asleep?"

"I reckon so!"

"Do you still have a plan to find Jeb?"

"I find him, and nobody gonna stop me."

Malinda gazed up through the pines at the harvest moon and realized she was just as afraid of the forest now as when she first vowed to conquer it. Despair gnawed at her stomach and filled her with dread.

An owl screeched in the woods. Jasmine groaned, flames from the fire flickering on her face. "That screech owl howlin' death?"

"They have to screech sometime. I guess he doesn't know we're here."

"I believes you, maybe. G'night, Malindy."

"G'night, Jasmine."

KNEE-DEEP INTO NOVEMBER

BY LATE THE NEXT AFTERNOON Malinda realized that the fever from the mosquito attack had taken its toll; their pace was too slow. Jasmine could not make it to Mobile on foot until her wound healed better. But the weather was turning against them; she had felt winter coming in the chill of the last few nights. If they stopped for a few days and the nights turned bitter, how could they survive with no shelter or warm clothes?

Jasmine was gathering cattails by the river. "Looky at all the logs washed up on the bank. That's a good sign, ain't it, Malindy?"

"It looks like our storm at Saint Stephens hit here, too. The waves churned up a lot of loose stuff, I guess."

"I like that. We be usin' it."

"It's too wet to make a fire."

"I knows that," Jasmine added gently. "I got other plans."

"Maybe I can catch a fish to eat with these cattails. But let's keep goin' till near dark, Jasmine—that is, if you feel like it."

"I feels like it."

Soon the ground rose away from the Tombigbee. A drizzling rain began, but they pressed on and soon reached a bend in the river. Malinda's throat tightened as she stared across the water.

"We'll have to walk two miles around this bend just to get over there," she said grimly.

"I reckon we can make it there before we stop."

As they followed the curve of the river, Jasmine's face brightened. "Looky! All that brush on shore." She pointed to the opposite bank.

"So what?"

"Malindy, let's hunt for a good stoppin' place in this here bayou. Tomorrow we's headin' for that brush."

Malinda plodded on ahead, too tired to figure out why the logs and debris washed up on

393

the shore excited Jasmine. Wishing the bank sloped gently from the water instead of rising so sharply, she leaned over the edge and looked down at the water ten feet below. She noticed a path through bushes growing out from the cliff and on impulse scrambled down, holding on to branches for support. Halfway down to the water, she found a cave and called softly for Jasmine to join her.

"It's not really a cave," she said, "but it's big enough for you and me and a fire."

"I's ready to move out of this rainy drip. I'll get the fire stuff, and you get the fish."

After Jasmine's foot had been redressed and they had eaten fish and boiled cattails, Malinda gazed at the drizzly black nothingness outside their shallow cave and measured her words carefully.

"I've lost count of the days, but it must be close to November. How much longer will the warm weather hold?"

"I ain't lost count." Jasmine pulled a stick from her pants pocket. "This here's nicked mighty near to pieces. We's knee-deep into November, not chin-deep, mind you, just knee-deep."

Malinda studied the stick Jasmine handed her, counting the nicks aloud.

"That be every day since we leave on the canoe. I can count, too," she said proudly. "Can you read?"

Malinda nodded. "Not a lot, but papa taught me all he knew. That's one reason he put me on the boat for Mobile—so I could go to a real school."

"What be the other reasons?"

Malinda averted her eyes and tried to smooth out the wrinkles in the once beautiful dress her mama had sewed for her. She had never had many clothes, but mama saw to it they had something clean to wear every day. Malinda and papa had kept up the washing the same way after mama died.

"My mama ordered this piece up by boat from Mobile," she said. "She sewed it last summer just before. . . Well, it was the last thing she did, and now look at it."

"You still got it, ain't you?"

"Yes, I still got it."

"Now, don't change the subject on me this time. I wants to know how come you never talks anything bad about your ma and pa. Was they angels from heaven?"

Malinda stirred the fire with a stick, flicking ashes away so the coals could flaunt their bright colors. "No, Jasmine, but now you've gone to meddlin'."

"Ain't meddlin'. I's tryin' to help."

"Why do you think I was askin' you questions? I was tryin' to help, too."

Jasmine poked the other side of the fire. "I reckon so."

"Anyhow, I can't remember anything but happy times, before last summer." Her voice, hoarse with emotion, lowered to a whisper. "And last summer I want to forget—if I can."

"I believes you not want to talk about it yet."

Tears rimmed her eyes at Jasmine's words. Would the day ever come when it would not be too painful to talk about mama's death and papa sending her away and her terrible fear? She could not imagine it.

"We got room enough to lay down." Jasmine surveyed the space on her side of the fire and promptly curled up as if to go to sleep.

"G'night, Jasmine."

"Oh, I ain't goin' to sleep. I's just gettin' my body satisfied so's I can tell you we got to make a raft tomorrow."

"You wouldn't dare get back on the river!"

"I sho is."

"Deliver me from a raft when you can't swim."

Jasmine snorted. "Deliver my feets from walkin' trails."

"A slow trail's better than drownin'."

"Malindy, you knows we ain't gonna make

it on foot. I feels winter creepin' in, and pretty soon me and you's gonna be cold, like lard chunked in spring water."

"I won't get on the Tombigbee again."

"We can build a raft tomorrow and get on our way after dark. It be savin' days, Malindy."

Malinda didn't answer, wanting to reject everything Jasmine had said and her own doubts about Jasmine's stamina.

"Me and you ain't dressed for out-and-out winter, Malindy."

"We ain't prepared for the 'Bigbee, either."

"We gets prepared."

Malinda curled up on her side of the fire, trying to avoid further discussion of a raft. "Jasmine, if Jeb really loved you, why didn't he come back and help you escape with him?"

Silence.

"Jasmine?"

"I's runnin' my mind on it, but I can't catch no answer. He musta tried." Jasmine rolled over, her back to the fire and Malinda.

"Is you askin' how come your pa left you if he loves you?"

Silence.

"Malindy?"

"I didn't think I was, but sometimes I wonder."

"I reckon me and you's in the same boat."

Malinda was silent for a long time.

"Is you asleep?" Jasmine asked.

"No. I'm tryin' to remember something mama told me once. She was talkin' about how someday I'd grow up and be independent from her and papa."

"I reckon that's right and proper."

"And I said no—never! But didn't she miss grandma and grandpa? And, Jasmine, she said—now let me remember just right." Malinda stared long into the fire, then repeated her mother's words. " 'Love doesn't depend on time or place, honey. They love us in North Carolina, and we feel it away out here on the Tombigbee.' "

The coals sizzled and popped. The rain outside the shallow cave crackled the fallen oak leaves, and a light wind rustled the trees.

"I reckon that be our answer, Malindy, if we needs a answer. Jeb, he love me right where he is."

"And papa, too."

Jasmine thumped her chest. "I got a feelin' right here about Jeb and your pa."

"What's that?"

"I feels they's tellin' us to use our common sense to build that raft and get back on the river!"

20

PREPARING FOR THE 'BIGBEE

THE NEXT DAY'S SUN was bright and warm. Malinda and Jasmine had risen at dawn and now were busy sorting out limbs from the debris by the riverbank and hunting vines to tie them together for a raft.

Jasmine wiped her face and looked at the sun. "Today be pretty nigh perfect."

"It's a good thing, because you're goin' in the water!"

"Who say?"

"You did! You said last night we'd get prepared for the 'Bigbee, and that means you have to learn how to swim."

"Oh, lawsy mercy!"

Malinda chopped at a limb with Eagle Eye's hatchet. "As soon as we get this raft put together, in you go."

Jasmine walked down to the edge of the river and peered in as if to challenge its depths. Suddenly she put a hand up to her face, feeling along her cheekbones and down her hairline to her jaw and chin.

"Malindy, I is pretty!"

"You're smart, too."

"Reckon I can go to school?"

That was a new idea to Malinda, but she nodded anyway. "And I can teach you a little about letters and words."

"Smart and pretty. With that I don't need no swimmin' lessons."

They hacked notches down the sides of two limbs. Several hours passed as they hunted for the right size of limbs for the crossbars and vines to strap them into the notches. By midafternoon, however, they floated their small raft with pride and exhaustion.

When they banked the raft, Malinda reached down and picked up a handful of smooth rocks in the edge of the river. She swished the sand off in the water and spread them out in the palm of her hand.

"Aren't they beautiful?"

"Every color of the rainbow and then some," Jasmine responded.

"Do you think they'll ever get to the ocean? Or maybe that they're kin to the pebbles that wash up on the ocean beach?"

"You is mighty serious, Malindy, but I sho don't understand you."

"I don't either, Jasmine. There are so many things I don't understand. I never heard of pebble tea, but those stones got me over the fever."

Jasmine hesitated as she started to get off the raft. "I suspects it be more than just old pebbles that make you well."

"Did you ever wonder if the stone you held in your hand was once a star?"

"Not before now.... Is you gonna save these stones, too?"

"I don't know."

"I keeps them for you." Jasmine tipped Malinda's hand and poured the rocks out into her own, pushed each one with her index finger, and then stuffed them into her pants pocket. As she did so, she began singing softly:

My head is wet with the midnight dew,
  Come along home, come home.
The mornin' star was a witness, too,
  Come along home, come home.

By nightfall Malinda had taught Jasmine

401

how to stay afloat in the water by paddling like a dog. First she had her hold on to the edge of the raft while she kicked with her feet and legs, then came the paddling with her hands and arms until at last Jasmine decided the water could help hold her up rather than drown her.

"It ain't easy!" she said with a note of triumph in her voice.

With the swimming lesson completed, they washed their clothes at the edge of the river, scrubbing the dirt and stains with sand. Malinda had always sprinkled sand over the floor at home before sweeping it. If it could get floors clean, it would help their clothes.

"Do you think the sand will clean us, too?" Malinda began rubbing some on her arms.

"We sho could stand something."

When they had rubbed themselves all over with the wet sand, they jumped back into the water. Malinda dived under and when she surfaced, Jasmine splashed her in the face. That was all it took to get a water fight underway—a cautious water fight. They did not shout or laugh, only chuckled.

What fun to play! They had almost forgotten how.

Finally they lay exhausted in the shallow water, their heads cradled by their crossed arms on the sand.

What fun to play! They had almost forgotten how.

"Won't it be fun someday, Jasmine, to shout so loud all creation can hear us?"

"I never knowed what fun it be when I do it anytime I want."

"Mama and papa and I used to have water fights in our creek. I bet you could have heard us for miles."

Jasmine chuckled. "We chilluns used to get cooled off in the waterin' troughs in the pasture. The cows and massa not like it a bit, but it sho was fun."

"And someday we can sing loud enough to fill up the whole forest."

"Sho enough?"

"Yes." Malinda brooded. "You know, I don't like the woods."

"That be strange. You live in them all the time."

"I liked them when Running Bull made his turkey gobble ring through all the trees."

"You talk about that Running Bull before. Who's him?"

As they lay at the river's edge at twilight, Malinda told Jasmine about Running Bull, the Choctaw who became papa's friend.

"Where he find him?"

"On the Georgia trail. Papa had packed all our belongings in a wagon in North Carolina, and we moved west, papa fiddlin' the whole way."

"He not too smart to fiddle through Injun country."

"He said he couldn't sneak by the Injuns, anyway, so he might as well warn them that Jeremiah Sharp was comin' through. He was goin' to the 'land of milk and honey' and wanted to sing about it. And everything was all right, too," she added, "until one day when a turkey gobble filled up the fog ahead of us."

"What be that?"

"It's an old defiant Choctaw call. Then a howl sounded through the forest. Papa howled back. 'I can't stand not to answer,' he said with a grin. An Indian with a fiddle under one arm appeared from nowhere and blocked our trail."

"What happened then?" asked Jasmine.

"Papa carried on a starin' game with the white-turbaned Indian. Finally the Indian said, 'My land don't need another fiddle in it. You go back to the land of your fathers.'

"Papa didn't blink an eye or say a word. Neither did the Indian. . . . Finally papa shouted, 'Every land can stand another fiddle.'

" 'Foolish man do not know Running Bull's fiddle,' the Indian replied.

"But papa didn't answer, only stared.

" 'Running Bull melt your bones down for fat.'

405

" 'Jeremiah Sharp cut your flesh up for blubber.'

" 'Running Bull make you swallow a thousand-pound gourd so you rattle when you walk.'

" 'Jeremiah Sharp make you swallow a thousand-pound bull to go with your name.'

"After that exchange the starin' seemed to last forever. Then Running Bull began to chuckle. When his rumblin' laugh filled up the distance between them, papa began to laugh, too."

"Lawsy mercy, he be lucky."

"Two stubborn men!" Malinda laughed. "Running Bull joined us on the wagon, and he and papa tried to out-fiddle each other all the way across Georgia and Alabama to the Tombigbee River."

"What happened then?"

"Running Bull wouldn't let papa settle on the east side of the 'Bigbee. He said that was Creek land, so we must join him on the west side—Choctaw country. And he stayed not too many miles from papa's clearin' until last year. If he could learn a thing or two about fiddlin' from papa, he said, papa could learn a lot about farmin' from him."

Finally Jasmine said, "I hopes your pa find him out West. Even a man need a friend in the wilderness."

"Because of Running Bull, I had to help Eagle Eye. Do you understand?"

"I does. I hopes we help our Injun. We sure not make him well."

Malinda smiled. Jasmine had said "our Injun."

They carried the pebbles in their hands and their wet clothes on their arms when they walked back to their hideout on the other side of the bayou. Now they could barely see as twilight gave way to night. Malinda realized she had hardly noticed their surroundings all day except as they yielded materials for the raft. The pines seemed larger than they had this morning, and a live oak's black limbs under its green coat seemed to stretch with knotty pauses into eternity.

"We worked quietly today, didn't we?"

"Uh-huh. Why?"

"We were so far back in the bayou I forgot to watch out for people. Could anybody have seen us?"

"No. We just naturally watches out without even thinkin' about it now."

"I hope so. Do you hear anything?"

"Just the regular squirrels and birds and foxes—"

"Is that a fox or a dog?"

Jasmine stopped and listened carefully. "It be a fox," she said.

Before they slept that night, they dried their clothes out by the fire.

Malinda ran her fingers through her hair in an attempt to get out the tangles. "I'll plait it," she said and asked Jasmine to part her hair in the middle for two braids.

"You does that real good." Jasmine watched with interest.

Malinda chuckled. "I should. About ten of papa's cows have plaited tails because of me."

"How come?"

"I learned how on them, that's how come. I bet I put fifteen tiny plaits in every cow's tail. . . . Those tiny things got so tangled up, most of them are still plaited together after four years."

Jasmine's eyes sparkled. "You has enough practice on them cows to do this good?"

"No. Mama let me braid hers, too—but only if I'd do them big." Malinda tied the braid ends of her hair into a knot. "Mama wouldn't redo her braids either—even when I got them crooked."

"Plaited cow's tails! I has heard everything now!"

When Malinda had finished, Jasmine got her to write out each letter of the alphabet on the cave floor.

"I'll write them out wherever you like until you can carry them around in your memory."

"Okay. Now we gets a little sleep before we poles on that river tonight."

It was almost dawn, however, when a congregation of mockingbirds awoke them. The crisp coolness, in contrast to yesterday's warmth, urged them onto the raft rather than waiting through another day for darkness. When they neared the raft, Jasmine held Malinda back.

"Stay here. Something's on them logs."

"What is it?"

They both stared at the raft.

"It's a bundle, Jasmine. It isn't ours."

"I knows."

They hid behind a bush and waited. When several minutes had passed and nothing happened, they ventured a little nearer the water's edge.

"Maybe it float up there while we was sleepin'."

A voice sounded behind them. "It didn't float up. I put it there."

Both girls jerked around. Malinda planted herself protectively in front of Jasmine. *Help me do the right thing,* she prayed, and hoped God was listening.

"Yes, ma'am. What do you want?" Malinda stammered as her gaze searched the tall plump woman, perhaps her own mother's age, who loomed in front of her. Her heart jumped like leap frogs as she waited for an answer.

"I sho am curious. What're you girls doin'?" The stranger's voice was firm.

This woman had to believe her. "We're . . . just on an adventure. Papa said I could explore this side of the river as long as I had Jasmine along."

"And where's your pa?"

"He's trappin' downriver a ways. We'll meet up with him in a couple of hours."

The woman smoothed out her muslin dress and her bright clean apron. *I didn't convince her,* Malinda thought. *And now I'm tongue-tied.*

"Honey, you don't have any cause to be afraid of me."

Malinda turned toward Jasmine for help.

The black girl poked her head around Malinda. "Mistis want to know how come the bundle down there?" She nodded toward the raft.

The woman folded her arms across her chest. "It's good strappin' vittles. Now I don't know where you two come from or where you're goin', but I do know skin and bones when I see them. You need all the vittles I put

410

in there and then some. So eat them up. And I put in some good liniment for your foot." She nodded to Jasmine.

"You saw us yesterday?"

The woman smiled broadly. "One of my young'uns strayed away from home and found you first. He fetched his pa, and his pa fetched me. We was afraid we would scare you off, but I knew you had to have some vittles. You sure you girls ain't lost?"

"No—no, ma'am. We know the Tombigbee."

"My man and me can help you get found if you're lost."

Malinda hesitated.

Jasmine popped out again. "Thanky, ma'am, but massa expect us back by noontime."

"I sho am curious." The woman shook her head slowly. "And you haven't satisfied my curiousness a bit."

"We don't understand, ma'am."

"I guess we can't keep you here if you're bound to leave, but I sho would hate to know we hadn't done our duty." She pushed back a strand of dark hair from her face. "If your pa is nearby, you tell him to feed you better, you hear? And if he isn't nearby, I just hope those vittles last you till you get home."

Malinda walked over and took the woman's rough hands in hers. "Thank you! You're kind.

. . . You're very kind."

"Git! Git!" Jasmine shouted and limped through the trees toward the river. "Thievin' old possum! Git!"

"You get, too," the woman said gently to Malinda. "We've fed that possum so long he ain't scared of nothin' when food's around."

"Yes, ma'am."

The woman still held Malinda's hands. "You take care. For my peace of mind, I got to believe you know where you're goin'."

"We do—we promise. Goodbye." Malinda sprinted after Jasmine who had not succeeded in chasing the possum off their raft. He crouched on a corner as if he would tumble off into the water any minute and watched them with beady eyes. Jasmine poked at him with one of the poles they had fashioned to push the raft, but he clung to the corner log by his long hairless tail and played dead until Jasmine turned her back. Malinda poked him with her pole.

Jasmine inspected the bundle. "We caught him before he got inside."

"It looks like he caught us, too. He isn't budgin'."

"Let's be a-pushin' off then. We can get rid of him later."

With their poles they moved the raft out of the bayou toward the open river, and waved at the woman until they rounded the bend.

"We sho didn't do so well yesterday after all. Three people were watchin' us." Malinda shivered.

Jasmine glanced at the food. "I sho is glad this time."

"I smell ham. I guess maybe we found one of those angels from heaven."

"Huh! I take her any day to a angel I ain't never seen."

The possum curled his tail around a log for support and fixed his eyeballs on the bundle as Jasmine began examining its contents. Malinda poled close to the banks heading downstream.

"I told you! Ham, Malindy, and corn bread and sweet taters and milk. Two jars of milk! We is rich!"

"Amen! With a possum thrown in."

Jasmine handed Malinda a piece of meat and then threw a scrap to the possum. She was humming a soft tune.

Oh go and tell it on de mountain,
  Jesus done bless my soul
Oh go and tell it in de valley,
  Jesus done bless my soul.

TRAVLER

THE FIRST TIME they hid out of sight from a boat, Malinda dressed Jasmine's foot with the liniment. The possum nudged at the pottery bowl and pot covering their remaining food with his long snout. They had decided it would be wise to stretch out their "manna from the heavens," as Jasmine called it, and not gorge themselves all in one day.

Jasmine hummed as they pushed down-river, sometimes singing softly, but always the same song.

Don't be weary, traveler,
  Come along home, come home.

414

Don't be weary, traveler,
  Come along home, come home.

"I never heard you sing before yesterday,"
Malinda said.

"Ain't nobody around. Besides, I's happy."

It *was* good to be on the river again, and
even the woods lining the shore did not look as
dark and sinister as they had earlier from
their canoe. Neither the day's chill nor the
frequent times they must take cover from
river traffic dampened their spirits.

By the end of the day Malinda, at Jasmine's
insistence, had carved all the letters of the
alphabet on the logs of the raft with Jasmine's
knife. The possum evidently thought she was
trying to play with him every time she squatted to work on the letters. He pushed his snout
towards her or scratched at her with a foot.
When she poked at him, he scurried back to
his favorite corner and played dead.

Jasmine traced each letter with a finger
when Malinda finished it. "How you make
Jeb?"

Malinda sounded it out slowly. "I think it's
J-E-B."

"This be *J* for Jeb." Jasmine pointed with
confidence to the right letter.

"For Jasmine, too."

415

The other girl looked startled. "Where be *E?*"

Jasmine traced each letter with her finger once again. Then she stood and resumed her poling but was soon outlining the three letters, *J-E-B,* with her big toe. "I got it now, Malindy."

Malinda was carving *Z.* "Where *is* Jeb?" she asked.

Jasmine frowned but said nothing.

"Do you really know?"

"I knows. But sometimes I forgets. Reckon these letters will help me remember if I sees it writ out?"

"Jasmine, is there really a Jeb?"

"I says so. Ain't that enough?"

Malinda gazed at Jasmine's big black eyes, her deep brown cheeks, her black bonnet of curls—all etched in Malinda's memory as permanently as the alphabet on their raft.

"Yes, Jasmine, that's enough."

Jasmine sighed heavily. "He passes word to me that all I gotta do in Mobile is get on most any boat, and it be takin' me north."

"What about the ones that go to New Orleans?"

"That ain't the sound of the place I's goin'."

Malinda fell silent. For days—weeks—she had pondered Jasmine's escape plan, but now she didn't want to think about it anymore. In

416

fact, it made her feel ill to consider their separation. She stared at her now, absorbed as she was in tracing her toe over *B,* and felt suddenly chilled.

"Jasmine, I didn't like playin' mistress this mornin'."

Jasmine straightened, stared intently downriver, and then looked at her. "Me neither. It ain't us."

"Of course, I know you nursed me back to life for me to help you that way, and I don't want to quit helpin' you. That's not it at all."

"You helps in lots of ways. But I had other reasons for gettin' you over the fever."

"You did?" Malinda brightened. "Like what?"

"Well, has you got to ask? I reckon the Lord sorta use me, as the preacher say, 'cause you be dead if I not find you."

"It sounds like you think God is takin' care of us," she said.

"Ain't I been singin' Jesus done bless my soul?"

Malinda nodded.

"I don't know much about this Jesus," Jasmine continued. "Most the time the preacher talk about how us slaves got to do what massa tell us. But sometimes a black preacher come around, and he be some preacher! Massa let us go down in the fields to hear him."

Jasmine gave out a deep, satisfied chuckle. "Massa just not know how that preacher talk about a freedom-lovin' Jesus."

"Our preacher came about four times a year," Malinda said. "But not a night passed that mama and papa didn't read the Bible. And I can remember how Jesus said, 'I am with you always.'"

"See there!" Jasmine clapped her hands. "He knows I could make you well, so I figures that's one reason I find you in the woods."

"What's the other reason?"

"He knowed I needed you, I reckon."

Malinda took a deep breath. "Next time we run across anybody, we'll just be ourselves —me and you."

"There ain't gonna be no next time. It be easier for us this way, all by ourselves."

Malinda shivered. "It's gettin' cold."

"You looks pale, Malindy. You better not get sick when we got good food for the first time."

Malinda shook her head, saying she felt fine when she really didn't—not as long as she was wondering what would happen to the two of them if they ever got to Mobile.

Soon after they started out on the river the next morning, Jasmine announced they were naming the possum Travler.

"For your song," Malinda said.

"Uh-huh. But if we ever gets on hard times, he gonna travel right into our soup."

As if they had not been through some hard times. The ham and sweet taters and corn bread—and the quiet Tombigbee—were making them forget. Malinda gazed deep into the forest as they glided past. It looked protective as if beckoning them to safety if the river turned against them. Did she no longer feel revulsion for the wilderness trail? She wanted to sing out that they had made the right decision to return to the river, but instead she joined Jasmine in her low song—just above a whisper.

Keep a-goin', traveler,
Come along home, come home.
Keep a-singin' all the way,
Come along home, come home.

Just where to go I did not know,
Come along home, come home.
A travelin' long and a travelin' slow,
Come along home, come home.

That night they could not sleep in the freezing wind that made their fire sputter and sucked all its warmth away. They built it as high as they dared and stationed themselves between it and the wind, but still they ached with cold. After two dreadful hours they returned to the raft, pushing their poles vigorously in the moonlight to chase away the cold.

Intent upon their task, a steamboat's shrill whistle from downriver startled and frightened them. They hunted for overhanging limbs of evergreens but, seeing none, had to ground the raft and hide behind tree trunks. The long wait for the boat to pass was agony. They ate a piece of meat and concentrated on savoring the strong, rich flavor of each bite, chewing slowly in a vain attempt to freeze out of their minds all sensations other than taste.

Once the boat was safely past, its lights unable to pick them out, they moved swiftly on the Tombigbee River as if frozen in position on the raft, moving silently—no song on their lips.

Daylight brought no relief, for the sun could not penetrate the heavy clouds. They stayed on the river fighting time and weather, but at last they were forced to stop from exhaustion. They jumped up and down and ran back and forth as they gathered brush for a fire, continuing to pile on limbs after the flames had a good start. They turned first one side and then the other to the heat, and only when they felt completely comfortable did they settle down to eat from their diminishing bundle and take turns napping.

Seated with her arms around her knees, Malinda moved her back dangerously close to the fire as she kept vigil. If only the sun would break through the clouds . . . But Jasmine wasn't asleep after all; she was mumbling although her eyes were closed.

"I's been a-wonderin', Malindy."

"What are you wonderin'?"

"About us—I mean, if we don't freeze and gets there, what is we gonna do in Mobile?"

Jasmine's question echoed her own.

"Is you got brothers and sisters?"

"No. Have you?"

"No. I has always wondered what it like to have a sister—and ma and pa."

Malinda twisted around slowly, gazing through the warm flames at Jasmine curled up on the other side. She lay so still, her eyes closed, that she could have dozed off to sleep. A damp log sizzled in the heat, and two redbirds high in a pine drowned out the mockingbirds with their song.

Her face cradled in her arms, Jasmine finally spoke again, her words muffled against her sleeve. "If I stays in Mobile, do you reckon

421

massa come lookin' for me that far away?"

What was she saying? That she would not head north? But she had just said yesterday—or was it the day before—that nothing would stop her from finding Jeb.

"I don't know. I saw a newspaper on the steamboat askin' for information about runawayers," Malinda said gently, miserable as she contemplated the end of their journey.

Suddenly Jasmine sat up and stared back at her through the flames. "But what about out West? Reckon massa find me there?"

Again Malinda shook her head. "I don't know. I thought you were goin' north to Jeb."

"I guess so. But first I got to know if you and your pa—well, is you ever comin' north?"

"I don't know that either, Jasmine. . . . Would you maybe stay in Mobile?" She held her breath for the answer.

Jasmine smiled. "Sho I would. Me and you, well—"

"We been through some hard times together. But I have to know, Jasmine, if we can stay just me and you when we get there."

"I reckon so. You sho don't act like a mistis—"

"I couldn't."

"I knows. And I be free, too. So that just leaves me and you 'cause I sho ain't gonna act like no slave. Your Aunt Eliza gonna like me, too. . . . You think our hard times is over, Malindy?"

Malinda hesitated a long time before answering. "I hope so, Jasmine."

She knew neither of them could yet predict their future.

COME ALONG HOME

THEY WERE ALMOST ready to stop for two or three hours of sleep, having abandoned their fire early in the afternoon and pushed out into the cold and continued long into the night.

"Soon's we get by this swampy place, let's stop. I sho could stand it," Jasmine said.

"And we'll have some greens and corn bread with the potlicker," Malinda said, beginning the fantasy in which they often indulged.

"And black-eyed peas and ham and chicken and blackberry pie."

"And buttermilk and hot sweet taters—"

"Aw, go on! Who wants them when we has cold ones?"

They began to laugh.

"I feels it, Malindy. Good things a-comin'. Me and you is gonna make it home, wherever home is, and I got a feelin' it be Mobile."

Malinda's spirits lifted.

Soon they were past the swamp and hunting for a good place to stop. High banks or stagnant swampland lined the river's edge. Finally they pulled the raft in between gum and cypress trees until it was out of the water and then gathered wood for a fire. Travler sat on the raft with their food. It seemed to take Jasmine forever to get sparks from the flint she was striking against the hatchet. When at last the long brown pine needles they had gathered were burning, it was a beautiful sight. They lit the dry leaves and needles under the heavier wood and blew on the tiny flames until the fire caught up.

Her teeth aching, Malinda rubbed her arms and legs until they hurt, trying to restore her circulation, and then she loped back to the raft for their food. In addition to a few berries, they would have half of a sweet potato and a hunk of ham, which would leave enough for one more day's meager feast.

The rest of the night was unbearably long, interspersed by feeding the fire, a little sleeping, and listening to wolves in the distance.

Once Jasmine asked, "Did your ma teach you how to make a dress like that?"

"No, she taught me how to crochet, and I've made a right pretty sampler—"

"Good! You teach me to read, and I teach you to sew—lace and ruffles and ribbons, too. You can sho stand a heap of cleanin' up."

"Your baggy trousers—"

"Yep, we gonna get rid of them, too."

"We're still on the Tombigbee. Let's not think about Mobile yet."

"That be okay with me, but sometimes my mind runs on in spite of myself."

With the first streak of dawn, they were back on the raft, a light breeze blowing from the south giving them hope for a warmer day. When the sun came up over the horizon, they wanted to shout but dared not.

They had not been traveling long before Malinda voiced her feelings. "I can't put my finger on it, but somethin's different down here, Jasmine. It feels like—well, like we're the only humans for a thousand miles."

"Somethin's different all right. What is them sticky things?"

"Palmettos."

"And there be a bobwhite."

Then they saw a pomegranate tree and headed for shore. As they picked as many as they could reach, they saw deer fleetingly in the forest.

"How beautiful!"

"It be a wonder nobody ain't huntin' them."

"These dense forests haven't been touched. We're alone in these parts except for the animals and birds—and it's creepy."

"I don't believes you this time, Malindy. Somebody is got to be in them woods somewheres."

Back on the raft, they each tore the skin off a large round pomegranate and nibbled on the sweet red seeds, spitting the bitter cores into the water once the sweetness was gone. At home pomegranate juice, cooled in spring water, had been a favorite treat.

"Look at the canebrakes ahead! They're as big as all out yonder!"

"We's gonna do without them!" Jasmine glanced at her foot, which was healing better now that she was not walking on it and was regularly using the liniment the woman had given her.

"This time we just gonna pole right by them," she said.

They had seen many patches of the bamboolike reeds growing three or four feet high in the swamps and bayous, but none covered such a wide area as these. Here the canebrake extended out from the shore so far that they were soon a good distance from the forest.

"We is way out here for the Lord and everybody to see."

"The river's widening, too. Look out there!" Malinda pointed ahead.

"That ain't no river. It be a ocean. What is we gonna do?"

"We'll keep the raft close to the canebrakes just as we've stayed close to the shoreline. Maybe we're gettin' near Mobile and the 'Bigbee is runnin' into the bay."

"What bay?"

Malinda told her what she knew about Mobile Bay. Ahead the water seemed to flow into a huge hole in the sky. It was difficult to see any shore on either side. How dreadful to be moving so far out to go around the canebrakes. But only small ripples pushed by a gentle wind marred the smooth surface. Travler slept. A turkey vulture sat in a leafless tree far ahead viewing the countryside.

They saw quail and doves in the cane. "If we just had papa's shotgun, we could grow fat on our eatin'."

"Uh-huh, and have the whole countryside out lookin' for who blowed off that gun."

Malinda gazed far into the distance where water and sky blended so well that she could not tell where one ended and the other began.

As they poled along sometimes they talked;

sometimes they didn't. Once Jasmine said, "I still likes this better than a-slavin' at the big house."

"You sure are spunky."

"I reckon you is, too."

Malinda looked toward the woods far away. "No, I'm not. I've been scared to death lots of times." It seemed easy to admit it to Jasmine now. She relaxed and watched the other girl's strong arms pole the raft along with the current.

"You not act like it, most of the time anyways."

"It's funny, Jasmine. I don't feel as scared anymore, but the night mama died—"

"Anybody be scared then."

"But papa was deep in the woods. Mama got worse, and I had to go find him, Jasmine. And I got lost—and—"

Malinda shivered. She couldn't tell her about the other runawayer.

Jasmine stopped poling to listen.

"And when . . . when I found him we rushed back to mama, but it was too late. He did everything he knew to do, Jasmine, while I just stood by and watched. But I was so afraid."

"Sho you was."

"Are you ever afraid?"

"Sho is. When I runned away, I thought

every noise in the woods was them devil slavers."

"How could you try again after bein' caught the first time?"

"Jeb! I just think about Jeb, Malindy, and the hate I feel for massa get me started again."

"Do you think Jeb knows you're on the way?"

Jasmine brooded over the matter. "I believes so, Malindy," she whispered.

After a long silence, Jasmine added, "When the steamboat exploded, I runned so fast a chicken could have sat on my shirttail. Then I hears somebody else crashin' through the woods, and I knowed them slavers find me again. Scared! Malindy, I ain't never been so scared."

"What happened?"

"It was you! I find you at daylight, and I praise God and promise him to make you well. I sho is glad he help me do it!"

"I am, too."

"The noises in the woods don't scare me, Malindy, when I be with you. So don't you think Jeb want me to stay with you?"

"He loves you, Jasmine. I'm sure he wants you with him."

Jasmine frowned, "I don't think so. You be a friend. . . . Why, Malindy, you ain't even white anymore."

"I know! Weather worn and dirty—that's what I am."

"That not be what I mean."

Excitement welled inside Malinda. If Jasmine wanted to, surely they could stay together in Mobile. Aunt Eliza would take her in, too, until papa came for them. They could both go to school; they could study together; they could play and shout and sing out loud, unafraid. Malinda pushed hard with her pole, eager to come to the end of their journey since they would not have to separate.

"All this big water is makin' waves." The surging river slashed against the raft as Malinda checked the vines that held the logs secure in their notches. "I wish they would quit."

"They maybe ain't gonna quit. Look, Malindy!"

Dark clouds were rolling in far to the south, although the sun was still shining where the girls were. Malinda checked the shoreline. As far as she could see, several hundred feet of gigantic cane separated them from the firm ground where the woods began. Suddenly the river current swirled them swiftly away, their poles as helpless as thin reeds.

"Watch out!" Malinda yelled.

The raft slammed into a boulder partially exposed above the water. They pushed away from it with their poles only to find that the impact had severed their logs from the notches enough that the river current ripped away the vines, tugged at the logs, and sent them peeling off in different directions.

"Grab a log! Grab a log!" Malinda was yelling almost before she surfaced after their plunge. Jasmine had already latched on to one.

"I's kickin', Malindy!"

Malinda snatched at a log whirling past, moving swiftly with the current. Jasmine stayed afloat on hers, just as she had behind the raft that warm day she had learned to swim. But now the river was as cold as spring water.

"Kick and try to work toward the cane!" Malinda yelled. Her wet skirt weighed her down, but the current was too strong for them to control their direction. Ahead the cane thicket extended farther out into the river, and they were headed straight for it.

"Watch for rocks!" Jasmine called. Seeing several jutting out of the water ahead, Malinda let go of her log and swam to them. Looking back to see that Jasmine was making it, she jumped from one rock to another until she was once again in the tall reed grass. When Jasmine joined her, they heard a rustling beneath them and jumped with fright back onto a slippery rock in the river. A soaked possum peered at them from the bamboo cane.

"That stupid possum is gonna be the ruin of us yet!" Malinda grabbed him by the neck and set him on her shoulder. "Now stay there!"

The logs from their raft swirled out again toward mid-river. Jasmine struggled to find a couple of medium-sized rocks.

"Just in case we needs them," she said as she heaved up one and then relinquished it for two smaller ones.

Malinda had used so much of her shirt for Jasmine's foot bandages that only the shoulders and sleeves remained, which she used as a belt to hold up her loose dress. She patted her round white pebble, knotted up in the end of one sleeve, and noted with satisfaction that it was not lost. Jasmine still carried the small Tombigbee pebbles in one pants pocket.

A boat horn sounded low and mournful in the quiet. Smoke rose against the distant sky.

"Malindy . . ." Jasmine sounded hesitant. "Did you hear a shotgun when that boat horn blew?"

Malinda shook her head. "Why?"

"I thinks I did."

"If there was one shot, I bet there would be others. I think it was just the horn."

"I don't know."

They walked side by side, each stepping carefully on the undergrowth and vines in an attempt to miss the prickles.

"It's impossible to get through this cane-brake," Malinda said.

"You just put one foot in front of the other and forget everything else."

Black birds were flying overhead, and geese skied across the water to land beyond the swirling current where the raft had broken up. Each step was a struggle. Malinda stopped so that she could measure with her eye how far it was to land and, watching the wild fowl, she suddenly felt hungry.

"Here! I got a piece of pomegranate." Jasmine had a difficult time getting it out of her soaked pants; but when she did, they divided it between them. They gave the peelings to Travler who still rode Malinda's shoulder.

"Jasmine, look how far we've come from the river. No way at all."

"We ain't looking behind us, Malindy. We keeps our eyes just on them woods ahead and what be under our feet."

They were more than halfway through the canebrake when something came crashing in their direction from their right.

"Run!" Jasmine yelled.

"I can't."

"You gotta!"

They didn't wait to see what it was. They tried to run. They swung at the reeds blocking their way and had no time to pick and choose where they were stepping. Malinda's foot caught in a clump of vines. She fell. At the same time she heard a wild squeal behind her.

"Run, Jasmine! Keep on runnin'!"

Through the cane rushed a huge, sandy-colored wild boar, its two long swordlike tusks and its two short stumpy ones, headed straight at her.

A rock zinged over her head from Jasmine's hand, and the boar squealed again. Jasmine, still clinging to her one remaining rock, yanked Malinda up as she struggled to rise. They were running, but what was the use? She knew how fast a boar could run. Papa had killed one once, but not before it had chased down a horse and cut it to shreds.

Malinda glanced back as she ran. The white tusks were gaining on them. Ears the size of papa's hands and red evil eyes, partly covered with shaggy hair, bore down on them. The canebrake was not opening up to let them through.

23
PROPER PAPERS

SO IT WAS ALL going to end right here in the canebrake. The past weeks—their struggles and fevers and fears and, yes, their songs and laughter—appeared before her like a mirage. The hovering forest ahead was the promised land. If only one of those trees were out here so they could scale it in a flash and be free of this monster.

She kept hearing Jasmine's voice as if coming from the far end of a rain barrel. . . "Me and you's gonna make it home, Malindy. . . . We keep our eyes just on them woods ahead. Me and you and the Lord, Malindy. . . ."

Through the cane rushed a huge, sandy-colored boar.

Throwing caution aside, she screamed for help, knowing full well there was no one to assist them in this desolate countryside. Jasmine's last rock flew over her head. It landed far to their right. The boar squealed. Then Jasmine dug the Tombigbee pebbles out of her pocket. She threw them in the same direction as the other rock. The boar veered off course and began butting the ground around the stones in fury.

The momentary relief gave Malinda a new spurt of energy.

"Run, Malindy!"

The boar was silent. The rocks had diverted him, but Malinda knew it would not be for long. She and Jasmine lunged forward toward the forest. The cane thicket clawed at them. With a violent squeal the boar plunged toward them again, and again Malinda screamed for help. She must get control of herself and use anything at her disposal to try to save them.

Anything! The heavy weight on her shoulder. She raised her hand to grab him by the tail and sling him into the canebrake to divert the boar when Travler made a flying leap and landed on the boar's bristled back. His cavernous mouth white with foam, the boar chased himself around and around trying to slash the possum riding him. The girls plunged ahead as fast as they could in the canebrake, but the possum never lost his balance until the boar rolled over on his back, his stubby legs in the air. Travler leaped off before he was crushed and dashed into the undergrowth. But in no time the swifter animal overcame him and slashed him to pieces with his long tusks.

Tears were streaming down the girls' cheeks as they ran. Now they had nothing: no raft or food or hatchet, or possum, or much strength or time. . . .

Once the boar had finished off Travler, he flew toward Jasmine and Malinda. Malinda kept her eyes on the trees. They were nearer, much nearer now—although she could hear the boar gaining on them. When Jasmine tripped and Malinda stopped to help her, they could see the white tusks flashing through the cane. *It's just me and you and the Lord, Jasmine,* she thought.

A single shot fired out from the trees. The sound pierced Malinda's consciousness, but she kept running. The boar had squealed wildly but was still crashing toward them. In another minute, however, all was silent. She turned her head long enough to see the boar's large body slumped in the canebrake, blood running down between its evil red eyes. Then she rushed toward firm ground as if still pursued. Three more steps would bring them out of the canebrake . . . now two . . . now one.

They ran well in under the pines before they collapsed on the soft brown carpet of needles, crying hysterically and hugging each other. Now their bleeding feet began to ache. With a tremor on their lips, they smiled at each other.

"Me and you and the Lord, we done made it, Malindy!" Jasmine gasped slowly.

Malinda looked up through the beautiful green pines to the clouding sky in thanksgiving. Perched high on a limb near the edge of the forest where the canebrake began sat a young man holding a gun. He was staring at them and smiled when he saw they had discovered him. He slid down the firm straight trunk of the pine and stood hesitantly where he landed.

"Oh, thank you!"

"Thank you!"

"Thank God!" he replied.

"The Lord sent you!"

"We's on speaking terms now and then," the stranger said in a deep rich voice. "But right now I gotta get you home so's Missy can take care of you."

"Where be home?" Jasmine demanded.

"I got a shack in these woods."

Jasmine brushed a tear off Malinda's cheek with a grubby thumb and gave her a brilliant smile. "See, Malindy, there was another human in a thousand miles—"

"Thank God!"

The man was helping them up. "I can't carry you both, but I ain't leavin' one of you here alone, so you both just lean on me and let my arms support you best they can. Let me carry your weight instead of your feet doing it."

"Wait!" Jasmine demanded again. "Who be at your shack?"

"Missy, she be my woman, and a couple of chilluns."

"Where the massa and mistis?"

"Ain't got none. I's free."

"You dead sure?"

The man smiled. "I's dead sure."

Jasmine was satisfied. "I lean on you then."

By nighttime—with torn feet bandaged and their bodies and heads scrubbed in a washtub and a supper of dove and peas and corn bread in their stomachs—Jasmine and Malinda rested by the fire in Missy's and William's cabin. The children were sound asleep in a big bed in the corner. The girls related their story, although Malinda could tell by her eyes that Jasmine was still suspicious. She kept asking them how long they had lived there, how they had come by their freedom, and could she see what a freedom paper looked like?

Once she saw it, she exclaimed, "Malindy, I still got the letters you taught me. They's written here, and I remember them."

Missy looked puzzled so they told all about their raft, and Jasmine repeated the alphabet without any prompting; then reported she could count, too. But when she rummaged in her pants for the piece of wood with a notch for each day, she discovered her secret pouch containing the stick and the piece of flint. Her knife was gone.

"What is I gonna do?" she wailed.

Missy smiled. "We take care of you."

"But me and Malindy got to go—" she stopped and looked cautiously at Malinda.

"We got to go home, wherever our home is," Malinda added, repeating the exact words Jasmine had stated so confidently—was it only yesterday?

"We have to get *you* to Mobile," William said to Malinda.

"How come?"

"Because your pa is turnin' the world upside down for you."

"What do you mean?" Malinda's heart pounded in anticipation.

"We been keepin' up with your pa in the papers," Missy said gently. And then it was their turn to relate how her papa had heard about the steamboat explosion some five days after it had occurred. When Malinda was unaccounted for, he went to his sister's in Mobile where he contacted the steamboat offices for traces of her. Now, he was still searching up and down the river.

"He say you learn from him how to survive like a Injun," William added admiringly. "And since you wasn't one of them accounted for among the livin' or the dead, he say you got to be alive somewheres. And hallelujah! You sho is!"

"I wouldn't be, though, if it weren't for Jasmine findin' me and nursin' me well."

"I's not be here to tell about it, neither, if Malindy not save me from drownin'."

"How you happen to come on Malindy so deep in the woods?" Missy wanted to know.

Jasmine's large eyes flicked once toward Malinda. If any telling was to be done, it was up to her; Malinda wasn't giving her secret away under any circumstances. Jasmine lowered her gaze to where her hands lay in her lap.

"I's a runawayer."

"I thought so," William said matter-of-factly. "You ain't got no pass, so you can't go to Mobile."

Jasmine was indignant. "I's with Malindy!"

"We're together. Nobody gonna separate us!" Malinda cried.

Missy leaned over and put an arm around Jasmine's shoulders. "Honey, Malindy can't help you. It be spread all over the countryside that she be travelin' alone on that boat. Ain't no way for her to pretend to be your mistis."

"I'm not her mistis. We're friends."

"Then we can go into town different ways—alone," Jasmine said.

"No!" William's voice was sharp. "You'd be picked up and sold right off the auction block."

"What does you mean?"

"Listen!" William put his face in his strong hands for a brief moment before he continued. "If you is alone somebody gonna demand your pass, and if it ain't real official—where you going and what for, when you left, when you return, and a unsuspicious signature of your massa—you gets took to the auction block."

"Even free blacks with proper papers has sometimes been picked up and sold," Missy added.

"It don't happen everywhere, but it do in Mobile."

"You said you're a shepherd and sell cattle and vegetables in Mobile," Malinda said. "How do *you* get around?"

"Me and a white farmer friend over yonder goes together."

"Do he have slaves?" Jasmine demanded.

"No."

444

"Does you have to pretend he's your massa?"

"No. Sometimes I has to show my freedom papers, but he always be there to help me. We never gets away from each other very far."

"Then I'll stay here, and you can go fetch my papa," Malinda said to William. She couldn't leave Jasmine; no one had better ask her to leave Jasmine.

William and Missy looked at each other for a long still moment. She rose and went over and stood behind his chair next to the fire, a hand on his shoulder. He put his hand up and patted hers as he spoke.

"Malindy, we can help you get to Mobile. And Jasmine, we can help you get away safe from your massa. But we can't bring nobody in here to us."

"Why not?" Panic was rising in Malinda's chest.

"Because we got ourselves and others to protect."

"You is talkin' in riddles!" Jasmine retorted. "Explain yourself!"

"We is so far back in the woods nobody ever runned across us," Missy replied.

"And," William paused and squeezed Missy's hand, "we helps lots of our people—just like we can help you, Jasmine—and we wants to keep on with it."

Malinda moved over close to Jasmine. William's message had finally gotten through to her. He had some way to help people like Jasmine escape to freedom, and he was not going to bring the world to his doorstep. "Is anybody suspicious of you?"

"Not at all." William spread his hands wide and smiled. "And I's gonna keep it that way—as I has for years now."

Malinda wiped unashamedly at a tear running down her cheek and salting her lips. "You sho don't give me and Jasmine much choice, do you?"

Missy poked at the coals and added another log to the fire. "They needs sleep, honey. Tomorrow will come soon enough. Then we can talk again."

"You's right," William responded. "Jasmine, I shift these chilluns over so's there be room for you on the bed. Malindy, you can have me and Missy's bed."

Jasmine drew herself up straight, her weight firm on her battered feet. "We is obliged for all you done for us, but we can't take you beds away, too. I reckon me and Malindy has bedded down by many a fire."

"Thank you just the same," Malinda added. "But we're gonna stay right here by this fire together."

FREE!

DESPITE ALL THE protection inside this home and all its cozy warmth, Malinda knew this was the cruelest fire she and Jasmine had shared. She knew it was to be their last.

How could it be otherwise? Now she had to face questions she had pushed harshly away. Separation sooner or later was inevitable. Even if they made the journey to Mobile successfully, how could they stay together for long unless they played maid and mistress? Soon the falseness and bitterness of that relationship would tear at their friendship, and they would be hating each other.

Tonight, in their first experience back in

civilization, even William had wanted to separate them—offering Malinda a whole bed to herself rather than offering it to them both. No, Malinda decided, despite the tears just behind her eyelids, there was no way they could be themselves—just Jasmine and Malinda—and stay together. If only they had lived in another time . . . another place . . .

She buried her face in the crook of her arm. Jasmine beside her on the floor moved, too. . . . Why must everyone she loved leave her? she wondered in desolate loneliness. And she could not go with Jasmine. If she did, she might never again find papa. She could see him in her memory standing on the shore, his hands in his pockets, while her own gripped the steamboat rail.

Malinda raised her head and gazed at the hot coals, the gray ashes, the black logs that sent out flames of red and purple and white and blue and green. When a hoot owl's lonely call sounded far away in the forest, Jasmine rolled over on her stomach and gazed into the fire, too. That was the way they spent the night—not needing to speak, lying side by side on the quilts and staring deep into the fire.

The next morning after the children were

outside playing, William explained how he could get Jasmine down the bay by boat, then transfer her to a ship on the Gulf of Mexico that would transport her to New York.

"What happens then? Will she have a home?"

"The cap'n on this ship will look out for her, and he has people in New York to help her as long as she needs them. She'll have a place to go immediately."

"How I know that boat not carry me back upriver to my massa?"

William was visibly stunned. "Jasmine, you can trust me."

"I ain't never seen you till yesterday, and you say I can trust you. *I* says I don't trust nobody! Once I got trusted right back to my massa's yard. This time I keeps to my own plan."

"You ain't got no massa!" William spoke with authority.

Jasmine stared at him speechless.

"You is free now. You ain't at nobody else's beck and call. I's just the instrument to see that you stays free, and you ain't free if you goes into Mobile."

"That be what you say. How does I know you tellin' me true? Besides, Malindy needs me through them woods."

It was Malinda's turn to stare, remembering again the time she had told Jasmine how she had been deathly afraid of the forest.

Had been . . . How beautiful it sounded! The small cabin could not contain her feelings. She escaped out the door and jumped down the two front steps, oblivious to her aching feet. As she landed on the ground she cried, "I'm free, too. I'm free! I'm not afraid of the woods anymore."

She had been freed and didn't even know it. Together she and Jasmine had beat back the wilderness and won.

Yesterday afternoon's clouds had spilled their rain, and now the resinous pines under which she walked scented the moist air. Cardinals were singing, and a distant crow cawed raucously. She could hardly keep up with her swift thoughts seesawing back and forth. She was not afraid of the reed grasses and canebrakes, and yet if William had not been there, they would have lost their lives in them yesterday. She had been terrified of the forest, but it had brought Jasmine and her together. Yesterday in their race against death, the trees had held out the possibility of life. . . . The wilderness had held tragedy for one runaway slave, but it had also protected another.

She gazed deep into the woods. The giant pines stood free of undergrowth across the land as far as she could see. The forest did not now torture her mind with the stench-filled fire and death of an unknown man. Instead it reminded her of the warm fires she and Jasmine had shared on their long journey, and of Jasmine's "G'night!" across the flames. Now she felt there was nothing in this wilderness she could not conquer if she tried.

I remember the very last words you told me, papa, she thought. *"You're going to come through on the other side." You had faith in me all the time.*

She was sitting on a log when Jasmine joined her. "How far is it to Mobile?" Malinda asked.

Jasmine flipped her head back toward the house. "He say not too far."

"I'm gonna walk all the way and see if my Aunt Eliza will keep me while I go to school."

"But your pa! He be here someplace looking for you. Ain't you goin' west with him?"

"Later maybe. But first I must grow up some and get more learnin'."

"I's comin' with you." Nobody wanted it more than Malinda. Her eyes ached as they met Jasmine's.

"I can't trust that William!" Jasmine said.

"How come? You trust me—at last. . . . And God, you trusted him all along."

451

"But I ain't laid eyes on William till yesterday."

"But Jasmine, he trusted *us*. He knows we aren't gonna tell anyone what he and Missy do, not even papa." She took a deep breath and blinked away the moisture in her eyes. "Besides, he killed that wild boar. And papa always said if somebody saves your life, that makes you blood kin. Can't you trust blood kin?"

Jasmine's eyes, getting bigger and rounder by the minute, clung to hers. They were both remembering the long fever days and the pebble tea and the storm waves and the overturned canoe.

Slowly Jasmine nodded her head, yes. Then she impulsively leaned over close to Malinda and spoke softly. "Love don't depend on time or place—I be rememberin' every word just like your ma said it."

"I'll be rememberin', too, Jasmine."

Jasmine smiled. "When I told you my name—well, it ain't really Jasmine."

"I know."

"You knowed all along?"

Malinda nodded.

"Well, I got to tell you my real name."

"You'll be Jasmine to me—always."

She leaned over and whispered her name in Malinda's ear, then drew back quickly with new understanding. "Oh, but I reckon I always be Jasmine to me, too. I give myself that name, and I likes it. It my *free* name."

"Will you keep it?"

"Sho I will."

"I'm glad, Jasmine, and I hope Jeb likes it, too."

Pain crossed Jasmine's face. "Jeb—he not make it, Malindy." She paused for a moment, looking through the trees. "He be killed when he runned away."

"But you said—"

"I knows. But I reckon I tells you what I wants to believe."

"Oh, Jasmine!"

"But don't you reckon maybe William can help me get where Jeb wanted me to go?"

Malinda nodded as she wiped away her tears. "I'm sure of it."

When William and Missy came out of the cabin, Malinda and Jasmine joined them at the steps.

"I wants to walk with Malindy through the woods when she leave," Jasmine said. "Then I do as you say."

"We is so glad you decided to accept our help," Missy said as she hugged Jasmine.

William added, "After we've given Malindy full directions and places where she can stop for help if she wants to—"

"And after I's fed her and wrapped up her feet and put some moccasins on them—"

"And I's gonna comb and plait her pretty brown hair—" Jasmine interrupted.

"Then we all walk with her as far as she needs us—but no more," William finished.

About a mile before the woods opened up into a clearing, William and Missy stopped and asked Malinda if she needed them any longer.

Trying hard to keep her voice even, Malinda said, "I can go the rest of the way by myself."

With their arms around each other, Missy and William watched her and waved as she kept going. Jasmine stayed by her side.

"Malindy, is you sure about these here woods? They can be mean."

"I'm sure, Jasmine. I'm not afraid anymore." The words tasted sweet as they left her lips.

Jasmine stopped, and Malinda turned to face her. They gazed at each other unable to take their eyes away.

Jasmine whispered, "We got good memories, ain't we?"

Malinda nodded.

"So we's rich."

Malinda nodded again.

She reached down in the pocket of her dress for her smooth white stone. It was wrapped in a piece of paper Missy had given her. Holding the warm pebble in her hand, she spread out the paper and gave it to Jasmine.

"Since your real name is Jasmine now, I wrote it out on this paper so you can spell it the way you learned to spell Jeb."

"How you know I wants to write my own name?"

Malinda gazed into Jasmine's black shimmering eyes. "I just felt it. Here!" Malinda took Jasmine's hand and put her pebble into it. Its crystals sparkled in the sunlight through the pines.

"What you doin'?"

"You gave this to me, Jasmine, a long time ago in some pebble tea. Now it's yours again."

"How come?"

"Because it's all I have."

Jasmine rubbed the stone with her fingers. "Maybe it be my star, too, Malindy."

"I hope so. It's daytime yet but, g'night, Jasmine."

"G'night, Malindy."

Malinda headed down the trail alone. She did not wave, but she knew Jasmine would be watching as long as she was in sight.

Betty Wilson Story is a native of Alabama, where *Summer of Jubilee* and *River of Fire* take place. Her novel *The Other Side of the Tell,* based on her husband's experiences in Israel on an archaeological dig, won the Indiana University Foundation Novel Award in 1975. In addition to writing, Mrs. Story frequently speaks at writers' conferences and in school classrooms.